MW00511361

The First
Mrs. Solberg
Volume Two

The First Mrs. Solberg

Volume Two

Michele Menard

The First Mrs. Solberg, Volume 2

By: Michele Menard

Designed by: Darlene Swanson • www.van-garde.com

Copyright © 2013 by The Four Menards

All rights reserved to include trademark on all graphics.
No part of this book may be reproduced, stored in a retrieval
system, or transmitted by any means, electronic, mechanical,
photocopying, recording, or otherwise, without written
permission from the author.

ISBN: 978-0-9891734-4-5

Published by The Four Menards Publishing, Asheville, NC 28816

TheFourMenards@gmail.com

Printed by Lightning Source, Inc., La Vergne, TN 37086

First and foremost, this book is dedicated to Mr. Roger Schram, teacher by his very nature and a professor in every sense of the word. A remarkable humanitarian with a dedication that could rival the angels! Benefits of your teachings and sense of humor have carried so many more than can ever be calculated over a half century and beyond. Known as the hallmark of excellence by many who were fortunate enough to have encountered your skill; changes for the better, literally circulate the world.

To Mrs. Marjorie Fulton and Mr. Lawrence Krepps, two more teachers who have left the few pleasant memories that I have of my school years.

To my father—thanks for the China doll and the giant lollipop, and all that they represented!

To both my sets of grandparents—I was too young to fully appreciate all that you did for us—so I send this thank-you all the way to Heaven!

To Nana, Aunt Lou, Aunt Joyce, and all of the Jamason boys—I have kept my promise.

Contents

Chapter One
The Extra Fidestrial

The last four and one half years had been wonderful in Miami, and Regina loved it there. While medical school was a grind, it was also filled with marvelous memories. Internship was more demanding, but at least Frank would be paid now. Occasionally she wondered if a move would be a good decision, and had discussed the possibility with him. The letter delivered by Eva Rodriguez months ago, lurked around every corner in her mind.

> "Frank, I must see you. I am pregnant and we must discuss what we are going to do about it; I will not have an abortion."

While she didn't believe the messenger was telling the truth, she was still bothered by the fact that this brazen woman lived in the same city as they did.

Eva Rodriguez was the granddaughter of one of Frank's former patients. She was infatuated with him to the point of making pop up visits around the hospital in an attempt to bump into him.

Although he had made it crystal clear that he was not interested in her, she persisted tirelessly, until she finally realized that the strategically placed blockades, were impassable.

There was North Carolina and its gorgeous mountains, which enticed her. Their close friends were here in Miami though, and it seemed foolish to run from something that would probably never even materialize. Her best friend, Jeannie, had a similar temptation to leave the area, triggered from a hospital employee who had relentlessly chased Chuck during the first year of medical school. Elena Garcia, a ward clerk at the hospital and the daughter of a prominent nephrology attending, couldn't resist married men. She went so far as to follow Chuck home using the excuse that her uncle lived in the same building. Finally she subsided, but Jeannie was never completely assured that she would not return to her old games. Having transferred from a nursing position, Jeannie was now working at the Child Enrichment Center affiliated with Jackson Memorial Hospital. She was delighted to be able to work with her new baby Charlie, but concerned that she could no longer keep her eye on things at JMH. Although she continually tried to reassure herself that her troubles with the prowler were over, the haunting attempts still came to mind on a regular basis.

The two girls shared their worries and had both concluded that their husbands were strong, faithful men and that moving would not guarantee that other women wouldn't chase them in another location. They had far too much to lose with all the beautiful friends they had in Miami and the golden opportunity for residency programs here, in a facility that was as well-known as Jackson Memorial Hospital.

Regina and her "second mother," Frances, were enjoying a cup of coffee after a very busy clinic.

Frank came bursting into her office excited by the news, "I have been offered one of the two spots for an Orthopedic residency here but," he added taking a deep breath, "I need to give George Easterlin my answer in 'six minutes!' The program is too competitive to wait for acceptance."

"Well what did you tell George?" Regina asked, annoyed.

"I told him that it wasn't only my decision, and that you were considering the mountains."

"I think it's ridiculously unreasonable for him to allow you six minutes to make a decision that lasts four years! They loved you in Chapel Hill and are willing to wait for your decision."

"So I'll tell him, no. Look, sweetheart, you have stood by me for almost five years, no questions asked. It's your turn to decide where we live."

"Don't tell him, no, Frank. What do you really want to do?"

"Stay here. The program is one of the best in the country and Chuck just signed up for his residency in internal medicine. Above all though, I want you and Frank Jr. to be happy."

"Then tell him, yes. Our friends are here, and so are both families."

"On second thought, I'll tell him, no." Frank laughed. "Are you sure, honey?"

"Yes, I am sure. We'll stay here at least for the next four years."

"Lamar will be pleased that we won't have to move now either," Frances laughed, but wasn't joking.

Hugging her, Frank practically ran out of the office to tell George Easterlin that he would gladly accept the position. Regina turned to Frances, "When I see George Easterlin, I'm going to give him a piece of my mind, attending physician or not! I don't care how great he is, he should be more considerate!"

"I can see why you're upset, honey," Frances answered. "The faculty around here can be downright snobs. They know we have the best program and make no bones about using that leverage. They have had their sights set for Frank since he was a first year student."

Moments later the door opened and George Easterlin walked in, his blue eyes dancing with delight. The attending knew that adding Frank Solberg to his staff was a valuable asset and that the Orthopedic Residency Program would benefit greatly by it. Moving toward Regina, he extended his hand for a warm welcome and congratulations. Regina stood, and shaking hands she said, "Thank you so much for considering Frank, Sir, he is delighted."

Frances looked up, smiling. Relieved that the Solbergs were staying in Miami, she laughed, "That's telling him!" The two women hugged each other as the confused attending stood by.

"Did I miss something?" he asked with a twinkle in his eye. "Men are born missing something," Frances answered gruffly but grinning. "I'm just glad I don't have to relocate since my adopted daughter and her husband will be here for at least another four years! Come on, Regina, let's go steal a few minutes with Frank Jr. while we tell Jeannie the good news."

Frank Solberg and Chuck Nugent had completed medical school, started Internship, and were now preparing for the second half of the haul toward the completion of their careers. Frank would specialize in Orthopedic Surgery and Chuck in Internal medicine. Wyatt Clements, another close friend, was thriving in his new practice as an Ophthalmologist, having finished his training only a few years ago at Bascom Palmer Eye Institute, where he met Regina and Frances. He and his wife Sylvia had a set of triplets. Sylvia had transferred from her work as a court reporter to the head of the infant nursery at the Child Enrichment Center. The center was recently opened at Jackson Memorial Hospital at the request of Leo Gerehauzer, for the three young couples' new babies as well as for the children of the house staff. The three younger couples were as bonded as any family might be and were extremely close to the two older couples that shared their group of ten. Leo Gerehauzer was the attending physician who headed the Orthopedic Hand Service. A former army Colonel, he and his wife Hazel adored the young Solbergs. Frances McNeal Mac Michaels was Regina's "second mother," and her husband Lamar, was Regina's step-father's retired former business partner and close friend.

The entire close- knit group was having dinner at the Rustic Inn Crab House tonight, accompanied by all five babies! Regina was closing the clinic area while Grandma Frances went to get Frank Jr., when the telephone on the desk rang. "Outpatient clinic, Mrs. Solberg speaking."

"Oh, hi, Regina, this is Carolee from Dr. Easterlin's office.

There is a gentleman here to see Frank," she whispered into the receiver, "I think that he is a process server."

"Well, Frank has left the hospital for the evening, may I help him?"

"No, he said it must be Frank."

"Well then it must wait until tomorrow," Regina answered calmly.

"Okay, I'll tell him. He's pacing the hall," Carolee whispered again.

The messenger was angry to learn that Frank's only home address on file was a post office box. Regina had taken care of that a long time ago, before Eva Rodriguez could get her hands on anymore of their personal information.

"I detest process servers," Carolee vented, "They're so pushy and intrusive."

Irritated to hear that Frank was not available, he demanded to know where Regina worked, as he figured he could follow her home, and serve him there. Considering the papers that he held in his hand, he'd run too if he were Dr. Solberg. "I can not disclose that information to you, Sir," Carolee advised coolly, "and this office is also closing. After you," she showed him to the door and turned off the lights. The man cursed and stomped out of the office, realizing that he would only be able to reach Frank Solberg among the vast population of the Jackson Memorial Hospital staff, when and if he could locate him.

The Rustic Inn Crab House was booming with business, and

people were amazed at the five infants who sat in their own high chairs and played happily with the "restaurant survival bag" contents that their parents always carried with them. Because of his fair coloring and bright blue eyes, Frank Solberg Jr. stood out like an alien. The image of his handsome father, he was not only adored by Frances and Lamar, but also the favorite of Leo Gerehauzer, who loved Regina as he would his own daughter.

Sylvia and Wyatt's adorable triplets were cappuccino-skinned with dark eyes and black curly hair. They were typically Jamaican and strikingly beautiful. Charlie Nugent had an olive complexion, huge brown eyes and a smile that would steal anyone's heart. The babies were a pleasure to take anywhere, as Regina had a strict rule about holding babies in restaurants and the other two mothers followed her example. "As he gets older, he'll stay in his own familiar seat and play with the toys that are introduced only in restaurants. Public high chairs may not be sanitized properly and are often unstable. Waitresses walk around with trays of hot food, and our children aren't going to be running around," she had firmly explained to Frank's parents, Dorothy and Raymond Solberg, in the past.

The two older couples admired Regina and understood exactly what she meant as they witnessed other children carrying on and running back and forth to the raw bar to get and throw ice. Everyone enjoyed a great supper and talked among themselves about the upcoming weekend. Spring was fast approaching and the grills were getting restless. Frank was watching his wife as she planned a Sunday menu with the other four women, and couldn't help noticing again how beautiful she was. There was a spiritual look about her, and a glow that he couldn't identify. Soft auburn curls fell gently past her small shoulders and her dark brown eyes were full of love. She was a missionary in every sense of the word, and adored God with all of her heart!

Leo was also watching the family of three. Frank Jr. resembled a small angel and always seemed to be smiling. His parents were known as "the hallmark of excellence," in everything they engaged in, and adored each other and their baby. George Easterlin had telephoned the Gerehauzers before they left for dinner to report the persistent process server. "I assume that this is hospital related, but I know of nothing that could have provoked it," the head of the Orthopedic Residency Program sounded concerned. Leo explained about the problem patient's visitor; that had encountered Frank several months prior, but added that he thought the issue was put to rest by taking Frank off the case.

George and Leo had been close friends for years in the army before coming to JMH. Both had numerous experiences with "over- zealous fans," and both their wives had endured the nonsense that the typical antics of these women on the chase carried with them. "From what I understand, Chuck Nugent had his fair share of troubles with Jorge Garcia's nymphomaniac daughter too," Leo shared, in a disgusted tone of voice. "Well, where do we go from here?" George wondered, and continuing, concluded, "It's really none of our business if it doesn't involve the hospital."

"I love Frank Solberg like a son, and I've stolen Regina as my own daughter years ago. If this could in any way effect his state of mind at work, it certainly is our business." As he watched Regina inconspicuously place her sweater on a shivering, elderly lady at the next table, he somehow knew that whatever the problem was, she was already aware of it and that God held her right in the palm of His hand as one of His cherished servants. He and Lamar had invited Frank to join them in a golf game on Sunday. Of course, there would be no personal questions asked, but he wanted Frank to know that they were there if he needed them. Frances listened to the news of the process server quietly, before the four older friends had left her home for the restaurant. She offered no information.

Sylvia was organizing the final touches on Sunday's menus when the group decided to take the sleepy babies and head for home. Hazel and Frances each grabbed a triplet, as Lamar grabbed Charlie. Holly and Hyacinth gladly accepted the lift, but Wyatt never shared Harper, the only boy triplet. Frank Jr. was retrieved by Grandpa Leo, as usual, and, to the Colonel's delight, reached up laughing as the tall (not-so-gruff-after-all), man approached his highchair. Arriving home, the Solbergs put their little son to bed and sat on the patio with Monique.

Tears ran down Frank's face, and as Regina sat quietly waiting for him to speak, she recalled the plaque she had seen in the gift shop, *"You are never given a wish, without also being given the power to make it come true,"* By Richard Bach. She had gone back to buy it the very next day, but it was gone and she had not seen another one. Frank turned to her and said, "There is a process server chasing me, Regina."

"I know it," she answered quietly. "He was at George's office this afternoon."

"I'm sure this has to do with Eva Rodriguez," he burst into heartbreaking sobs.

Regina immediately held him. "Look Frank, whatever this is, we can and will get through it."

Unable to speak, he shook his head. "She came to the on-call room that night that I went in to see her grandmother. I was asked to stay for an emergency patient in transit, and thought I'd grab a power nap. She locked the door behind her and got into bed," Frank was crying so hard he couldn't talk. "I was half asleep, but she got me. Now I'll be punished for the rest of my life, and I deserve to be."

Regina was very calm and knew exactly where she was getting her strength from. Closing her dry eyes, she thanked Him silently. Her husband loved her and he loved their son. He had been set up to fail, and while he had fallen hard into carnal temptation, he had been trapped nonetheless.

"I must ask you, Frank, was it just the one encounter?"

Frank felt like she had stabbed him in the heart. "Yes, Regina, it was the one encounter. I couldn't blame you if you left me, but I beg you to let me be a part of our son's life."

The street-smart missionary answered immediately, "Frank, this is no time for your monumental self-pity. This lady is a calculating, cold-hearted schemer, as far as I'm concerned. Do you want to fight this together or not?"

Frank was in shock. Was he dreaming this conversation? He must be.

"What will your family think? What will mine think, and all of our friends?"

"Well after seeing the information trailing behind the Goodyear Blimp and hearing the news on television, they probably won't want to have cookouts anymore," Regina's typical sarcasm surfaced. "Who do you think we are, Frank?"

Puzzled, he waited to be enlightened as to who he thought they were. "We're ordinary people and we have an ordinary problem to deal with. There is no need to broadcast our issues."

"I have committed a terrible sin, Regina."

"That is between you and God. Personally, I doubt that He would think us wise to tell the whole world the details. Do you think that you're the first or last to have this happen to you? The rest of the group will follow our reaction. You made a mistake in a moment of weakness when you were half asleep. What are the chances that this woman could be pregnant anyway? And why, do tell, Matey, would you even entertain the idea of showering family or friends with the gory details?"

"She told me after the fact that she had been monitoring her ovulation, and waited for just the right night." Frank put his head in his hands, crying harder than before.

"If she is pregnant, which in itself is still doubtful, it is God's doing. He doesn't always explain why He allows things to happen, Frank, but then, He doesn't have to," the missionary smiled. "The situation is here, but how we react to it, is our choice, and her certain downfall if she is intending to trap you."

Exhausted, Frank looked up at his wife. She was an unshaken

tower of strength compacted into a small graceful body. She belonged to God first, and He held her in His own arms tonight. "Where do we go from here, Regina?"

Laughing softly, his little redhead from the Bronx spoke, "We run that process server's backside off, keeping in mind that somebody must be paying him, and it isn't us!"

"What do we tell our friends, or do we tell them?"

"That is your choice, but I would tell them that we have another Elena Garcia on our hands, who is alleging that she is pregnant. I think that you will find our friends very supportive. I would certainly not enlighten either set of our biological parents to what is going on. Frances and Lamar will be on our side as always, and Leo and Hazel will be right beside them! If she is pregnant, there's still a huge question that the baby is yours. We'll cross those bridges as we come to them." Frank was riddled with guilt and sorrow. He sat in silence and shook his head.

Frank could not and would not let everyone think he was innocent. Regina was a walking saint, and he would follow her "to the end of the earth," as they say.

Bowing his head, Frank could not bring himself to speak to God for a few minutes. "Father, I have done the most horrible thing to Your daughter. I know that You will forgive me, but I will never forgive myself."

He went to the dining room table to unpack the baby bag from the last dinner he would ever enjoy with their friends. "My God, I wish things could be as they always were before I made this horrible mistake." He took the empty bottles to the sink to wash them, but beside them was a small parcel wrapped in tissue paper. Opening it, he read, *"You are never given a wish without also being given the power to make it come true."* By Richard Bach.

"Where did this come from?" he asked his wife. "I don't know," Regina looked delighted but surprised. I saw it in the gift shop weeks ago, but I didn't have any money with me. When I went back the next day to get it, it was gone." Frances! Frances knew that Regina had seen the plaque and didn't have the money for it.

Watching Regina brush her hair, he was reminded of an exotic angel. He couldn't touch her and he told her so. "I can never forgive myself, Regina."

Once again shocked by her response, he thought he was going to collapse.

"Don't be such a jackass, Frank! The first thing you better do is forgive yourself.

It's not as though you had a deliberate affair with someone. You were set up by a calculating malicious party, who wanted to fulfill her own selfish wishes.

She is going to come out with egg all over her face, no matter what the outcome is. We have been given a problem to deal with. Together, we can make it a beautiful adventure, to which," she said approaching him, "there will be no sequel!" He took her in his arms and held her. They laughed quietly, but the tears still rolled down Frank's cheeks. Could it be possible that this would serve to strengthen their marriage? As though she knew what he was thinking, the sleepy spitfire mumbled, "That's the power to make the wish come true."

Frank never could keep his mouth shut and told Chuck and Wyatt what had happened. Both were an amazing source of support and understanding. Wyatt laughed and said, "That slut is in for a real surprise when she comes face to face with Regina!" Chuck added, "I bet she never pictured the scenario that she has created for herself. She probably figured she would at least shake up your marriage, if not destroy it. We need to have some protection from these stalkers. Visitors shouldn't have a clue where the on call rooms are."

The two older men were as understanding as the younger guys, if not more so. When Frank suggested that he must let Dan know, Lamar advised him, "There's a reason why Regina didn't want you to do that, Frank. This whole thing could be a trap, or, if she is pregnant, it may not even be your baby. I would tell nobody. If you still feel that you must tell Dan, I would certainly leave the other three parents in the dark. This wasn't exactly deliberate on your part, and while it may have been an error, there were also extenuating circumstances that must be weighed into the picture before you go beating yourself to death over it." "That's right, Frank," the army colonel was as kind as any close friend, "this type of nonsense comes with our line of work. I think we need far more security regarding doctors' lounges, on call rooms, and the availability of our personal information. Your Regina is right; you aren't the first or last to have this terrible burden inflicted on you. We'll get through it as a group. Regina is the ace in the hole, so you've already got that."

Lamar couldn't help laughing, "I feel sorry for the stalker! Our women will have her for lunch!"

Dan met them later in the day. He was deeply concerned about the young Solbergs, but he understood Frank's situation and loved him no less for it.

He asked if they might see his daughter, and Leo answered that the gang was all coming to dinner. Frank lowered his head as Dan put his arm around his shoulder, "We're all on your team, son. Considering Regina's reaction, I have a feeling that this is going to be very entertaining. I would not disclose this to your parents or to Elizabeth and Andrea, though. Let's wait and see what happens first, then you and Regina can decide when, if, and how the families should be told."

Dan had always been a good-hearted man, and adored his stepdaughter. Obvious that she was his favorite of the eight collective children that he and Elizabeth had, the middle aged architect had never made any attempt to hide it. He and Regina had always shared a deep love and respect for each other. Dan would oversee this obstacle to the extent that his involvement was needed and wanted.

Chapter Two
Wild Goose Chase

The close friends and Dan were far more concerned about Frank than Regina. She was clearly viewing this despicable act as exactly what it was: a trap. Typically, when anybody posed a threat to someone she loved, Regina was all action, and this scenario was no exception. Around the dinner table that evening, it was Wyatt who spoke first, "Frank, the first thing you need to do is to realize that you have been set up. When someone is half asleep and attacked by an intruder who locks the door behind them, they can hardly be held responsible for their actions; or in your case, reactions."

Everyone agreed, especially Regina, who spoke next. "That's exactly right, and I'm still convinced that Eva will rue her conduct far more than you will, Frank. She has put herself in the position of being charged with trespassing, and sexual assault. Acting on those would be unwise for us, but she doesn't know that. Does she?"

"That's right," Sylvia was more vocal than the group ever recalled her being, "And the threat of a counter-suit will scare the daylights out of her, especially since we have witnesses. She even came to the nursery one day!"

"Let's make a plan," Jeannie was ready for adventure. "What does this woman look like?"

"'She'd have to sneak up on a glass of water,'" Leo answered, clearly recalling Eva Rodriguez. "If she really is pregnant, the extra weight certainly won't enhance her challenged appearance, either," he added bitterly.

Regina and Dan were both laughing, as Regina continued the "plan."

"The first thing we do is run this process server on a wild goose chase."

"In the morning, you have George Easterlin tell Carolee to let the process server know where Regina works," Frances indicated Leo. "We'll take it from there, but everybody must stay in contact with each other."

"Frank, do not answer any unscreened pages," Leo was already glad to be part of the next predicament that found its way to the feisty women in his extended family. The army colonel noticed that Hazel, Dan and Lamar looked disappointed. "You three are on prank standby." The three faces lit up, glad to be included.

The next morning, the process server approached the desk at the outpatient clinic. "I am here to see Frank Solberg, and I will sit right here and wait all day for him if necessary."

"No law against waiting," Frances answered brightly. Paging Frank, she advised him not to come to the clinic today, but to meet Regina for lunch at the Bascom Palmer Eye Institute cafeteria across the street.

Five o'clock came and the process server, intending to locate Mrs. Solberg and follow her home, stood up to leave. Regina, wearing no name tag, went out the back way to the Child Enrichment Center, picked up her baby, and left without a trace of a trail, to the disgruntled stalker's disgust. Eight hours wasted. Calling Eva, he sounded exasperated, "Look, this is ridiculous. Can you give me any ideas or clues?" Eva relayed the information about where Frank Jr. went to daycare. The next day, the process server would roost there.

Spying him bright and early the next morning, Sylvia and Jeannie were instantly hot on his trail and sounded the alarm to Frank, who called Regina. "He's at the childcare center." Hazel brought Frank Jr. to the center, calling him "Seth." Approaching the process server, she asked, "May I help you?"

"I'm waiting for someone," he snarled. Afraid that he would miss something, he sat there all day, missing lunch.

At five o'clock, Hazel picked "Seth" up and brought him to Regina in the clinic.

Eight more hours wasted.

The next day he presented himself again with his lunch. Everyone repeated the same plan, but at five o'clock, the Chairman of the Board of Directors had the infuriated process server escorted out by security with a staunch warning, that if he returned he would be arrested for loitering. Eight additional hours wasted.

The next day, Leo walked into the clinic and approached the short-fused process server, inquiring as to who he was. "I have noticed you around here, and I wondered if you were being helped," Leo had been careful to remove his name- embroidered lab coat before entering the waiting area. "I'm looking for Frank Solberg, Buster, and I'll sit here until I find him."

The Colonel didn't appreciate being called "Buster," but it made the itsy bitsy little white lie easier to tell. "Well slap my dirty rotten mouth for asking," he laughed, jovially smacking the process server so hard on the back that it knocked him off balance. "Listen, Pal, you need to be waiting in Nebraska! From what I understand, Dr. Solberg transferred from here last month. Personal problems," Leo added in a loud whisper.

"Where in Nebraska is he?" The outraged messenger asked through his teeth.

"Let me see if the gals at the desk know," Leo faked sympathy.

Regina had once again removed her name tag before entering the complex, in case the dupe ran into her and had gained knowledge of her description. Looking directly at her, and straining to hold back the laughter, Leo asked loudly, "Say, Samantha, do you know where in Nebraska, Dr. Frank Solberg is?"

"Yes Sir," Samantha" answered sweetly, "He is at Mt. Marriah Hospital in Forest City."

"Is his wife and son with him?" the process server wiped his forehead.

"Are his wife and son with him," Frances corrected, "And no, I believe they may have gone to New York."

Walking briskly out of the clinic, the recharged process server took his new notes, and slammed the door, as the three pranksters laughed uncontrollably.

Calling Eva, he was revived to have gained the new where-
abouts of the runaway suspected father-to-be. Eva was ecstatic!
"You are great! I heard that you were great, and I'm happy that
you are working on my case! I will go with you. They have split
up, and I will have the chance to get my baby's father to take me
in." Arriving in Nebraska and finally locating the hospital, the
couple first had to change the complaint forms to the new location. The local attorney charged $500.00 to file the papers, and
agreed to follow the case if Frank refused to cooperate with a very
pregnant Eva Rodriguez. Sighing, Eva wrote the check and then
paid the process server while she was at it. "Can I get reimbursed
for these fees? She asked her new counsel."

"As long as he is a Timberland County resident, and the prov-
en father of your child, you can," the attorney advised.

From the new lawyer's office they went to the hospital and
began their search. Hours later, needless to say, the travelers were
stricken with anger and resentment upon realizing that they had
been tricked. The nice lady in the reception area referred them to
the Intern/Residency offices two buildings over, where a search
was run for Dr. Frank Solberg, an Intern from JMH in Miami. After
two hours had passed, the lady presented them with the information that Dr. Frank Solberg was still at JMH in Miami, Florida.

The next process server hired by Eva's attorney was a "stop-at-
nothing/go- getter." He hung around JMH relentlessly, which
gave Dan his shot to join in the fun! Leaving his meeting in
Miami, he happened by the clinic with a huge bag of Chinese
takeout. Spotting the process server, he mocked a call from the

desk. The process server seized this clever opportunity to catch Solberg once and for all. "I'll take that, Sir. I'm meeting Frank Solberg as well," he smiled at Dan, reaching for the bag.

"Not so fast, Fella, I need $194.00 for this order before I'm leaving it with anyone."

Peeling off two one hundred dollar bills, the smug messenger said, "Keep the change, good man!"

Chuck stepped into the clinic wearing Frank's coat, and approached the process server, "Looks like you've got our lunch!"

"Indeed I do," the man answered, handing him the bag and the papers while snapping his picture.

"Hey, thanks," said Chuck, passing the bag to Regina, who passed it to Frances, who took it to the lounge where they would all be enjoying the contents.

Acting surprised to see the papers, Chuck laughed and said, "I'm not Frank Solberg, and you've just been hoodwinked. Thanks for the lunch, though."

The second process server stared in horror as the tow truck backed out of the parking garage with his classic Mustang in tow. Lamar grinned as he walked past him with the empty roll of contact paper that had been applied to his windshield, requesting that he observe patient parking signs in the future.

As the group passed around the fortune cookies, Dan smiled at his daughter. She was adorable, and there was no arguing the fact that she was enjoying every minute of this "wild goose chase."

Reviewing the picture, Eva was livid. "You idiot, that's not even Frank! You are fired."

"That's fine with me, lady; you are out your money, as I'm already short $200.00 bucks for Chinese food and $125.00 for my car."

"Who pays $200.00 dollars for Chinese food, you senseless boob?" She screamed.

The second process server, who was already disgusted, yelled over his shoulder, "Maybe you should find a donor who isn't married next time, lady," as he walked to the corner to wait for his cab.

The third deliveryman was from the Sherriff's department, which only intrigued the girls more. The officer could already see that Frances was not impressed by his badge, but asked anyway, "Madame, would you be so kind as to locate Dr. Frank Solberg for me? I have official papers to hand him."

"That's your job, Sonny, and good luck."

The officer had no personal gain in the endeavor and had been a patient himself in this clinic. "Well, can I have a sandwich anyway?"

Regina laughed and prepared a to- go plate for the appealing turncoat.

"Thanks," he said leaving, "If you see Dr. Solberg would you give him this number?"

"Sure we will," Frances answered, holding up the trash can, "Just leave it right in here." Setting the paper in the circular file, the officer left, taking a bite of his turkey salad sandwich as he walked out of the clinic.

Weeks passed with no further attempts to serve Frank. Finally, Sylvia went to the door of the nursery to see a huge Eva

Rodriguez sneering at her. "I will need an op-lication for my son to go here. I understand that this center is for the doctors who work at JMH, and this baby," she rubbed her stomach lovingly, "is Frank Solberg the third!"

Sylvia wanted to slap her across the face, but restrained herself. "You are not entitled to place your baby here unless you are house staff yourself, and even then, only if we were to accept your 'op-lication,' she mocked uncharacteristically.

"I'll just sit here and wait for his brother's parents, then," the fat obnoxious lady grinned.

"Fine, you can be escorted off the premises just as easily as your moronic process server was," Sylvia was riddled with anger, "I just hope they don't drop you off at Sea World by mistake."

Eva waddled out of the childcare area, foolishly hoping to have Sylvia fired.

Relaying the incident to Regina, Sylvia reassured her, "There is no way we would be obligated to enroll her child. Additionally, the Court won't grant the name to wit, without proof that the child is Frank's or if she is found guilty of trying to jeopardize Frank Jr., as he and you are both injured parties."

Regina was unruffled, as usual. "She is also not taking into consideration the fact that we have perfect grounds to file for custody of this baby, and collect child support from her."

In a final attempt to serve Frank, yet another party stalked the cafeteria at the hospital. The Sheriff's department had informed Eva that they were doing their best, but could not find him without a physical address. Eva and her lawyer hired yet another man to serve Frank with papers announcing the paternity suit. Picking up sandwiches for herself and Sylvia, and noting the gentleman on watch by the door, Jeannie called Frank. "I don't know if this guy is a process server or not, but he has paperwork and is certainly checking out every name that he sees on a white coat." Frank and Chuck were grabbing lunch there and Wyatt had come to join them.

Hanging up the phone, they saw the man at the door combing the crowd. Wyatt quickly changed coats with Frank, and walked up to the man. The process server immediately called the name, "Frank Solberg."

Wyatt looked up but did not answer. The process server thrust papers in his hand and snapped the picture. Smiling and nodding his head in satisfaction, he left the cafeteria, and Wyatt made no attempt to correct him.

He delivered the photo to Eva, who was nearly outraged. "Look closely at the man in the picture! Look at him, Fool. He is a black man, not a six-foot blonde as I told you Frank Solberg is!" Her voice shook with anger.

"He was wearing a coat that said 'Dr. Frank Solberg' on it," the disappointed process server appealed.

"I don't care if he was wearing a toga, you should have been more careful. I demand my money back."

"You can demand until the cows come home, lady. That's why our agency gets paid up front and in cash."

Eva was frustrated and angry. Her plans continued to fail and her dream of being a doctor's wife evaporated in the realization that Frank Solberg had no obvious intention of leaving his wife. Her family was infuriated with her, as they were strict Catholics, and knew that the father of her baby was married to someone else. Her mother, Mercedes Rodriguez, tearfully begged her to stop chasing Frank and raise the illegitimate child on her own. "It's not right to interrupt his marriage, Eva; you knew very well that he was taken."

Finally Eva went into labor and presented herself at Trinity Hospital for delivery. Although the ultrasound technicians had been unable to determine the sex of the baby, they assumed it would be a boy, by the sheer size of the bones. Eva was pleased by the fact that she would be able to finally inflict well-earned punishment on her child's father. Two sons named Frank would surely do it, and she would enjoy seeing him suffer the consequences over many years to come. Struggling through the last push, she was surprised to see what a large baby she had delivered! "Whoa, ten pounds, eleven ounces and twenty-six inches long," the doctor said. Smiling, Eva responded, "He's a big boy, like his Daddy."

"Like her Daddy," the obstetrician corrected. If the baby was in fact Frank's, taking after his mother, Dorothy Solberg, she had an extra large head and long, heavy bones. Eva tried to name her Gabriella Solberg, but was quickly informed that until the father signed admission of paternity or was determined by a court to be the father, the baby would bear the last name Rodriguez.

Eva loved her baby, even though she was disappointed that the gender plot had also failed her. While she had no other child to compare her to, the infant seemed much bigger than she had expected even a boy to be. Learning that Gabriella was the largest infant in the nursery, her curiosity about Frank Jr.'s appearance multiplied. She sent a letter to JMH to inform Frank that the baby had arrived, and that she would pursue him at any expense.

Regina retrieved the letter and made no comment. All babies were beautiful to her, and she was happy that this little girl's mother seemed glad about her arrival. Supposing that it was certainly time to take the next step, she shared the letter with Frances.

Dear Frank,

Our daughter, Gabriella, was born last week. Enclosed is her picture. You are very good at avoiding me, but I will find you and force you to shoulder your responsibility in the care of our baby. She is beautiful, and I would like for you to meet her and to be a part of her life. (I don't wish to create trouble for your wife). I love my baby and I want the very best for her as you should also. I am willing to work out finances and I will let you see her at my house only. Please do not make this difficult for any of us. I would not tell your wife if I were you.

I can be reached by letter or personal visit at the above address. Modern couples work things like this out all the time. You can still be her father and Frank Jr.'s too.

Love,
Eva

Reading the letter, Frances shook with laughter. Tears rolling down her cheeks, she could hardly get the words out, "Look at the picture of this moose! That's just what the outcome ought to be. If this child is Frank's, the mother has been graced with a baby Goliath! The kid will probably drive herself home from the hospital."

Frances took the photo to the childcare center where Leo was having a visit with Frank Jr. "Damn!" he commented, "I see no sign of Frank Solberg in that photo, and I'm glad that she is stripped of any opportunity to duplicate Frank Jr.'s name. So it's a girl, huh? She's huge!"

"They better get an attorney lined up in case she does pursue this chase. He definitely needs a three tier DNA test to establish the likelihood of paternity," Sylvia advised, also laughing at the picture.

Since the baby's blood type was O+ while Eva and Frank were both A-, Frank began to relax a little, but Regina realized immediately that this was entirely possible. She was O+ herself, and so was Frank Jr! Since babies get two genes for blood types – one from each of the parents, if Eva was AO, and Frank was AO, each could have contributed the factors that would account for another O+ child. The child also resembled Dorothy and Adam, which oddly amused her. They made an appointment with Sylvia's friend, Attorney Eleanor Greenberg, on Coral Way.

Regina was stronger than ever, but appeared to have no feelings of resentment or malice. She liked Eleanor as soon as they met and appreciated her candor. The attorney immediately acquired the complaint that was never successfully served, and sent papers ordering a paternity test, and demanding that Eva present herself and her baby for cooperation with the same. Eva's lawyer, Eduardo Suarez, was the recipient of the order. According to Eleanor, Eva did have the right to use the name to wit, "Solberg," if paternity was established. Frank was upset by this, but Regina seemed unthreatened. "So what? The child is a female and won't be able to carry the name on. Just thank God that she didn't have a son. Let's wait and see what happens, honey," Regina suggested.

Eleanor had a deep admiration for Regina and told Frank so. She reassured Frank that he had many options on his side. First of all, he could counter-sue for trespassing and sexual assault. He could also torture this Cuban mother by going for custody, as she seemed pretty attached to her infant daughter. At the very least, he would be allowed generous visitation, and at his own place, not Eva's. "Cuban mothers hate to have their babies out of their sight. They worry about them and she would definitely be court ordered to stay clear from the place of visitation."

Regina was not necessarily relieved at the ability to use an innocent baby to get revenge on the mother, regardless of what had transpired in the past. It fell under the category of *un-necessary roughness*, in every sense of the definition.

As a dedicated lay-missionary, she lived by a code and did not intend to make an exception in this case.

Dan was in Miami at a meeting, and Frank was on call. Hazel and Leo stayed with Frank Jr. while Regain met her stepfather for dinner. "Wow!" Dan reacted to the photo. "If that baby is

Frank's, she sure doesn't look it." He and Regina looked at each other and laughed. "Well, at least her little plan to name her baby Frank won't work," Regina sighed. Dan looked thoughtfully at her, "Honey, I'm sure this is heartbreaking, and I admire you for standing by Frank."

"My mother and the Solbergs will be a problem if the baby tests out as Frank's."

"I'll handle your mother, and the Solbergs won't have a prayer against Frances!" Dan laughed, as his blue eyes twinkled. Regina seemed to be holding up very well, and was determined that this was not going to destroy her husband. "I'm concerned about Frank, Dad. He will still be devastated if Gabriella is in fact his daughter." Dan noticed that Regina called the baby by her name, and that there was no anger in her voice. He looked into her dark brown eyes, filled with concern. "Look, honey, Frank has a full support system and we will decide how to tell the families if there is a need. There are plenty of ways of doing it without giving out details. The fact that you are reacting as you are, will be the biggest curve. Keep me informed," he added.

Regina looked up and smiled, "I love you, Dad," she stood up and went over to him. He hugged her and whispered, "I love you too, Pandemonium, and so does God. You know, He doesn't call on just anyone to deal with tasks like this."

Chapter Three
"The Unrightable Wrong"

A gentle rain tapped softly against the glass doors in the master bedroom as the intercom from the nursery added to the symphony. Frank Jr. was laughing and making his usual noises to acknowledge his "friends" in the big top décor of his room. It was a rare Saturday when everyone in the group was off and would be going out to dinner together; and Regina lay quietly, counting her blessings. Frank was stirring next to her, as little Monique surfaced from under the covers and stretched in satisfaction, ready to start another day.

The DNA testing had been started, and everyone was anxiously awaiting the results. Regina prayed that whatever the outcome was, she and Frank would be given the strength they needed to see Eva's baby and Frank Jr. through the upcoming proceedings. The three adults would each have to settle their own feelings and hopefully end up finding peace in their hearts. Frank reached over and pulled her to him. "I had a thought," he said, "Let's take Frank Jr. to the Crandon Park Zoo. Then after his nap, we can get ready to go over to Frances and Lamar's and we'll all leave for dinner together." Regina moved closer and whispered, "That sounds wonderful. You are such an outstanding father, and I don't think this rain will last, if it's even still raining now. "

Listening to his little son laugh and jabber, Frank was taken back. "What if that baby is mine, Regina? What will our plot be?"

"Her name is Gabriella, Frank," Regina was always able to laugh, "and if she is yours, she is also your son's half sister, and mine too in a sense. We're all in this together, and I'm confident that we'll be guided to act in everyone's best interest."

"Well I want Eva to pay and pay big for what she tried to do to our marriage."

"Getting even with Eva is a natural desire, and believe me, I've thought of some great ways to do it myself, but it isn't our place to judge anyone. Eva already has paid big for her attempts. The process servers alone," Regina laughed and continued, "were enough to break the bank! Adding to her dismay, our marriage is stronger because of the challenge that we were faced with, and will overcome."

"Will we go for custody, Pollyanna? Eleanor said we have an excellent chance."

"If necessary; I think that it's far too early to make those decisions, since we are not even sure that she's yours."

"Okay, so what if she is? What if she is mine?"

"Then I think you'd have to assess the entire situation and decide how you want to proceed. Do you want to be part of this baby's life or not? If you do, to what extent do you want to be involved?"

"Are you willing to be involved in her life, Regina? Are you willing to allow me to be?"

"Involvement in her life would be based on how you feel about her. Setting aside your feelings for her mother, would you feel any moral obligation to the child?"

"I owe her nothing!" Frank was angry. "I'll give her nothing."

"You owe her mother nothing. If paternity is established, you'll be required to give her child support and medical expenses, but probably nothing more."

"Eva is a cold, calculating animal, Regina. I want nothing to do with her."

"You would never be required to have anything to do with her, as far as the law is concerned."

"You read her sick letter. 'She will let me see her at her house only?' Who does this woman think she is? She is not in a position to give orders."

"No, Frank, she's not, but she'll try to give orders until she is told by the court that she has no authority to continue to do so. Eva is definitely in for a rude awakening, and believe me, she will get it, without any help from us."

Regina didn't relish dealing with Eva anymore than her husband did, but feeding into mounting hatred would only work against them, and she wanted to avoid any un-necessary obstacles. "We must understand that we will have contact with her if you have custody or even visitation, and we must be able and willing to let go of some of the anger that we have for her in order to successfully act in the children's best interest."

The telephone rang and Eleanor Greenberg apologized to Frank for calling on a Saturday. "I just wanted to share this happy moment with you. I am here in my office catching up, and I just opened a letter from Eduardo Suarez. The tramp of a woman that trapped you is apparently being educated about your rights, rather than just your obligations. As I suspected, she is very bonded to the baby. She cried when they told her they had to draw Gabriella's blood for the test, and attempted to withdraw her complaint and drop the matter. The lab technician advised her that there was a court order in effect and that she had better cooperate. The report goes on to say that the mother broke down as they put the needle in her baby's arm. Her lawyer was foolish to tip his hand with this letter, as it just confirms the attachment we strongly suspected. If her child is yours, she will drop dead when she gets served with custody papers!"

Dear Ms. Greenberg,

As we await the results of the paternity testing, I am sure that you have made Frank aware that he will be ordered pay child support. My client wants Gabriella to have <u>no visitation with her father and especially no contact with Mrs. Solberg.</u>

She will make concessions to keep child support reasonable as long as he relinquishes the right to see the child. I have reassured her that we can probably arrange that. Please advise me as soon as you get Dr. Solberg's consent to this, so that we may reduce it to writing.

Sincerely,
Eduardo Suarez

"That's great news, Eleanor!" Frank was smiling from ear to ear. "When will we have the results back?"

"Not until next week, but I love the way they are already making offers about child support."

"Well, keep me posted, and it's great to know that we have her over a barrel!"

Relaying the conversation to Regina, Frank seemed relieved.

"It certainly serves as ammunition for our side." Regina was surprised at the opposition's carelessness in relaying the information, and by the amusement that their own counsel found in a mother who was hysterically trying to protect her baby.

Frank Jr. rode in a giraffe stroller at the zoo and hollered out gleefully to every animal they passed. He was a beautiful child and always seemed to be happy. His bright blue eyes and light blonde hair were the only distinctions between his baby pictures and those of his father. Regina bought him a chocolate ice cream cone, which wound up all over him as he happily ate it. Frank snapped picture after picture of him before Regina cleaned him up. Hot and tired, the little spectator clutched his stuffed aardvark from the gift shop as he rode the elevator up to the apartment. After a welcome bath, Frank Jr. drifted off to his long nap.

Regina and Frank were on the patio talking when Chuck and Jeannie stopped in.

"Any news about the blood tests?" Chuck seemed more anxious than Frank.

"No, but good news from Eleanor Greenberg," Frank relayed his conversation of earlier that morning. Jeannie and Regina left Frank Jr. sleeping in his crib, put Charlie in his stroller, and went to Diamonds. Jeannie was looking for arts and craft supplies for the center, and that store was the best supplier in Miami.

Shortly after they started shopping, they were distracted by a loud scream two aisles over, and went to investigate the problem. "Help my baby, Oh, please help my baby," the mother cried frantically. Her baby was in a stroller and was turning blue and gasping. Regina noticed the base of the pacifier missing the nipple and acted immediately. Grabbing the child, she placed her in the proper position and with one efficient thrust, dislodged the nipple, causing a loud cry. She handed the child back to the mother, while customers applauded, as the EMT arrived asking for details. Regina explained that the baby's airway was blocked but that the child had never lost consciousness. Jeannie made a note to have all childcare teachers updated on their CPR/First Aide classes, and held Charlie as though he was the one that was just rescued.

Arriving home, Charlie and Frank played happily on a blanket, while Monique and Dodger, both of the babies' dogs, pirated any of their unsupervised toys. The group was going to the Doral

Buffet tonight, and the babies' restaurant bags were being carefully stocked by their mothers. Sylvia telephoned to borrow Regina's 30-cup coffee maker for a church function the next day. "Sure, I'll stick it in the car, and give it to you after dinner," Regina promised, taking the pot from the pantry.

Dinner was a blast as usual, and the babies were full of the dickens. They played and laughed in their high chairs, since Grandpa Leo got the bright idea to give them each a small condiment cup of chipped ice! Seeing Regina return to the buffet, he joined her. "Well, any news yet?" the Colonel asked.

"Not yet, but we should know next week."

"You two seem to be holding up well. Am I right?"

"Right as rain," the redhead grinned.

"'A penny for your thoughts', then."

"Well, I figure that what's done is done. There is really not that much to do until we know whether the baby is Frank's or not. I am very glad that she didn't have a boy, though! If Gabriella is his, he will hopefully assess what obligations he has to her, and how he intends to fulfill them. I just have to back him, so my part's relatively easy."

"Walk over to the fountain with me, for a minute, will you?"

"Of course," Regina wondered if he had some news for her.

Leo reached in his pocket and retrieved a velvet box. He handed it to Regina, and walked away. Leo couldn't allow himself to cry, especially in front of two young residents. Opening the box she found a little card that said: *To the strongest soldier I have ever met.* The medal was Leo's and it was a brilliant gold eagle suspended from a dark blue ribbon, supporting the sign Valor.

The United States Army Medal of Honor
The Nation's Highest Medal for Valor
I will Always Place the Mission First.
I will Never Accept Defeat.
I will Never Quit.
I will Never Leave a Fallen Comrade.

Regina went into the ladies room, followed by Frances. She hugged her second mother as she wept. "Someday, this will be handed down to Frank Jr.," his mother shared her intentions for the beloved gift.

The week started off with a bang as the clinic patients poured in. Frank appeared to be shaken, as he and Chuck came in for lunch. Handing Regina the test results, she read – *high probability*. Frank motioned for her to pass them to Frances. "Okay," she responded, "You two better contact your lawyer."

Eleanor Greenberg filed the papers for custody, which started World War Three.

Eva wept bitterly and begged Eduardo Suarez to cancel the whole thing.

"We can't, Eva, it's too late. There is confirmed evidence that Frank is the baby's father."

"But we instigated everything and we have the right to cancel it," the panicked mother screamed.

Eva's mother, Mercedes Rodriguez, was even more frantic than she was, "Why would Mrs. Solberg even want custody of Eva's baby? She's mental and she could kill Gabriella because this baby is a symbol of her husband's infidelity! That is the plan! She'll murder her and make it look like an accident. Mrs. Solberg is not going to be anywhere near this baby," her small body was shaking as she shouted at the top of her lungs.

"Look, ladies," Eduardo tried to explain sympathetically, "I don't think Dr. Solberg can get automatic custody. You are a good mother, Eva, and we will fight it every step of the way; BUT, he will definitely be awarded generous visitation and Mrs. Solberg will be included in that whether you like it or not."

"Fine," Eva snubbed, "but they will see Gabriella at our house where we can be sure that she is safe."

Shaking his head, Eduardo answered, "You will not be allowed to dictate where they see the baby, Eva."

"Then it will be in a park and we will stay far away, AND for three or four hours," Mercedes wept as she hollered in Spanish.

"It will be what the judge orders," the lawyer answered calmly.

"We can tell the judge that Mrs. Solberg plans to kill my baby, and get supervised visits through the court," Eva yelled, hoping that she was right.

"There is no evidence that Mrs. Solberg would harm the baby, ladies, and the judge will not appreciate a slanderous allegation like that. If you interfere with visitation, it will only serve to make their custody battle stronger."

Now both weeping uncontrollably, Eva and her mother held each other.

Eva shook her head desperately, "Mama, I should have listened to you. Now, God will punish me."

"Okay, I have an idea that will make Frank think twice about custody, and it will also show the judge how bonded to you the baby is," Eduardo encouraged.

"What?" Eva asked, exhausted from crying since the papers arrived the day before.

"You know how Gabriella screams when strangers pick her up? Well, when we meet them in the court room, I will snatch her from your arms and force her into Frank's."

"I don't want to traumatize her, Eduardo, but if you think it will help our case, I will do it. Could that stop visitation?"

"No. It won't stop visitation. Remember that she also has a sibling, and her older brother has a right to know her as well."

"I want him in court when we go. I want Frank Jr. there too," Eva sobbed again bitterly.

"We cannot order the Solbergs to bring their son to court with them, Eva."

Regina tucked her baby into his crib and kissed him. Frank Jr. smiled at her as the soft nursery music played. Joining her husband in the living room, she read the Notice of Hearing that he handed her. "This is great!" Frank laughed, "That scumbag will be in a rage when she reads this. Eleanor said that she probably never imagined this scenario."

Regina set the papers on the coffee table. "I know that you are very angry with Eva, and so am I. Custody is a tremendous step, Frank, and we want to be sure that is not out of spite that we choose this path."

"What do you mean? Do you not want custody?"

"I mean that we love our baby, Frank, and we should consider the possibility that Eva loves hers too."

"She brought this all on herself!"

"Perhaps, but we should see how everything goes and be open to make adjustments if we need to."

"Listen, if you don't want Gabriella here, then you should say so."

"It's not that I don't want Gabriella here, sweetheart. She'll be here for visitation even if you are not granted custody will she not?"

Frank was momentarily silent. He hadn't even thought about that. Finally he answered, "Yeah, I guess she will."

"Sometimes attorneys can get so caught up with winning that their efforts cause everybody involved to lose."

"Eleanor said that we have the power to bring Eva to justice."

"You also have the power to 'right the un-rightable wrong,' and it comes from a much higher place than Coral Way. If someone had threatened to remove Frank Jr. from our home, would we not have suffered terribly already? Do we really want that on our consciences? Are we even considering the pain and worry that Eva will be forced to endure with visitation alone?"

"She brought it all on herself, Regina, she deserves to suffer!"

"I understand exactly how you feel, Frank, and I feel the same way, but we don't necessarily have to compound the problem. We must also consider the feelings that your daughter will have down the line. Let's see what happens in court."

Frank walked over to Regina and pulled her to her feet so he could embrace her.

"I have deep feelings of hatred for Eva, Regina. They will never resolve. She tried to destroy our marriage."

"She tried. Period. She also failed miserably. She, in fact, has been a force that strengthened our marriage," Regina whispered softly.

Frank looked into the dark brown eyes and saw no ill feelings. He quietly asked for her position. Smiling, Regina answered, "Do you remember our wedding song, Frank? *Bridge Over Troubled Water.* Like the song says, 'I'm on your side!'"

"Then what about custody?"

"I would ask you to be very honest with yourself and with me in answering why you want custody. If you were worried that the baby was being harmed or neglected in some way, there would certainly be just cause to remove her from her mother. If we want custody to spite or hurt her mother, then we should ask ourselves if that course of action is fair to any of us."

"I hate her mother, Regina, and I want to see her wretch in pain."

"You are a physician, Frank, and an excellent one. Please re-evaluate your intentions keeping that in mind."

Chapter Four
We Meet Again

Stepping off the elevator at the courthouse, Eva immediately recognized the lady who had rescued her baby in Diamonds weeks ago. Similarly, Regina recognized Gabriella at once, but she didn't recall seeing the angry, bitter, expression that she noticed now on Eva's face.

Eva was of average height but she had a very heavy frame. Her over-processed, copper-toned hair was parted on the side and hung just above her shoulders in rigid, brittle strips. One of her angry brown eyes wandered, and she had a very poor complexion. She glared at Regina with a hatred that was chilling to observe.

Gabriella was in her arms and appeared to be oblivious to any ill feelings among the parties. She was an adorable, chubby baby with a typically deep Cuban skin tone. Straight, black hair framed her little round face as the large, dark-brown, almond shaped eyes took in her surroundings. Regina noticed the baby's serious expression and her heart went out to her.

As previously planned, Eduardo Suarez grabbed Gabriella from Eva and thrust her into Frank's arms. The baby did not cry, but turned her attention to Regina's necklace. Passing the baby to Regina, Frank noticed the look of sheer panic on the Plaintiff's face, and he thoroughly enjoyed it. Eleanor nodded and winked at Frank, goading him on, as she saw tears of anger well up in Eva's eyes. Fighting the temptation to join them, Regina spoke, "She's a very content, bright little girl, isn't she?" Eva lunged at Frank, demanding her baby back. Regina, quietly returning the baby to her mother, reminded both parents that they were all in a court of law, which was being called to order; as the their attorneys stood in silence.

"Please rise," the bailiff announced, "Court is now in session, the Honorable Marcus Leonard presiding."

Judge Leonard was a middle-aged man with a pleasant but no-nonsense expression. During this initial hearing, both Eva and Mercedes were corrected for their out-of-control conduct, and warned that they would be held in contempt for the repeated behavior in the future. The judge ordered Frank to pay child support of $100.00 per month and a visitation schedule to start immediately, consisting of two overnight visits weekly and every other full weekend. Eva shrieked and started screaming before being escorted out of the courtroom. Mercedes Rodriguez raised her hand crying loudly, "Jour Honor, please, may I be heard?" The judge sat back in his chair and addressed the attorneys. "Mr. Suarez, I would suggest that you arrange for counseling for your client and her mother. They both have some serious adjustments to make and the sooner they resign themselves to that fact, the better for all concerned." Standing, the judge repeated himself, "Court is adjourned."

Frank and Regina left the courtroom with Eleanor. Walking out to the elevator, the threesome passed Eva and Mercedes holding the baby and each other, crying as though Frank had already been awarded custody. Eleanor was delighted with the outcome of the first hearing, and told the Solbergs so. "I have no doubt that you two will get custody. Those two women are hysterical and the judge already sees that. When you go to pick Gabriella up Tuesday night, I want you to take notes and keep a careful record of anything we may be able to use against them." The Solbergs shook hands with their counsel and thanked her before reporting to work.

Regina went straight to the Child Enrichment Center to see her own little boy. He and Charlie were playing happily with colored toys that stacked. Frank Jr. rushed over to his mother as though he was being pulled on a string and reached up to her, laughing. Regina picked him up and hugged him tight. "Father," she whispered, "We have to do better than this. What happened in the courtroom today was not a victory at all. Please touch our hearts and give us what we need to extend the fairytale setting we stand in now, to the cold and heartless lobby that we just left. After all, My Abba, they don't call me Pollyanna for nothing!"

Sylvia noticed the tears in Regina's eyes and asked how the hearing went. "Well Regina, she's getting exactly what she deserved. I hope you and Frank do get custody; then you'll be rid of that louse forever," Sylvia responded mercilessly.

"Hardly," Regina answered calmly. "Eva would certainly be

granted visitation, which will ascertain continuous contact with her and Mercedes. This woman wanted a husband and a baby. She went about it in a despicable way, and there's no question about that, but we don't need any more questions. We need answers."

Jeannie had just come into the room with Frances. "I saw Frank on his way through the clinic," Frances started, but noticing the tears in Regina's eyes, she paused. "He was whistling, so I assumed that everything went well."

Regina shared the courtroom experience with Jeannie and Frances. Indicating Sylvia, she added, "I can understand why you left the courthouse. It is a terrible place to be."

"Yeah, but you guys won!" Jeannie looked confused.

"We may have succeeded in devastating Eva and her mother, who is another injured party, but we really didn't win anything."

Frances looked thoughtful, "Sweetheart, she tried relentlessly to destroy your marriage, and still would, if she was given the chance."

"Oh, I know she did, and she's no piece of cake to deal with. Jeannie, do you remember the woman in Diamonds with the choking baby?"

"I sure do, I'll never forget that day."

"Do you remember what she looked like?"

"She was ugly; but she was so grateful to have her baby rescued, that she almost looked attractive."

"Well, I introduce Eva and Gabriella."

"No!"

"Yes, except in the courtroom, Eva had a horrible, hateful stare about her, and the baby's grandmother was riddled with anger as well."

"Did she recognize you, Regina?" Sylvia rejoined the conversation, as Frances just listened.

"I'm not sure, but I think so."

"So she's an ungrateful tramp!" Regina's second mother wasn't giving an inch.

Regina put her arms around Frances. "Perhaps, but a very frightened and bitter tramp."

"I remember when she came here," Sylvia recollected. "She made my skin crawl. She's evil, Regina, and I hope she does lose her baby."

"Well, let's see what happens Tuesday night," Regina said, praying silently again, "Uh, Abba, I need some backup down here. I assume they just need time to vent and enjoy the 'victory,' but please escort my extended family women back to Your side with me."

Frances was watching her "adopted" daughter with both admiration and intense worry. "Don't tell me she is going to attempt a civil relationship with this tramp, Father. Please enlighten her!"

"What about the Solbergs and your family, Regina?" Jeannie was as worried as Frances.

"Well my Dad has another meeting here late this afternoon, and we will figure those details out at that time."

"What time are we all supposed to be at my house for dinner, Pollyanna?" Frances was already moving over toward the Right side.

"I have a huge pan of lasagna, since it's a work night." Regina was grateful for the support that, moments ago, she was afraid she had lost.

"Okay, everyone can meet at my place." Frances was taking notes.

"I'll bring a big Cesar salad and some garlic bread," Jeannie was in.

"I'll handle desert," Sylvia was also ready to help solve the problem.

"I'll call Hazel from the clinic," Frances took Frank Jr. from Regina, gave him some juice, and set him back down with Charlie.

"We better get back to work, before the Colonel misses us," Regina laughed as she turned around and found him standing right behind her!

Leo hugged his stolen daughter, "So, I hear things went well in court today."

"Yeah well, you heard wrong, Colonel. Pollyanna is concerned about the level of hatred she encountered today," Frances corrected.

"These things are never simple, but at least the judge ruled in Frank's favor," Leo put his arm around Regina's shoulder. "We'll work out the small stuff later."

Clinic was a welcome distraction from the torment of the morning, and Regina was delighted to see some smiling faces. The humming cast saws and chattering technicians rolling new plaster were therapy for the missionary, who appeared carefree, but was deep in thought.

Dan came down for dinner and the group was delighted to see him. "So the first visit is Tuesday?" he asked.

"Yes, we are to pick Gabriella up at 6:00 pm and keep her until 7:00 pm Wednesday. Then the same on Thursday." Frank seemed to be genuinely happy to be spending time with his daughter.

"Are there any risks involved?" Dan was concerned.

"I don't think so, Dad," Regina answered, "They are angry and upset, but I don't think they're violent."

"Be careful anyway. You guys are threatening to take the baby away, and they're not likely to greet you warmly." Dan was still not convinced that all would be well.

"Frank, what do you think we should tell the families?" Dan wanted to know where to begin.

"The truth," Frank answered. "It was an extenuating circumstance," he moved to Regina and put his arms around her. "We are choosing to right whatever we can right in spite of those circumstances, and I'm proud to have the kind of wife that I do. Gabriella has the right to a happy, normal life. I hope the families understand that."

"You could tell them that it was a surrogate mother situation that went sour." Jeannie suggested.

"Or tell them nothing at all, and just say you are adopting the baby and allowing the birth mother visitation," Sylvia added.

"Why tell stories when the truth is so righteous?" Wyatt wondered.

"Stories all come out in the wash anyway," Leo confirmed as Dan nodded in agreement.

Lamar spoke quietly, "If Frank was going to hide anything, he would have been better to just pay monthly child support and have no contact with, what's her name again?"

"Gabriella," Regina laughed.

"Well, Gabriella," Lamar continued, "I give him credit. He cares about that baby and is willing to be a part of her life. Regina and Frank are both outstanding young people, and they have nothing to hide."

"Agreed," Dan picked up his coffee cup.

"I'll call my parents later," Frank dreaded the idea.

Following Frank's phone call, Dorothy Solberg had to be taken to the Emergency Room in West Palm Beach. Raymond just cried and shook his head quietly. When Dan went home and told Elizabeth, she wept and relayed the news to Regina's younger sister, Andrea. Like Dan, Andrea didn't see the need for making a big deal. After all, Regina and Frank had the situation under complete control, and in a most exemplary way. Elizabeth ranted and raved about the "lousy Solbergs," as Dan continued to calm her. Regina's Uncle Bub and Aunt Sis reacted much like Dan and Andrea.

"You see no fault in this?" Elizabeth screamed at her brother.

"We don't know the details, Elizabeth, and I think we should give Regina credit for supporting her husband."

"Well, I will have details!" Elizabeth continued, "I am going to Miami unannounced."

Both sets of parents arrived at the young Solbergs' home the next evening, each unbeknownst to the other in advance. The party was greeted by Regina, who minced no words with any of them. Dan beamed with pride as his stepdaughter announced that Frank was not yet home from the hospital. When attacked by the three other parents, she remained silent, demanding attention before answering. "Let me be the first to inform all of you, since nobody else has, that this is none of your business. Your options are extremely limited, so it won't be a mind-boggling choice for you. You may either welcome your new grand-daughter or you may reject her."

The Solbergs and Elizabeth stared in shock, as Regina continued. "The circumstances that brought Gabriella into this world are both extenuating and classified. Any display of disrespect toward my husband will be met with a joint and ferocious rebuttal, and you can kiss all of us good-bye, until it sinks in that you are not in any position to pass judgment on matters that you cannot possibly understand. Smiling sweetly, she added, "So, who wants to engage?"

The three stood dumbfounded as Dan laughed and entered the nursery to play with Frank Jr. Slowly, the three other parents moved into the living room to take seats. Crying, Dorothy said, "Regina you must understand that we are most certainly going to question our son about this." Calmly but sternly, she answered her mother-in-law. "Forgive me, Mom, as I obviously didn't make myself clear. You will question your son about none of this, as it is none of your business. If it is alright with me, his wife, in case you have forgotten, it will have to be alright with you." Raymond recognized the underlying threat of another feud and backed down instantly. "We will be able to speak with Frank in general though, right honey?"

"Certainly," Regina answered coolly.

Elizabeth had to get into the act, "Wait a minute," she waived her hand, "You're mine," she said angrily.

"And Frank is mine!" Regina stood as solid as a rock.

"You are all in my husband's home, and you will all kindly remember that."

Dan emerged from the nursery pulling Frank Jr. on a ride on train. "All aboard for Shorty's Bar-be-Que when Frank Sr. comes home; or would you prefer to be excluded?" he grinned. Mr. and Mrs. Solberg Sr. waived white napkins and finally Elizabeth followed suit. Everyone suddenly began laughing, still totally shocked at Regina's fiercely protective demeanor, which they knew would not subside.

When Frank walked in the door, all four grandparents were playing with Frank Jr. on the floor. They rose one by one to hug and kiss him, making no reference to the original reason they had visited. The seven all went to Shorty's and enjoyed a great meal, while Frank Jr. entertained the entire group. The only talk about Gabriella was when and if they would meet her. Surprisingly, the parents were relieved to see Frank and Regina in close tact and were consequently forced onto the road to recovery themselves.

Tuesday night came and Eva refused to allow Frank and Regina to pick the baby up. She accused Regina of trying to kill her baby and slammed the door in their faces. Although she was advised by her lawyer to let the baby go with Frank as ordered by the Court, the hysterical Cuban mother refused. The same scene took place on Thursday night, during which time Eva threatened to toss a pan of boiling water into Regina's face if they did not leave her property. Eleanor Greenberg was furious and filed a Motion for Contempt,

"Perhaps if the mother wasn't so disturbed, we could deal with her without the courts, but it will be necessary to force her to comply with the Court Order," the agitated lawyer stated coldly.

"Perhaps if we weren't threatening to take custody, the mother would be less disturbed," Regina answered quietly. Eleanor was livid, "Regina, you are also going to have to get some help dealing with this."

"Not to worry, Eleanor," she answered in a sweet but serious tone, "I have all the Help I need."

"Frank," Eleanor continued, indicating Regina, "she must be willing to fight with us if we want to win. We will rehearse prior to the hearing," the concerned attorney added.

"We will not rehearse for court, Eleanor," Frank smiled sincerely. "The best she can be is what she already is. I pray that the Judge will see that."

"And when you are put on the witness stand all alone, Regina?"

"I am never all alone, Eleanor," Regina answered confidently.

"I understand, dear," the lawyer softened, "but if we want to win custody, we must move in a very aggressive manner."

"We must first decide why we seek custody," Regina spoke sternly. "Are we striving to enrich the child's life, force cooperation from the mother, or ----- ," she hesitated, "are we simply trying to spite Eva or get even in some way? And once we have custody, what effect will this broken woman have on her own baby? What effect will all of the drama have on Frank Jr.?"

"Regina, do you two want custody or not?" Eleanor asked sternly.

"We want what is best for everybody," Frank answered calmly.

Continuing, he added, "If the threat of custody forces Eva to co-operate, then so be it."

"My question," Regina remarked, "Is what would we be dealing with if we backed off the custody threat and reassured the mother and grandmother that we just want to fulfill our moral obligation to this child?"

"Get real, Regina!" Eleanor snapped. "This isn't a fairy tale, you know."

"Not yet, anyway. But the potential is definitely there," Regina smiled.

"Ridiculous!" Eleanor answered, nearly outraged. "Exactly what are you thinking, Regina?"

"I am thinking that we have a heck of a problem to solve with two babies involved. One happens to be ours; the other, only half ours. I am not suggesting a cake walk by any stretch of the imagination, Eleanor. I am simply wondering what would be, if one side could set aside their hatred and try finding a positive solution; as positive as can be expected under the circumstances, of course."

Eleanor removed her glasses and rubbed her eyes. "So if you are put on the stand, what will your position be?"

"The same position as yours, Eleanor; we want visitation and we are entitled to it, but we are willing to assure the mother of the child that no harm will come to her baby and that her fears are without just cause."

"Yes, without any cause!"

"But fears, nonetheless! Any decent mother would have concerns under these circumstances. The child is still a baby," the understanding missionary explained.

Chapter Five

Order in the Court!

The morning of the Contempt Hearing was hectic, to say the least. Hazel came over to play with Frank Jr. and Frances accompanied Frank and Regina to court in case a witness was needed. When the Solberg party arrived, Eva and her mother were already there with the baby.

Eva's attorney looked worried as the court was called to order. Both she and Mercedes were sporting very defiant, angry expressions, and Judge Leonard did not appear to be the least bit entertained by the early return of the parties. He began the Hearing by defining what a Court Order is and by stating that they are to be obeyed. In spite of what their attorney had told them about making slanderous remarks in court, both Eva and Mercedes verbally attacked Regina.

Eva began by telling the Judge that she feared for her baby's life, and had had several nightmares in which her daughter was killed by Regina. Mercedes told the Judge that some American woman called their home and said she was going to hurt the baby. The caller spoke no Spanish, but Mercedes still understood the threat. As Mercedes continued her lies, another thought popped into her mind! "Gabriella doesn't hear English and will be confused in a house where only English is spoken." She tried to point out that the baby needed to be visited at their house where there would be Spanish in the background. Certainly the Judge could not expect Regina to be permitted in their home, so Frank must visit alone. The Judge was clearly irritated, but allowed the Hearing to continue.

Frank testified that he was complying with everything he was ordered to do, and that he felt he had a right to see his baby under the terms set by the Court during the last Hearing. Eleanor called Regina to the stand and questioned her.

"Please tell the Court your position in this matter."

"Your Honor, Counsel, Mrs. Rodriguez, Ms. Rodriguez : My position in this most difficult situation, is by my husband's side. My main interest is the same as his, to ensure the emotional safety and well-being of the two minor parties, who are in fact injured parties, through no fault of their own."

Eleanor continued, "Have you ever hurt anyone, Mrs. Solberg?"

"Not to my knowledge."

"Do you feel anger or resentment toward Gabriella Rodriguez Solberg?"

Looking at the baby, Regina involuntarily broke out in a beautiful smile. "No, Ma'am. None."

Frances slipped Eleanor a note.

Eleanor gratefully continued, "Do you speak Spanish, Mrs. Solberg?"

"Yes."

"Have you ever telephoned the Rodriguez's?"

"No."

"I have no further questions, Your Honor."

Eduardo Suarez was next to question Regina. He couldn't help noticing the peaceful and loving expression on this witness, and was distracted by it.

"Mrs. Solberg, do you understand how the Rodriguez family must feel?"

Eleanor was on her feet in a flash, "Objection. Irrelevant!"

"Sustained, (approved) the Judge ruled."

"I'll rephrase the question, Your Honor," Eduardo continued, though obviously shaken, "Do you think that you can care for Gabriella when she is with your husband without it upsetting you?"

Regina answered softly and with a glow of love that shocked everyone in the room. She was working for Abba and her position was as clear as a flashing name tag would be. "I don't think the issue is whether or not it upsets me, Eva, or Mercedes, but rather what is best for Gabriella in obtaining a relationship with her father, who happens to be married to someone other than her mother."

The Judge sat back in his chair. "Go on, Mrs. Solberg."

"If Eva and Mercedes fear that I could or would hurt the baby, I am willing to set their minds at ease."

"How?" Asked a very interested judge.

"Well, Your Honor, we could schedule a Psychiatric screening to determine if there are any anger issues; if there would be any risk involved."

"And you would be willing to do this, if I ordered the Rodriguez family to pay for it?"

"I would, Your Honor. If the Rodriguez family has no objection, we could probably get it done at Jackson Memorial for free."

"No! screamed Eva, you will pick someone you know!"

The Judge looked at Eva and spoke sternly, as her attorney shook his head in disgust. "Ms. Rodriguez, we are here on a Contempt Motion. If you speak out of turn like that again, the consequences will not be pleasant."

Eva burst into tears, and Regina was filled with sorrow for her. "Dear Father, please help us. All of us," she prayed.

Eduardo continued his questioning, "Mrs. Solberg, do you know the physicians at Jackson Memorial Hospital?"

"Not in the Psychiatric area."

"Why would you be willing to undergo such an evaluation?"

"Because I am a very protective mother myself, and I understand the same in others."

"Would you be willing to allow the Rodriguez family to choose the physician?"

"No. I would be willing to allow the Court to assign one, though."

The Judge smiled and answered. "The Court will assign an examiner and the Plaintiff (Eva) will pay for it as well as all court costs and attorney's fees related to this Hearing. Mrs. Greenberg will schedule the evaluation as soon as possible, followed by another immediate Hearing."

Turning to Regina, the Judge asked, "Do you feel that you would like Ms. Rodriguez to be examined as well?"

"No, Your Honor, I don't request that." Now it was Eleanor who shook her head.

Frances watched Regina and smiled proudly.

While still in court, Eleanor made arrangements to which Eduardo Suarez did not dare to object.

Regina was to see Dr. Arnold Merchant the next morning at 10:00. Eleanor scheduled a deposition (questioning of a witness, in the presence of the attorneys from both sides of a dispute, to obtain testimony for court evidence) to follow, which Eduardo would also be attending, all at Eva's expense.

Dr. Arnold Merchant was extremely impressed by Regina, and stated the same in his report. He likened her stability to a stone wall, and added that she was a delight to examine.

Another hearing was scheduled for the following week. Eva was livid and ordered her attorney to bring the doctor to the hearing as a witness. "I want to know if he ever knew her prior to this examination. You were too stupid to ask that in the Deposition!" Eva added, reading the printed copy.

Dr. Merchant was irritated at the receipt of the subpoena ordering him to court.

The hearing also had to be postponed to accommodate court protocol and the doctor's schedule conflict. Delayed by another week, Eva was falsely delighted.

Frank was furious, "How does she get away with this nonsense? I want her punished, Regina."

"Frank, she will not be successful in court. The Judge is already irritated with her. We are only delayed a week."

The Senior Solbergs were also furious. "We have a right to see our grandchild," Dorothy was edging her way into the act. "Dad and I would like to be at the next hearing." Frank informed them that he absolutely did not want them there, to Regina's delight. Frances was disgusted, "That's just what we need! Now all of a sudden they must see their bastard grandchild! I suppose it's just as well Goliath gets to know her. She'll be the only one who can lift her once she starts walking." Regina laughed and hugged her.

Leo was plenty irritated himself, when he learned that any court dared to suggest that "his" Regina be questioned, much less evaluated! Frances explained that Regina offered the solution to lay aside the fears that the Rodriguez family were inventing. "You don't say," the tall Colonel got taller, "and just where is 'Pollyanna' at the moment?" Frances laughed, "She is with a patient, but I'll tell her that her second father wishes to see her."

"Sir, yes Sir!" Regina walked up to Leo and gave him a big hug. "I have taken the liberty of fixing your lunch," she added, nodding to the plate on the counter.

Fighting a smile as best he could, and with his twinkling eyes giving him away, the Colonel responded. "What's this nonsense about a psychiatric evaluation?"

"I've already had it done, and they find no reason for the Rodriguez family to be concerned," the small-framed missionary smiled.

"Regina Louise, you are never to compromise in this manner again! Understood?!"

"Sir, Yes Sir!" Regina responded in her best soldier mimic.

Leo hugged her so hard that he lifted her off the floor. "Thanks for the lunch," he smiled.

Eva presented herself to the Child Enrichment Center again that afternoon in another effort to get a look at Frank Jr. Sylvia called security immediately and had her escorted off the grounds, while Leo called Eleanor Greenberg to obtain a Restraining Order. "That will look great in court!" Eleanor laughed.

Dorothy was digging for information from her home in West Palm Beach, and was more than a little disgruntled upon being told that no information could be disclosed to her, by both Eleanor Greenberg and the Department of Psychiatry at Jackson Memorial Hospital. Calling Regina, she demanded to know the name of the doctor who had examined her. "I believe that Frank already asked you to stay out of this," she replied coolly.

"We have rights Regina, and I wonder what you did to make our son find satisfaction outside of his marriage!"

Regina closed her eyes and fought back tears of hurt and anger, "Dear Abba," she prayed, "please stay with me. This is getting much harder than I ever thought it would." Taking a slow, deep breath, Regina answered her menacing mother-in-law. "You do not know any details, and as a favor to you and a supreme sacrifice to God, I'm going to pretend that hideous remark never left your lips. I suggest that you refrain from making any similar comments in the future. My patience is not unlimited," Regina quietly hung up the phone.

Eva Rodriguez exhausted herself in a frantic search for information about Regina. "There must be something that could delay visitation and restrict her from seeing Gabriella altogether." Her attorney had advised her to stay away from Jackson Memorial Hospital and control herself, or he would be withdrawing from her case. Mercedes hired a private detective to find any information he could. After a few days, the detective called with the vague information that Regina Solberg was, at one time, involved with the prison in Miami. Eva jumped up and down laughing and shouting victory. The detective had no details, but Eva could call the prison and get them herself. Angry because no one would help her, she went in person and demanded to know if anyone there had ever heard of Regina Solberg. Pouring her heart out to the clerk at the security desk, she was told that Mrs. Solberg was well known there and had been there several times. The hateful Cuban woman literally danced down the front steps. Returning home, she advised her mother of the great news, and was relieved that this woman never got her hands on Gabriella. Mercedes tearfully suggested that they call Eduardo and see if they could not have Frank Jr. removed from Regina based on their newfound information.

"I don't know about that Eva, but I apologize for getting cross with you. If this woman has done time on multiple occasions it may be enough to have supervised visitation or exclude her from visitation altogether," the shocked counsel replied. Eduardo shifted in his chair and continued, "I will search for records so that we are sure of the facts. Eva, do you know Regina's maiden name?"

"No. I don't know how I would find that out."

"Can he file something with the Court?" Mercedes was ecstatic, and yelled into the phone from across the room.

"I could, but why tip our hand? Let's put Mrs. Solberg on the stand and let her hang herself."

"She's also known as Pollyanna," Eva continued. "What kind of a sick name is that?"

"No idea," Eduardo answered. "Where did you hear about that?"

"The detective said the people in the clinic all call her that."

"I wonder if Pollyanna was some infamous criminal or nut case," Eduardo perked up.

"I don't know, but I'll find out!" Eva was on the womp path all over again.

"Okay Eva, now be very careful not to be anywhere near Jackson Memorial,"

Eduardo warned. "We've most likely got them!"

"Do you think I can get more money?" Eva asked hopefully.

"We can probably have Dr. Solberg forced to pay for all of my time, the psychiatric evaluations, and all of the court costs, if we are correct. As far as higher child support - probably not, until he finishes school."

"But my baby is safe from that criminal?" Eva was being goaded by her mother.

"Yes, I think we can definitely put some restraints on the phony missionary."

Eva searched every source she could think of, but found no "Pollyanna." She called the prison once again and sweetly inquired, "I am the concerned mother who called prior regarding a Regina Solberg. Can you tell me if she was ever called Pollyanna while she was there?"

"Oh yes," the clerk answered, "Regina Solberg is also known as Pollyanna."

"How did she come by that name?" Eva was on a roll.

"I have no idea," the puzzled clerk answered.

"What is Mrs. Solberg's maiden name?" Eva sang sweetly.

"I have no idea," the receptionist appeared to be getting annoyed.

"Well it's still a prison name," Eva relayed the information to her mother.

"Thank God you are so smart," Mercedes was in tears. "Gabriella could be dead by now."

"She grabbed Gabriella in Diamonds Department Store that day!" Eva recalled.

"We could have her charged with assault," Mercedes added thoughtfully.

Calling Eduardo again, Eva relayed the new information.

"Why didn't you tell me this before?" The lawyer asked, sounding a bit concerned.

"I never thought of it. I didn't know it was her."

"Did she know you, Eva; and why did she grab Gabriella?"

"Gabriella was choking and I screamed. Regina and her friend from the Child Enrichment Center were shopping and came over to help."

"Well, that won't serve you well in court. That's not assault, Eva, it's a rescue."

"Even if she struck the baby?"

"Did anyone else see this happen?"

"Yes, but I don't know any names. The Emergency Medical Service showed up, so there must be some record."

"The problem is that if this is a good thing, it could muddy the waters, and cause the Court to see Regina in a good light."

"Well I want the records! I have my receipt from Diamonds Department Store which will have the date on it."

"Okay, but be careful who sees the report until I review it myself."

Over-zealous and falsely excited, Eva fished out her receipt and called the EMS.

Quickly and hysterically stating far too much information, she was assured that the report would be generated and forwarded. What Eva did not realize was that the report was being sent to the Court under the case name, which meant that neither attorney would have knowledge of it being in the file.

Eva poured Mercedes and herself cold glasses of soda and they settled into their chairs to have lunch. They had finally won and for the first time since the court battle had started, she could relax. They hated Regina and hated Frank for staying with her. Gabriella was his baby, by trickery or not, and he would either leave his criminal wife and allow Eva to see Frank Jr. with Gabriella, or else. She munched comfortably on her sandwich, and smiled at her mother. Mercedes also found new hope in their findings and wondered if the strain of all of this would shake the Solbergs' marriage and lead to Eva having a happy life with Frank after all.

She drew her rosary beads from her pocket intending to ask God to help with their new plan.

Dorothy paced the living room floor and fumed. She did not appreciate being left out of the excitement or the spotlight. She was also disgusted that, once again, Regina had managed to smear the family name. She looked up at Raymond who started crying, as she called Frank's brother. "I want you and Marge at dinner tonight," she snapped.

"It's our anniversary, Mom," Adam quivered.

"Tough tomatoes!" Dorothy shouted, "You and Marge will be here by six or you'll both be plenty poor and very sorry that you didn't show up."

Hanging up the phone, Dorothy planned dinner. She had every reason to feel confident that the "kids" would be there at six, if not before.

Marge was disgusted, as usual, but had to comply, as Adam did. They were far too indebted to the Solbergs' to even hope to see independence. They had already heard about the baby born out-of-wedlock, and how no details were available, but that Regina was standing behind Frank like a Sherman Tank. Marge was amused to see that this, too, was now being blamed on Regina, and wished the feisty redhead was going to be at dinner with them. Dorothy walked up and down the living room floor as though she was the Queen of the United States. "I want answers! I want support! I want some say-so!" Adam nodded along subserviently while Marge fought the urge to drop to the floor laughing. "Our family has been wounded, and we need representation in court that will support all of us," the large matriarch continued. "Regina is trying to play the saint because she is probably responsible for your brother's stray from the marriage."

Adam, puffed up like a big shot, responded, "You are absolutely right, Mother, and we deserve to be informed about the entire situation. This 'no details' is not about to fly in this family!"

"Oh, sure," Marge snickered, not realizing that she was barely audible.

"Is this in fact my brother's child?" Adam did his best to sound important.

"So the DNA tests show," Raymond answered in disgust. "Regina is not going to upstage us with her little missionary behavior. We are behind Frank too, and we suspect that this is not his fault."

Marge placed her face in her hands to keep from being divorced. She thought to herself, *"I wonder if Regina's genetic material was found in the test!"* Barring a faulty surrogate mother plan, it most certainly was a Frank Solberg botch-up.

Dorothy looked at Marge and after a moment of observation, questioned her. "Marge, what do you think about all of this? You have known Frank for years."

Marge looked up, pulling her face out of shape with her hands to keep from laughing, "Whatever," she responded. "Not good enough," Dorothy hammered, "I want a better answer."

"Well, I don't know the circumstances either," said Marge, "So I would rather not say."

"Comfortable," Dorothy glared, "real nice and comfortable."

"Tough," Marge said to herself, "real nice and tough." She glanced over at her spineless husband, who was still shaking his head as though he had never erred in his life. "Adam, will you call your brother?" Raymond pleaded.

"Certainly, Dad, I can call him now if you like." Dialing the phone, he was already polishing his favorite son medal. "Frank, Adam here. Say, listen, what are the details about this baby? It really is my business, Frank and our parents' as well. What caused you to impregnate another woman? Was it to be a legal deal or what? Yes, I know that Regina is behind you, but we want to know how and why it happened. That's fine, if that's the way you want it, but..... Frank, Frank, hello....." Adam paused, doing his best to look shocked. "He hung up, Mother."

"What did he say before he hung up, you idiot?" An outraged Dorothy broke her glass right in her hand. "He said that the circumstances were extenuating, were between Regina and him, and were none of our damn business!"

"Well we'll see about that!" Raymond yelled. "That girl has caused this family more trouble than I ever would have imagined."

"Oh, sure," Marge caught herself and disguised her comment as a cough. Adam was not budging from his mommy's side, as that was where the money was.

Dinner was served with little conversation, as everyone was deep in thought. The Solbergs' knew better than to push Frank too far, especially by criticizing his wife. Marge envied Regina's position, as she quietly ate her dinner. The Senior Solbergs would never have succeeded in ruining Frank and Regina's anniversary dinner plans, just as Adam would sooner slam his head in a commercial oven than tell his parents to mind their own business.

Chapter Six

Psycho Free Guarantee

Regina and Frank Solberg sat at the breakfast table finishing their orange juice, while Frank Jr. was eating his Cheerios in his high chair. The adorable blue-eyed baby would laugh out loud all through the day. The image of his father, he was the young Solbergs' pride and joy. When Hazel and Frances came to the door, the baby squealed with delight. Hazel would babysit while Frank and Regina returned to court, with Frances accompanying the couple again, in case she was needed.

When they arrived at the courthouse they found Eva and Mercedes sporting smug smiles and gloating as though they knew they were going to win a huge prize. Gabriella was not with them, and Eva walked briskly up to Frank, positioned herself three inches from his face and said through gritted teeth, "What's the matter Doctor Solberg? Are you thinking that the pig you married will ever see our daughter again?" Walking away with a sickening laughter, she rejoined her mother. Regina squeezed her husband's hand.

"Don't let her take you out of control, honey," she whispered. Dr. Arnold Merchant came into the room, addressing neither attorney and appearing to be thoroughly disgusted about his upcoming command performance. Eva and Mercedes talked behind their hands, laughing as they poked each other. Frank looked questioningly at Regina, who was a pillar of strength. Her calm and quiet demeanor helped him relax, while Eleanor asked him what the other side might be up to. Frank responded with a shrug as he glanced over at a smiling Eduardo Suarez, who had just joined his client.

Frances was ready to strangle Eva and her mother, which was nothing new. Suddenly, Warden Robertson came into the courtroom and whispered to Frances, who immediately introduced him to Eleanor Greenberg. Eleanor was practically doubled over with muffled laughter as the court was called to order. The Hearing was started in the usual courtroom protocol, each witness swearing in and being questioned by both counsel and sometimes by the Judge, himself.

On the witness stand, Dr. Merchant was asked by Eduardo Suarez if he had evaluated Regina.

"I did."

"What did your results reflect?" Suarez continued.

"What you read in my report, assuming that you can read, that is."

"Your report, Sir, does not indicate whether or not you knew Mrs. Solberg prior to the evaluation," Eduardo continued, "Did you?"

"If I knew Mrs. Solberg prior to the evaluation, my report

would be non-existent, as I could not have performed the evaluation for court purposes. Are you new, Sir, or just an idiot?" Dr. Merchant was clearly aggravated.

"Dr. Merchant," Judge Leonard reprimanded firmly, "Please answer the questions in a professional manner."

"Apologies, Your Honor," the doctor answered.

Eduardo Suarez continued, "Did you know Mrs. Solberg prior to the evaluation?"

"No, I did not."

"Do you feel that she would be capable of hurting the baby that her husband and Ms. Rodriguez had out of wedlock?"

"I do not feel that Mrs. Solberg is capable of hurting anyone, at anytime, or for any reason."

"Did Mrs. Solberg share her criminal background with you?"

"She did not," the doctor looked surprised.

Eleanor Greenberg addressed the court, "I have no questions, Your Honor."

The hearing went on as a confused judge listened intently.

Regina was called to the stand, and remained calm during the questioning. Her dark brown eyes were shining with warmth and her thick auburn hair hung in soft curls tumbling well past her shoulders. Frank noticed that the Judge watching the witness, appeared to be deep in thought.

"Mrs. Solberg, did you ever touch or grab Gabriella Rodriguez prior to our first hearing?" Suarez began.

"I did, Sir. The baby was choking in Diamonds Department Store, and her mother screamed for help. I was in the store with my friend and we ran over to her to dislodge a nipple that had detached from a pacifier which was blocking the baby's airway."

"Did you have the mother's permission to touch the baby, Mrs. Solberg?"

"I did not. The baby was blue and the mother was frantic. I did not know that the baby was Gabriella at that point in time, or that the mother was Eva."

"But you did grab the baby without the mother's permission?"

"The mother, Eva Rodriguez, was screaming for help. Noting that the baby was turning blue and couldn't breath, I interpreted that as a request to help. The EMS (Emergency Medical Services; an ambulance) was called to the scene as well."

"Just answer yes or no, Mrs. Solberg!" Suarez was annoyed by the witness rattling his plan.

"Yes," Regina smiled, "the EMS was called to the scene, and yes there is a report on file, as they contacted me a few days ago and stated that they would be sending it here." The Judge flipped through the file in front of him, and was now reading the report. He raised his eyebrows and combed the small group of people that sat before him. Eleanor and Frank looked at each other and shrugged their shoulders. Eduardo Suarez shot Eva an angry look, and continued.

"Mrs. Solberg, have you ever been at the prison in the city of Miami?" Eduardo grinned sickly.

"Indeed," Regina answered calmly, "many times."

"For what were you incarcerated?" The lawyer nagged on.

"Oh, I wasn't incarcerated, Sir, I was working there."

There was a loud mumble from the Rodriquez family to which the Judge put an immediate stop.

"In what capacity were you working?" the attorney persisted.

"I suppose Community Outreach would best describe it," Regina smiled.

The Judge suddenly gave a knowing look to the Warden and then to Regina.

"Were you called Pollyanna while you were in prison?" Suarez taunted.

Infuriated, Eleanor was on her feet, "Objection, Mrs. Solberg was not IN prison."

"Sustained," the Judge supported Eleanor.

"I'll rephrase the question, Your Honor," the lawyer was once again shaken.

"Were you called Pollyanna at the prison, Mrs. Solberg?"

"I am not sure."

"Where did you get that name?"

"From the clinic at Bascom Palmer Eye Institute."

Frances whispered to Eleanor, who nodded smiling.

"Why did they call you Pollyanna?"

"I am not certain."

Eleanor followed the questioning, "Mrs. Solberg, have you had CPR and First Aid Training?"

"Yes, both infant and adult."

"When you touched Gabriella in Diamonds Department Store, was it to save her life?"

"Yes."

"Did the mother ask you to help?"

"She was screaming, 'Someone please help my baby.'"

"Did she stop you?"

"Oh, no. Eva was hysterical, as any mother might be in that position."

The Judge smiled, unaccustomed to seeing a witness in Regina's position answer so kindly in the opposition's defense, even though they were launching an attack on her.

Eleanor declined further questioning and called Frances to the stand.

After being sworn in, the questioning began again. "Mrs. Mac Michaels how do you know Mrs. Solberg?"

"I met Mrs. Solberg at the Bascom Palmer Eye Institute here in Miami."

"Did she acquire the name Pollyanna there?"

"Yes, I started it. Pollyanna was an orphan girl who brought joy and sunshine everywhere she went. It is an American story and was a very popular movie."

"Why was Mrs. Solberg named so?"

"Mrs. Solberg came into a depressed clinic and turned the place into a sun shower. Suddenly people were laughing, loving, and caring about each other. Mrs. Solberg spent weeks in the community gaining resources for the poor patients. Her selfless efforts and personal expense provided lunches, snacks, toys, and magazines to the impoverished clinic patients who have long hours of waiting in a crowded area. Now people come in smiling, happy to be there."

"Do you think that Mrs. Solberg would ever hurt a baby?"

"Mrs. Solberg is not capable of hurting anyone; even those who have deeply hurt her." Frances glared at the Rodriguez ladies.

Mr. Suarez declined questioning.

Warden Robertson was called to the stand. After swearing in he smiled at Regina, as Eleanor questioned him.

"Warden Robertson, do you know Mrs. Solberg?"

"I do."

"How do you know her?"

"Mrs. Solberg took our ice-cold prison and, with the help of her husband and other missionaries, created The Musical Cons Marching Band. There has been a constant warmth and love there since she did so, to say nothing of a deep mutual respect. Regina changed every life she came in contact with for the better, including mine. She is also known as 'Can-Do,' by the way."

Mr. Suarez declined questioning.

The Judge ordered a recess, during which Warden Robertson visited Regina and Frank along with Frances and Eleanor Greenberg. "That Rodriguez lunatic came to the prison trying to find out just who Regina Solberg was. She had hired a private detective to find out anything he could to use against you guys in court. When the clerk came to me, I checked the court calendar and decided to show up in case you needed me," he said. Nodding toward Eleanor, he continued, "You know Attorney Melinda Thompson Robertson, I trust?"

"Of course," Eleanor smiled.

"She is my wife, and a good friend of the detective that that nut-bar hired."

Court was back in session and Judge Leonard was all business. He called the two attorneys to approach the bench. He then addressed everyone. "We return to court today to evaluate the previous concerns of Gabriella's safety with her father and his wife. I will have to say that, based on what we have learned today, no threat to the baby exists. Ms. Rodriguez, the report that you had sent over from the EMS clearly states that Mrs. Solberg saved your baby. She could not have done that without touching her. Oddly, this hearing has somehow turned out to be an attempted attack on 'Pollyanna,'" he smiled at Regina, "who stands accused of bringing 'sunshine and love' into multiple dark places, and whom this court finds guilty of the same." The judge removed his glasses and continued.

"I find Eva Rodriguez in Contempt of this Court. Ms. Rodriguez will pay all related attorneys fees, any costs from the evaluation, and the appearance of Dr. Merchant in court today. In addition, she will pay related costs, if any, resulting from the Warden appearing as a witness. While the custody suit continues, visitation is to resume immediately as previously ordered. Any violation or deviation from this Court Order will result in the removal of Gabriella Rodriguez from her mother's custody to her father's primary residential responsibility until permanent custody arrangements are determined. Mrs. Greenberg, please prepare the order."

The Rodriguez women left the courtroom quickly and in tears. They did not even address their lawyer, who struck an awkward pose while leafing through a file.

Frances and Warden Robertson hugged each other and then Frank and Regina. Eleanor was glowing, obviously enjoying their success. "You know, in all of the years I have practiced, I have never seen a witness remain so calm and so beautiful, while being falsely accused of such horrible things. Regina, you sat there all alone on that scary stand without a shred of anger or spite in your eyes."

"I wasn't alone, so there was no need to be frightened or angry. What they were saying wasn't true and would only serve to make them look foolish, so there was no need for spite either," the Defendant's wife smiled. Frank grabbed Regina and hugged her. Frances smiled at the young couple and closed her eyes in prayer, "Thanks so much for being here, Father. Thanks so much for everything."

The following day, Frank and Regina went to pick Gabriella up. Eva was upset, but handed her over to Frank, as ordered. Mercedes glared at Regina, as Eva demanded the phone number to the location where her baby would be. "That's not your concern," Frank grinned and answered coldly. "There is no provision in the Court Order for you to have our number." Eva broke into tears, as Regina asked her for her number. "Perhaps we could call in and let Eva rest assured that Gabriella is doing well."

When Eva handed over the paper with her number on it,

Frank stared ahead in disgust. Leaving, he said, "You have a short memory, Eva. Did you forget what you said to me before court, and that you called my wife a pig? You can sit and wonder about Gabriella now. Here Gabriella, let's meet your new Mommy."

Eva burst into louder tears as the door closed, and Regina was fighting tears herself, while Frank placed the baby in her car seat. Eva and her mother rushed back out to be sure that Gabriella was fastened safely. Regina nodded her head to communicate that all was well, and smiled at them. Frank pulled away quickly, still angry about their attempts to malign his wife. "They can just suffer," Frank snapped angrily. "They are getting just what they deserve. They're bad losers," he laughed. Regina remained quiet. "What's wrong, honey? Aren't you glad to have the baby?"

"We have not focused on the baby for one second since we got her, Frank.

We are what one might call 'bad winners.'"

Regina turned to smile at the little girl in the back seat. Gabriella was sitting quietly with no apparent reaction to her new surroundings.

The rest of the ride home was silent. Frank Jr. welcomed Gabriella as he would any other baby, since he was used to playing at the Child Enrichment Center. Gabriella was very solemn, but joined in the fun with the toys on the floor, as Hazel looked at Regina and shook her head. "There's a difference of night and day in the children, even considering the age between them," she remarked.

Frances came in with Lamar, who noted the same thing. Regina slipped into the bedroom to call Eva. She reassured her that Gabriella was playing with her brother in a completely safe environment. Eva was crying too hard to converse, but Mercedes took the phone and asked Regina in Spanish, if she would call when Gabriella was in bed for the night. "Certainly," Regina answered in their language. "Is there anything that I should know to do for her?"

"Eva sings to her at night," Mercedes wailed. "Okay," Regina answered softly, "how about *Que Sera Sera?*" Mercedes laughed softly through her tears, and thanked Regina as she hung up. "Maybe Mrs. Solberg isn't all bad," she said, still crying.

Eva went to the Child Enrichment Center the next morning, in spite of the Restraining Order. She asked Sylvia not to call the police but to please call Regina. Sylvia called Frances and relayed the message. Frances called security and had them stand by, and then told Regina what was going on. Regina finished with her patient and walked over to the nursery school. Eva placed both palms up crying, "I am not harming anyone, Mrs. Solberg. May I please just look at Gabriella?"

"Gabriella is not here, sweetheart," Regina answered quietly, "She is home playing with her brother. We will be bringing her home tonight at 7:00."

"Thank you," Eva sobbed. "You don't know my pain, because you still have your baby," she suddenly shouted.

"I do know your pain, and you still have your baby too, Eva. She is just visiting with her father and her brother right now."

"And calling you Mommy!" the exhausted Latin woman collapsed into a lunchroom chair, sobbing loudly.

Regina put her arms around Eva Rodriguez and held her

close to her. "What would you like Gabriella to call me?" she whispered.

Eva looked up at her, surprised. Was that love in Regina's eyes? No, it could not be, but at least she wasn't having the nearby security remove her.

"How about Sati?" Eva answered, snubbing.

"Sati! I like it," Regina smiled. "Where does it come from?"

"It's what I called my stepmother," Eva answered.

"Okay, Sati it is. I must return to work now, Eva."

Eva nodded sadly and left the building.

Jeannie and Sylvia, who had been silently observing, hugged each other, and returned to work as well, both misty-eyed.

Dorothy and Raymond called and were happy that court had gone well for their son, but were still annoyed by the fact that they had no details. They planned to come down for the next visit with their granddaughter. When Frank and Regina took Gabriella home, Frank Jr. was also in the car. Both Eva and Mercedes rushed over to get a look at him. Frank held his hand up to stop them, but Regina pleaded with him. "Darling, they mean him no harm. Let them see him." The two Cuban ladies raved about the little blonde-haired, blue-eyed boy who smiled at them and offered them some animal crackers. Mercedes looked into Regina's eyes and thanked her for letting them know how Gabriella was during the visit. Regina answered that it was absolutely no problem and would be the case each visit. Frank demanded a translation and was not too happy about "Pollyanna" being kind to these women. "Did you forget that they tried to smear your name in court, Regina?"

"Nope. Did you forget that they lost hands down?"

"I want them to pay for everything they did to you; to us."

"My debt reflects a credit, and I suggest you let yours go as well, as a favor to both your daughter and our son."

"You want to be their friends? Please tell me you're not suggesting that!"

"I'm not. What I am suggesting is that this animosity is harmful to both babies and the adults involved as well."

"What do you expect me to do, 'Can-Do?'"

"Stop making fun of me, Solberg. I expect all of the adults involved to be civil and decent to each other."

Frank Jr. laughed out loud as though he knew what was going on. Both his parents joined in. "You do notice that your daughter doesn't laugh like that?"

"Yes, that's because of her ignorant mother."

"No, Frank, that's because she senses tension and anger."

"Okay, Polly, I will try harder, but only because I love you so much."

"I truly appreciate it, darling."

When Frances heard that Dorothy and Raymond were coming down the next day for visitation, she called Hazel. "Let's have a grandparents' supper at my house; that way if Goliath starts running her mouth, we can be there to rescue Regina and Frank!"

"You got it," Hazel agreed wholeheartedly.

Dorothy was irritated and voiced her protest. "Frank, this is not their grandchild, but ours! I don't want them around while we bond."

"They are our close friends, Mother, and Leo Gerehauser is my boss."

Dorothy and Raymond were outside of the hospital before Frank and Regina came out with Frank Jr. They barely acknowledged their grandson, and were openly rude to Regina.

"We will take Frank to get Graciella while you go ahead to Frances' house with the baby," Dorothy said sweetly through her teeth. She was determined to learn the details of this whole sordid mess.

"That's fine," Regina answered, and kissed her husband. "Her name is Gabriella by the way."

Frances was already prepared for Dorothy's nonsense, and Hazel was right behind her. Leo came in to the living room and took Frank Jr. Flying him around like a plane, they landed on the floor with the new trucks that Grandpa Leo had brought him.

When they arrived at the baby's home, Dorothy gave Eva a cold stare and reached for the baby. Gabriella screamed and held onto her mother. Mercedes was livid, "You have no right to be here," she said in broken English. "Where is Mrs. Solberg?"

"I AM Mrs. Solberg," Dorothy grimaced, "and I have every right to this baby. We are going to make a little hell for you, lady," the large matriarch continued.

Dorothy tried to pry the baby away from Eva who shoved passed her and handed Gabriella to Frank.

Frank grinned and handed a kicking and crying baby to his mother, as Eva fell to the floor in hysterical tears. "Byeeee!" Dorothy called over her shoulder.

The baby would not stay still long enough to be placed in her car seat, so Dorothy turned her over, gave her a hard slap on her bottom and forced her into it. Mercedes, who had come out to observe, screamed.

"You sit still or I'll wallop you again," Dorothy shouted, glaring at the baby. Seeing Mercedes staring in horror, she grinned and said, "She will need a bathing suit this weekend – we are taking her to the pool."

Mercedes ran in to get Eva, and Dorothy repeated her remark about the bathing suit, so it could be translated, as Frank and Raymond laughed. "You are sick monsters," Eva shouted, "and so is Mrs. Solberg! Where is that pig? Why did she not come with you? To torture us? You are going back to court, Frank, you filthy animal!" Eva dropped to her knees on the front lawn and cried, banging her fists into the lawn in front of her, as the car pulled away. Dorothy, Raymond and Frank were laughing hysterically, but Frank was not too sure about his actions. He looked into the rear view mirror and saw Gabriella crying and hiding her face. He suddenly stopped laughing, and wasn't sure just how he felt.

Chapter Seven

Hate Plate with a Side of Guacamole'

Arriving at Frances' house, Dorothy yanked Gabriella from her car seat and gave the kicking baby another hard smack on her bottom. Pointing a large finger in her face, she ordered her to stop her crying at once. Regina had gone out to the car to greet them, and Gabriella reached for her desperately. Dorothy pointed her finger at her again, "Stop it!" she warned once more. Regina moved quickly to the passenger side and took Gabriella from her. The baby clutched onto her and cried harder. "What happened, Frank?" Regina asked in a no-nonsense tone that Frank recognized all too well. "She was spanked, first for refusing to get into her car seat and again now, as she and Mom must set boundaries together." Raymond answered, smiling.

"I believe I asked Frank! Hear this all of you," Regina shouted, liken to the Colonel, who had come out carrying Frank Jr. "You are never to lay a hand on this child again! Since when do we spank any baby, Frank? This baby is to be treated exactly as

you would treat Frank Jr. Do you understand? And just as a re-
minder, we do not use negativity but positive reinforcement!"
Regina turned on her heels and walked into the house. Gabriella
babbled noisily as she settled into her arms and quieted down.

Frank Jr. shook his little head and added to his mother's stern
lecture. Pointing his finger at his grandparents, he spoke, "No, no!
You be nice. We do not hit or push," rubbing his small hand on
Leo's cheek, "niiiice," he repeated to his father and visibly disgusted grandparents. Frank Sr. couldn't help laughing and hugged his
son, while the outraged grandparents went inside demanding to
know who Regina thought she was. Frances was ready for action
and so was Hazel. Leo and Lamar took both babies out of the
room and away from the brewing storm, as everyone noticed that
Gabriella went to Lamar without any problem.

"Please tell me what happened at Eva's house that caused
Gabriella to react the way you described," Regina asked her husband.

Dorothy answered, "She was ki – ….."

"Nobody asked you, Goliath!" Frances was hot on her trail.

Frank relayed the events as Regina and the others listened
quietly.

"Why did you try to grab the baby, Mom?" Regina asked
bluntly, "Especially when you saw that she was clearly not comfortable going to you."

"You listen here to me, Missy," Dorothy yelled, "Yo ….."

"Shut your gigantic mouth, Dorothy!" Hazel spoke quickly and very out of character. "You have upset Regina and your
granddaughter."

Regina continued, "So you left Eva crying hysterically on

her front lawn as her baby watched?" Regina indicated the three adult Solbergs.

"Well I guess we all just got caught up in revenge, and in retrospect, I'm sorry it happened," Frank approached his wife. Hugging her, he brushed the tear from her cheek and solemnly promised that it would never happen again.

Regina hugged him back, understanding how he was likely goaded to behave in the irrational manner that he truthfully described.

Frank spoke to his parents and the two adopted grandmothers in the room as he continued to hold his wife. "We have made a terrible mistake this evening, and we need to correct it and be sure it never happens again. We are trying to enrich Gabriella's life, not destroy it."

"We have rights, Frank, and they are not determined by Regina," Dorothy fumed, "Graciella is not even her baby!"

"There is no Graciella here, moron," Frances was irate, "and Gabriella is Frank's child, not yours!"

Frank suppressed a smile and answered quietly, "Gabriella will be treated just as Frank Jr. is. Anything less would be highly inappropriate."

"Raymond we're leaving," Dorothy stomped toward the door.

"Wait a minute, honey," her usually chicken husband responded, "we are all adjusting to a totally new and highly irregular situation here. Let's all just calm down for a minute."

"Regina, we only wanted to defend you and Frank, which is why we were trying to un-nerve Eva," Dorothy spoke next.

"Frank and I don't need or want to be defended. As we have told you, the circumstances are extenuating and probably not at all what you are concluding."

"Well then I think we have a right to know what caused this situation to be!" Dorothy persisted.

"Unfortunately for you, we don't think you have that right. You may either enjoy your little granddaughter in an appropriate manner or you may chose not to acknowledge her. But <u>you will not be permitted</u> to strike her or harm her emotionally, by Frank or by me." Regina stood her ground.

"Well, Regina, do you think that we have the right to see Gabriella as her grandparents?" Raymond asked.

"I believe that's why you're here, Dad, is it not? Now, if all of you will excuse me, I am going to call Eva and let her know that her baby is okay."

Regina left the room and made the call. Eva screamed and yelled into the phone. "You are a pig and a stinking monster! You bring my baby home now, or I'll see that your life is ruined!"

Mercedes took the phone, "Rahgeena, you are una persona with two faces! I think you were deeffrent, but you are no deeffrent."

"Pick a language and stick to it, will you?" the tired missionary answered, "I just called to tell you that Gabriella is fine and playing with her brother. I will give you my number so you can call to check on her anytime you want, after you calm down; that is."

Leo stood at Lamar's office door smiling. "Regina, I'm proud of you. It's time you started laying down the law. Come on now, honey, we are serving dinner."

When Regina entered the dining room, both of Frank's parents hugged her and apologized to her. "We will try to love this child as our grandchild," Raymond said.

"Good, since that's who she is!" Hazel snapped, as Leo looked shocked.

Later that night, Eva called to see if the baby was in bed. "Yes, she is sound asleep," Regina reassured. Eva started crying and told Regina that she did not want Gabriella swimming on Saturday. "It's too cold and she could drown, Mrs. Solberg."

"First of all, my name is Regina, if you don't mind. Secondly, nobody is going swimming this weekend. Third, when any child swims here, they have a one-on- one adult with them and wear lifejackets that zipper up the back the entire time they are around the pool."

Eva was laughing and crying at the same time, "Frank's mother was very cruel today, Regina."

"Yes, well that has been dealt with and will not occur again, Eva."

"I wish this terrible mess never started!" Eva cried again.

"Eva, why don't you and Mercedes meet me for lunch on Saturday? Let's say Francisco's at 12:30?"

"We don't have the money for that."

"Don't worry about that. Frank will be delighted to treat us. We can all sit calmly and see if we can't make this new adjustment better for all of us."

"I don't know. Do you think we can?"

"Why, I bet we can turn this into something fun! After all, we are three Latin women who have been thrown into a life together."

Eva translated to her mother, as Mercedes' eyes grew wide with fear. "I don't think that is a good idea, Eva."

"Mama, we will talk later," Eva answered. "Where will Gabriella be, Mrs. Solberg?"

"Napping, Ms. Rodriguez," Regina laughed easily as Eva joined her. "Regina, will she be safe without a woman there?"

"Not to worry, I'll have my second mother, Frances, there. She is not only the best second mother anyone could ever have, but a top-notch grandmother and an RN."

"Where will Frank be?"

"Which one?"

"Both," It was good to hear Eva relax a little.

"Frank Sr. will most likely be on the golf course and Frank Jr. will be at home."

"Does Frank Jr. love his sister, Regina?"

"Frank Jr. loves everybody, and how could anyone help but love Gabriella?"

"Will Frank's mother be there?"

"No, and believe me, nobody messes with Frances."

"Okay, we will see you at Francisco's at 12:30."

They were waiting in the foyer of the restaurant when Regina arrived. Both ladies looked like they were ready for a fight. Regina typically whispered a prayer before approaching, "Father, these two are no treat to deal with, so please stay with me. We need to set this straight for the children involved, as well as the three parents." Walking up to the ladies, Regina smiled and extended her hand. Both shook it lightly and skeptically. Greeting the hostess, Regina requested a table for three and slipped the waiter a small note. Mercedes saw the note and grabbed Regina by the hair, yelling, "Call the police!"

Regina pried the lady's fingers from her long curls with the help of Eva. Glaring at her, Eva remarked, "We knew we couldn't trust you, Regina. We knew you were just an actress." Puzzled and angry, Regina strained to answer calmly, "What is the problem, and what's with you Cubans pulling my hair?"

"Show me the piece of paper she gave you!" Eva shouted at the waiter.

The police entered the restaurant in response to a call from the hostess when she witnessed the physical confrontation. The waiter waved both hands trying to explain the note, but finally handed it to the police officer. "It's in Spanish," he said, handing the small piece of paper to his partner. Sgt. Lopez translated,

Please be sure I get the bill, for these are my friends and I am treating them to lunch.

Mercedes started crying and explained that she had since learned Regina's maiden name. They were afraid that Regina Foglietta Solberg was connected with the Mafia and was attempting to have them both killed; so that she and Frank could have Gabriella without complication. Regina looked surprised and then laughed. "You guys are worse than any Italian Mafia ever thought of being! I haven't anything to do with the Mafia."

"You do look very prestigious," defended the police officer.

"Oh, well I am the daughter of the King, but then; so are they."

"Where do we go from here?" the officer asked.

"Lunch. Care to join us?" Regina answered as though nothing had occurred.

"Oh sure, Ma'am, I'll just have the hate plate with a side of guacamole!"

All five people laughed, along with the hostess and the waiter.

"Okay, if everything is under control, and there are no assault complaints, we'll go."

"I pulled her hair," Mercedes turned herself in.

"She was only trying to style it," Regina smiled.

The three ladies were seated and Regina broke the awkward silence by suggesting they get drink orders and appetizers under way.

Eva and her mother lowered their eyes as Regina smiled. "What can we do now to fix this, Sati?" Mercedes asked in broken English while sobbing quietly.

"Well, you can start by looking up and recognizing a funny story that we will tell our children one day, after they are all grown up."

Both ladies looked up at her. "Now I am going to reach into my purse for a paper and pen. I have no gun, so please don't freak out on me."

Eva and Mercedes looked at each other and began laughing. Regina handed the pen and paper to Eva and said, "Write what you think would make a perfect world, given the fact that we must all get along. Get along nicely," she added.

1. Gabriella must never call you Mommy. "Done: she will call me Sati," said Regina.

2. We want to be able to call and check on her. "Done. Already done, but agreed formally."

3. Frank's parents are never to come to my house again. "Done. You lucky duck!" Regina laughed.

4.   Frank's parents are never to be alone with Gabriella. "Done."

5.   The custody battle must stop. "Done." The two ladies transferred there business expressions into grateful tears and said together, "It's a wonder."

"It's a wonder that you two don't dehydrate. No more crying, now.

My turn," Regina took the paper and pen.

1.   There is to be no more hysteria, especially in front of the children. "Okay."

2.   There is to be civil and polite communication with Frank and me, and absolutely no more name-calling. "Okay."

3.   Visitation is to be fashioned in the form of a Consent Order to allow both parents fair time with Gabriella. "What's a Consent Order?" Eva asked.

"An agreement between the parties outside of court, but filed with the Court and therefore a Court Order."

"Okay, but what would the times be?"

"Well, I don't think we should take Gabriella for Christmas or Easter or other major holidays. If things work out well, perhaps we could all meet for lunch or something the day before or after. After all, she is your only child and we have Frank Jr."

"Sati," Eva began slowly, trying to control herself, "Eleanor Greenberg told Eduardo that she was confident that you and Frank could get shared custody, if not custody in full."

"Eleanor was not invited to this lunch. Leave Frank to me. He will want what's best for all concerned, and I think reasonable visitation is best, with Gabriella having one home; your home. She simply visits us often. How do you feel about that?"

"Fine," both ladies answered as the appetizers arrived. Ordering lunch, they continued their planning, while munching on nachos and guacamole.'

"We have a huge tree of avocados at our home," Mercedes finally relaxed.

"I know," Regina smiled, "that's part of the deal," she added laughing.

"As many as you wish!" Eva laughed, relieved.

"We have seen where you live, Eva; do you think you and Mercedes would rest easier if you see where we live?"

The ladies looked at each other in shock. "Would Frank allow that?"

"I think Frank will be very receptive to our new arrangements. We just need to give him a little time. He is at a disadvantage, you know."

"Because of the trap," Eva said sadly.

"No, that's old stuff," Regina answered. "Because he's a man," she winked mischievously.

Mercedes asked the next question, "I am keeping Gabriella when Eva works. She pays me to, so I have income. Will you like her to pay you when the baby is no with me?"

"No, that is not necessary. Gabriella will not be spending weeks at the time with us. We both live in the same city, so there is no need for the 'Even Steven,' act."

The ladies chatted easily during lunch. They became more comfortable with each other and hopeful that all could be resolved.

Regina paid the check and all three ladies hugged each other. "Is this really possible, Sati?" Eva asked, teary-eyed.

"If we all work together, it's a certainty."

Regina went home and was delighted to find both babies asleep and Frances waiting. "Well," Frances smiled, "Someone looks happy."

"I am, but I am not sure I'll have the support I need to pull this off."

After explaining the whole story, Regina finally sighed.

"Well, I think you are a saint! And I'm behind you all the way," Frances poured the coffee. Regina hugged her second mother and drew a small box from the drawer under the doll cabinet. Handing it to Frances, she said, "Open it."

The box contained a gold locket with *Somebody Special* engraved on it surrounded by a beautiful flowered border. Inside were pictures of Regina and Frances at Bascom Palmer. The back of the locket was engraved in smaller letters that said, *I love you, but then, everybody does!* Frances hugged Regina and wept.

"I never knew what love was until you served me that plate of food in the clinic!"

"Yes, that's where I became known as Pollyanna." Both women laughed as the intercom announced the two little nappers!

Chapter Eight

The Clash of the Cultures

After putting Frank Jr. and Gabriella to bed, Regina and Frank had their dinner out on the patio. The breeze from the river softly rustled the palm trees as Monique sniffed the air. The little dog was exhausted from the vigorous play with the two children, and seemed to enjoy the quiet break. Regina shared the events of the lunch meeting, omitting the hair pulling incident. "They aren't terrible people, Frank, and they are your daughter's family. If we could make this work, it would be better for everyone concerned, and would eliminate the agony and expense of litigation."

"I am entitled to at least shared custody, Regina."

"Okay, nobody is disputing that, but why do you want it?"

"Because I deserve it."

"Indeed. You also deserve to be loved and respected by your children and grandchildren as the loving and considerate father that you are; remembered for being understanding rather than spiteful, and forgiving someone who is not easy to forgive."

"Well, I guess you're right, but I do have deep feelings of ha-tred for Eva and her mother, and so do my parents. They know only that we were tricked and I think they believe we attempted a surrogate mother deal because of your last pregnancy."

Regina laughed, "Well that's fine! That's all they need to think."

"I invited Eva and Mercedes to come over to see where Gabriella visits. I think it will set their minds at ease."

"Oh great, Regina, maybe we can send them on vacation to Europe too."

Frank grabbed his wife and pulled her into his lap. "Do you have any idea how much I love you?"

"Yes." She kissed him, "almost as much as I love you. I'm not suggesting that we all become close bosom buddies or extended family, as we are in the ten-pack. I'm only thinking that we could be civil and decent to each other, rather than pursuing the hatred that naturally exists in situations like this. We have a long way to go for a very long time, Frank; an entire lifetime. Why not make the best of it?"

Wyatt and Sylvia were hosting a big coming out party for Gabriella the weekend after next to include all of the Miami friends, Dan, Elizabeth, Andrea, and Aunt Sis and Uncle Bub. Attempting to eliminate typical upset, Frank suggested that the Solberg Sr.'s be removed from the guest list, along with Adam and Marge. Regina told him that the choice was his, considering that tension would spoil the party that their friends were kind enough to plan. Everyone was meeting at the Gerehauser's house tomorrow night so the girls could discuss the menu. Regina decided that she would take that opportunity to inform the group that Eva and Mercedes would neither be regarded as enemies, nor as close friends. Placing firm but comfortable boundaries to insure the personal space each of the parties needed, she truly hoped to accomplish the goal that she and Frank discussed. Praying to have the support of their friends, she was particularly concerned about telling the Colonel about all of this.

Arriving early, Regina met Hazel and Frances in the kitchen, where Leo grabbed Frank Jr., who giggled with delight. Frances had already told Hazel about the new understanding, and reassured Regina that the Colonel most likely already had some idea about it. "I doubt he was the least bit surprised, sweetheart," Hazel smiled.

"Who was surprised about what?" the Colonel boomed from the kitchen doorway. Frank Jr. was on his shoulders, patiently waiting for his ice pop. "Grandpa Leo, he hasn't had his dinner yet," Hazel laughed. Regina answered quietly, "I was concerned that you would not support my attempt to get along with the Rodriguez family and to try to understand them better." The Colonel tried to be as serious as possible when he answered. "Well I don't!" he blasted, "Those people do not deserve to be understood. You, however, do, and I love you enough to cooperate, so you have my support." Regina hugged him and sobbed. "You have no idea what that means to me," she temporarily lost her army voice. Leo hugged her back and then shouted, "Now where is my grandson's ice-pop?"

"Sir, Yes Sir!" Frances replied, removing a cherry Disney pop from the freezer.

The entire group agreed that, if Regina wished, Eva and Mercedes would be included in the festivities, since the party was for Gabriella. She appealed to Frank, who also agreed. "It will give us something to talk about while we clean up," Jeannie laughed, as Chuck raised his eyebrows in warning. Regina called Eva and extended the invitation, but both Eva and her mother were apprehensive about accepting it. "Oh, please do come," Regina encouraged, "it will be fun and there will be no references of the past made by any party. I might add that Frank's parents will be sitting this one out." Eva mentioned that her own father would be in town, and when he was also invited, she asked if they could bring something. Regina graciously accepted and the planning went on.

The party was a smashing success and Eva's father, Juan Rodriguez, was a delight to meet. Although he was divorced from Mercedes, they had all managed to maintain an amicable relationship. He fell in love with Regina at once and congratulated his daughter on her wise choice to accept the invitation. Wyatt and Sylvia were spectacular hosts and welcomed one and all. Frank Jr. was the baby "ring-leader," and the others played in coordination with him. All six babies were amazing to watch, but Charlie in particular was amused by Gabriella. Slowly, Eva and Mercedes relaxed and appeared less self-conscious. Dan was his usual easy-going self, and socialized with the former enemies for his daughter's sake. Regina loved him for it, as he also kept Elizabeth in check. Andrea and Eva met each other and chatted pleasantly, as did Uncle Bub and Aunt Sis, joining the two of them.

Lamar's son, Brain, had ridden down with Dan and Elizabeth, and had his eye on Andrea the entire evening. Frances winked at Regina and smiled. Before desert was served, Mercedes went over to Sylvia and Wyatt. Wyatt asked for everyone's attention and gave her the floor. In broken English, the frightened, tiny, Cuban grandmother addressed the group. "We weesh to bring honor to Raygeena, who we all call Sati. Thees medal of St. Crease-to-pher has been in our fomily for many years. St. Crease-to-pher, with Baby Jesus on his shoulders. Regina has walked forward with all of us on her shoulders to ask for God's grace. She called on Him to make us all unite for the beautiful babies here. Frank, may we present thees humble geeft to your wife?" Frank escorted Regina to the front of the room, while everyone applauded. Sincere hugs and kisses circulated the party as Elizabeth rolled her eyes. Dan smiled at her and whispered, "You do notice that Dorothy and Raymond are not here? We want to be a part of our grandson's life, Elizabeth. If this is all okay with Regina, we must accept it."

"I still feel that we are entitled to the detailed explanation from Frank," Elizabeth answered.

"Well, I am afraid that Regina has labeled that as 'classified.'"

"Do you think that's fair, Dan?"

"I think that's Regina, Elizabeth."

"Do you not see how strange these people are? They are dressed for a circus, and so is that baby. Since when does a baby wear gold bracelets and earrings? They have enough perfume on her to choke a horse, and have no right to speak Spanish here. Eva is a Cuban pig, Dan, and so is her mother."

"Elizabeth," Dan answered quietly, "they are from another country with very different customs than we have."

"Well they are here now. I just wonder why Dorothy and Raymond aren't here!"

"They weren't invited."

"That baby will suck on a bottle until she's in high school. I see Cubes walking all over the grocery stores at home with four and five-year olds sucking pacifiers. That one will be no different," Elizabeth gave a disgusted gesture toward Gabriella.

Mercedes made her way to Elizabeth and thanked her for having such a beautiful daughter. "Her soul is so beautiful because it belongs to God," she added. Elizabeth asked for the details of what happened between Frank and Regina and Eva, but Mercedes deliberately did not understand the question. She and Eva had been advised by Regina beforehand that nobody had or was to receive details. "I wonder if Regina is afraid to get pregnant again," Elizabeth pursued. "No se (I don't know)," the wise Mercedes answered. "Well somebody certainly knows," a very annoyed Elizabeth muttered to herself.

Making her way to Regina, Elizabeth finally caught her alone. "There was a time when you told me everything, Regina," she mumbled. "Funny thing, time," Regina answered, and continued, "time is what changes children into adults, or adults into adults in many cases; adults who have become independent thinkers and problem solvers; individuals who are able to assess a situation and act in the best interest of all concerned. Knowing exactly what that course of action is, can't always be easy. That's when it's wonderful knowing that we can get help in an instant. That's when we can be certain that God is, and has always been, right by our side. Surely you don't expect to know every intimate detail that exists between my husband and me, Mother. Frank and I agreed that we would offer the best explanation that we could, and we have done that. I hope you can accept the explanation in the true intention in which it was delivered. We both love you and Dad very much."

"I will never consider that little spic one of my grandchildren. I hope you can accept that." Regina closed her eyes and bit her tongue. "I believe the distasteful term you just used, pertained to the Puerto Ricans when I was growing up in New York. Gabriella is half Cuban and half the same as your grandson. I can only hope she never knows how you truly feel about her. After all, she is completely innocent." Elizabeth felt her anger rising, but answered anyway. "That's more than I would say for her father." Regina's eyes filled with tears, but she remained in control of herself.

"Look around you, Mother, and tell me if you should be behaving the way you are right now." Regina was relieved to see Dan approaching. He immediately calmed both women and commented on how well the Rodriguez family had spoken of Frank Jr.

"And why shouldn't they?" Elizabeth demanded, "They aren't the ones who have been smeared. It is Regina who has been. The entire Solberg family stinks, if you ask me."

"Which we didn't," Regina smiled and moved toward the remaining guests.

Elizabeth was ready to burst into tears of frustration. Her confusion, and perhaps the sheer need for understanding, did not go unnoticed by Dan. He put his arm around her shoulder and walked her outside to finish their conversation.

Dan's voice was very gentle as he began, "Listen, sweetheart, Regina is not asking us to love Gabriella as we do Frank Jr. She certainly doesn't expect the Rodriguez family to be blended with ours, either. They are not even going to be socializing with the intimate group of friends that Frank and Regina have here in Miami. They are here only because this party is for Gabriella. Regina is simply asking that we allow her and Frank to love Gabriella in this unique and special way, to best serve the situation that has occurred."

"And what situation is that, Dan? How is it that this baby has Frank's last name? What caused this? How did it happen?" Elizabeth sobbed as she continued, "What blame or consequence is the great Dr. Solberg taking in all of this?"

"We don't know all of those answers, Elizabeth. We know that Regina needs us. She needs our support, and so does Frank. Sure, it seems difficult, but in the big picture, she asks us to accept Gabriella to avoid a tremendous burden that would be the alternative; a burden that would affect your grandson. Regarding any blame, that's not for us to determine. Regina has never been one to 'cast the first stone.'"

"Who's throwing stones out here?" The Colonel's voice was loud but kind.

Walking over to Elizabeth, he put his arm around her. "You have raised a wonderful woman, Elizabeth. Don't make too much of Gabriella. We are not expected to love her as our own, and it's a damn good thing that we're not, because I won't! Her grandparents won't love Frank Jr. as they do their own, either, but we can all love her, just the same, as they have come to love Frank Jr. This is a tough situation that takes someone like Pollyanna to handle. God is overseeing the whole set up, which is why I'm cooperating," he laughed.

Elizabeth and Dan laughed too. "Well I better leave. I am all upset, and I'm sure I wasn't very thoughtful of Regina today."

"Nonsense," the Colonel continued. "You were upset; big deal. So you run into the ladies' room and return to the party like nothing happened. Regina knows this isn't easy. She knew it would be awkward in the beginning for us."

"So who has been supporting her? Who is looking after Regina?"

Dan and Leo answered at the same time, "He is."

"God, God, God! How could He allow a thing like this to happen?" Elizabeth burst out crying again.

"God grants all of us free will, ma'am, and everything happens for a purpose," the Colonel's voice was firm and defensive. "Now quit crying and get back to the party, Elizabeth. Everyone wants you back there."

"I don't speak Spanish," Elizabeth laughed lightly.

"Yeah, well they don't all speak English either," Dan replied. "Eva's dad seems nice enough. Did you have a chance to meet him?"

"No. Darn it! I may never be the same," Elizabeth was still not in the mood to cooperate.

Leo smiled at them and returned inside. He could see where Regina got her irreverent sense of humor, and laughed to himself.

Elizabeth dried her eyes and asked Dan one final question, before joining the other guests: "Do you think it's right that Regina converses with these low-life people in Spanish?"

"Si," Dan laughed, and Elizabeth couldn't help laughing too.

Relieved that she was only being expected to be friendly to Gabriella and her family, Elizabeth took a deep breath. She was also happier to find that she wasn't the only one who didn't intend on simply blending with the Cubans.

Remaining at the party until the end, she was also getting caught up in the excitement of Andrea and Brian. Eva approached her and complemented her on her two lovely daughters that looked so much like her. That helped a little, but Elizabeth still looked down on Eva and graciously snubbed her. This Rodriguez and her motley family were beneath the Mc Brides, whether Dan believed it or not. As far as Elizabeth was concerned, Regina's life was ruined unless this truly was a surrogate mother situation that went sour and the facts to prove it were brought out in the open and dealt with the way they should be according to the highest of snob standards. The fact that Elizabeth and her children barely existed on welfare before Dan came into the picture was of no importance in this scenario. The Mc Brides were of better breeding than the Rodriguez family and Elizabeth continually told herself that she was not acting like the Solberg seniors in any way by believing that.

Watching Brian put a flower in Andrea's hair, Dan whispered to Elizabeth, "Eight down, none to go."

Chapter Nine
Beware of Watch Hog!

The fall came bursting in and everyone seemed to welcome the excitement with open arms. The Saturday before Halloween there was to be a huge party, hosted by Jackson Memorial and Cedars of Lebanon Hospitals. The event was booked at Daphne's International Restaurant, and the ten-pack were all going, along with Sylvia's parents, who had relocated to Miami from Jamaica. Sylvia's mother, Hyacinth, was the head of the hospital volunteers, and chaired the committee for the party.

Jeannie, Sylvia, and Regina had secured three top-notch baby-sitters from the Child Enrichment Center, all of whom had to pass Leo and Hazel Gerehauzer's, and Frances and Lamar Mac Michael's inspection. Frank and Regina were dressing as Darth Vader and C-3PO from Star Wars, Chuck and Jeannie were going as Bonnie and Clyde, Sylvia and Wyatt would be sporting Adam and Eve costumes, Frances and Lamar would scare it up as Dracula and a witch, Hazel and Leo were using professional clown costumes, and Roger and Hyacinth were dressing as an adorable pair of hedgehogs. The whole group was meeting for a cookout at Frances and Lamar's house tonight to discuss the fun, and start celebrating early.

The patio table was bursting with wonderful dishes, including honey baked ham, sliced roast beef, butter-rum flavored turkey breast, macaroni and cheese, green bean casserole, fifteen bean salad, Caesar Salad, honey knot rolls, and relish trays. Dessert was a mango cheesecake and assorted butter cookies. The three older couples doted on the children, now very active toddlers, while the three younger guys talked football and their ladies gossiped.

Sylvia told Jeannie and Regina about a young nurse who had a huge crush on Wyatt. She worked at Cedars of Lebanon on the surgical floor. Born in the Philippine Islands and moving to Miami as a child, her name was Fortunada, and she called herself, "Fort for Short." The situation had a few of the same signs that Jeannie's and Regina's former problems did, as far as calling about ridiculous symptoms for patients and personal aches and pains. Consequently the potential scenario kept both Sylvia and Wyatt watching very carefully. "Little Philippino called our home to see if Wyatt was going to the party," Sylvia laughed, "Wyatt, mind you, not Wyatt and his wife."

"What did you tell her?" Jeannie asked nervously.

"That is was not her concern," Sylvia answered brightly.

Regina just laughed and shook her head. "I am amazed at the gall these women have! Who do they think they are?"

"Well, 'Fort for Short' is known to chase doctors and will one day meet her match," Sylvia reassured, "one of the parents of a child in the toddler class had a problem with her when she worked at Jackson. She kept track of her little antics and finally had little 'Fort for Short' dismissed for questionable behavior. That's how she migrated over to Cedars to begin with."

Jeannie was uneasy, "Isn't there something the hospitals can do to prevent this stuff?"

"Not really," Regina answered, "it's up to the individuals to set limits and maintain their private space, according to Mindy in Risk Management."

"The important thing is for the husband and wife to stay alert and stick closely together," Sylvia looked pensive, "so far she has made no attempt to visit Wyatt's office or see him anywhere other than on his rounds at Cedars."

Looking up and seeing the three older ladies move toward the patio area, Sylvia changed the subject. She did not want to worry her parents, who were unaware of the possible matter at hand.

The Saturday before Halloween came quickly. After the babies in the three younger households were settled in with their caretakers, Leo piled the "ten-pack" into the hospital van with Roger and Hyacinth, and headed for the party. The restaurant was exquisitely decorated like a haunted mansion, sporting seven long tables of hot and cold food from all over the world. The magnificent buffet lined the entire perimeter of the room. Paper sacks of candy were stationed at each place setting on the tables for all of the guests, while jack-o-lanterns burned brightly in the centers. After a brief greeting period, the dance floors were packed and the party was in full swing. Chuck and Jeannie danced up to Frank and Regina, telling them to try the sausage puffs and crab pockets. Sylvia and Wyatt were busy at the dessert tables, and the three older couples were seated comfortably, sampling all of the goodies. There was a candy apple tree display that looked like glass, and intricate chocolates decorated like Halloween characters, that were almost too gorgeous to eat. The bowls of punch were designed to produce "fog" from their delightful contents of fresh fruit juices, Ginger Ale, and exotic sherbet flavors. Regina could not resist this opportunity to close her eyes and quietly thank God again for her beautiful life, her husband and baby, and their wealth of close friends. Everyone seemed to be having a ball, and very few guests were able to recognize Leo and Hazel!

Suddenly the bandleader, who had been coaxed to make an announcement, did so, and "The Empress of the Universe," entered in full costume. None other than "Fort for Short," she was bedecked in an $875.00 gown of gold sequins, cut all the way up one side and fastened by spaghetti cross straps, that clearly revealed the fact that the empress had left her undergarments at home. The other side of her glamorous gown was slit to the upper thigh. The "empress," wore an exceptionally high crown of glistening rhinestones to enhance her hair, which was done in an elaborate upsweep. Commenting to one and all that she had spent all day in the beauty shop followed by a trip to the cosmetic studio to have her detailed makeup applied, she circulated the room, behaving as though the party was for her. Once she met Sylvia Clements, her radiant expression instantly faded. Sylvia was beautiful, and not the portly mother of triplets that Fort was anticipating. Fort involuntarily glared at Sylvia but caught herself. "Why, Adam and Eve," she laughed lightly, "what darling costumes! You please the Empress," she tried to joke her way out of her obvious discomfort.

"Why, thank you, but do tell us how you decided to be the Empress of the Universe, and have yourself announced as the same?" *Eve* responded coldly. Wyatt stood smiling and wondering what would happen next, when the music started again and Frank and Regina summoned them to help start a mixer. Fort stood staring at the two couples for a moment before continuing to circulate.

Trying every which way she could to get a dance with Wyatt, Fort failed. The girls were wise to her and watched her every move. Finally, when Wyatt and Sylvia were sitting comfortably on a couch beside the dance floor, Fort moved forward and positioned herself on the arm of the sofa. Next to Wyatt, with the slit side of her gown against him, she nuzzled closer. "You two are so cute together," she began, as she rubbed Wyatt's neck. "Where did you learn to dance so well?" Out of the corner of her eye, Fort saw the spiked coat just before feeling the cold sticky wave of the sherbet punch bowl drench her crown first, and rush down her dress. "Adam" saw the flood coming and grabbed "Eve's" hand, jumping out of the way, as the little hedgehog spoke, "Oh, I'm sorry, dahlin. I tripped! Must have had my eye on somebody else's mahn."

The *Empress* was outraged and shook with anger and humiliation, but didn't speak. More remarkable than that, was the fact that nobody moved to help her wipe the punch and melted sherbet off. Wyatt and Sylvia returned to the dance floor, and Hyacinth to the kitchen area to turn in the empty punch bowl. Fort ran for the door, catching her heel on a chair that had been pushed out. The sticky empress tripped but caught herself. While she did not fall, she did manage to rip her gown farther along the slit and left the party screaming.

Silently, waiters came forward with no reaction, and cleaned up the floor where 'Fort for Short' had dripped, and the couch area where the "accident" had occurred just prior to her dramatic exit. The only comment several minutes later was by Leo Gerehauzer, when he announced quietly to his own table, "I believe that the ten- pack is now the twelve-pack!" The group of ten applauded to the confusion of the other guests at the party, who appeared to have no reaction to the very discreet punch bath, and the celebration continued without further incident.

The ride home was hilarious, however, as the five women cheered for Hyacinth. Frances was a radiant witch and enjoyed the party to the hilt. "I've been in the hospital business for too many years and seen too many marriages split up! Broken hearts seem to be a given in the medical profession – that's where they get these ideas for all of the soap operas! I absolutely love to see women like Fort get what's coming to them," she laughed. Roger shook his head, "I feel sorry for any lay-dee that messes around wit dis group of weemin!"

Regina just smiled quietly and hugged Frank.

The Halloween festivities continued on Halloween night as the twelve-pack Trick- or- Treated with the five toddlers. Dorothy and Raymond came down for the event, as did Elizabeth, Dan, and Bub and Sis. Andrea and Brian Mac Michaels, who were now dating regularly, rode down in his car.

The large crowd of twenty-five walked around the Doral and Isla Del Mar, seeking goodies at every door. Frank Jr. was dressed as an Indian Chief, Charlie was Peter Pan, and the triplets were the Three Blind Mice. The little group recited Five Little Pumpkins and enjoyed the applause from their fan club. Each of the babies was outstanding and they caused heads to turn wherever they went. Frank Jr. wore his black wig and full headdress proudly, his pale skin and blue eyes setting a whole new look for the Native Americans! The olive-skinned and dark-eyed Peter Pan was in a similar position.

The parents had talked about switching the costumes, but the little boys had each chosen their own, and that was that! The Three Blind Mice were exquisite, and marched along as little Hyacinth bossed the whole crowd around. Followed by her sister and brother, she meant business, and was obviously named correctly for her role.

The evening was filled with love, fun, and laughter, as the little ones played with their hard-earned candy and nibbled on a good bit of it while they were at it. The night ended with a trip to the Pizza Palace, where Eva and Mercedes met up with the crowd, carrying a very tired Gabriella, who was dressed as an adorable ballerina. Frank Jr. was seated by "Grandpa Leo" and Dan, as usual, but was grabbed for a few minutes by Mercedes, who couldn't resist hugging him. Dan and Regina had exchanged loving smiles the entire day, and supported the affection that Eva and Mercedes had for Frank Jr.

Dan visibly admired his step-daughter and also loved both Frank Sr. and his grandson. In fact, everyone, except Dorothy, Elizabeth, and Mercedes, seemed comfortable, and enjoyed a great supper followed by rounds of grand hugs good-bye. Dorothy and Mercedes were still bitter enemies while Eva was indifferent to both of her baby's paternal grandparents. She was cordial. Period. Elizabeth was thought to be a snob without cause, and was consequently overlooked by the Cuban women, but certainly not disliked.

Going up the elevator, little Frank Jr. was sound asleep, still holding on to his candy treasures. Two tired, bright blue eyes opened in protest when Regina attempted to pry the bag of candy loose. "Mine. My candy!" Frank Jr. sleepily stood his grounds. "Yes, Chief Frankie, the candy is yours," Regina laughed and hugged her baby, who had become a little boy before her eyes. "Let's set your candy here by the big clown and let him watch it for you while you sleep."

"Not by the el-phant, Mommy, 'cause he will eat all of my candy and get berry sick," the little chief finished as he drifted off to sleep.

Joining Frank and Monique on the patio, Regina nibbled on a Halloween cookie, while she admired the sky filled with brilliant stars and a glorious moon. The happy couple held each other and enjoyed the cool breeze from the river, watching Monique devour a captured lollipop that had dropped from Frank Jr.' s bag on his way down the hall to bed. "Our lives are a fairy tale, Regina," Frank whispered, "and we owe it all to Him," he added, indicating the breathtaking sky.

Dan and Bub chatted on the way home, both noting Elizabeth's silence. Sis finally broke the mood by asking, "Elizabeth, are you okay, honey?" Following a deep sigh, she answered, "No, I am not. I am not okay with the Cuban scum simply joining us like there is nothing wrong. I am not okay with not knowing the details, and I am not okay believing that Dan knows the whole story and won't share it," she added tersely.

"What's the damn difference?" Bub asked no one in particular, "Frank and Regina are fine with everything."

Elizabeth answered, "Well, the difference is that Regina is my child and I have a right to know what the hell is going on, Bub." The group was silent when Dan answered gently. "Regina is nobody's child, Elizabeth. She is your daughter, and a tower of strength. Whatever the circumstances were, the outcome is beautiful. Eva and her mother adore Regina and Frank Jr. Nobody has pure knowledge of what happened, but I think a blind man can see that God has made everything okay. We should be proud of Regina and in awe of her deep faith. We must also be very aware of how much she loves her husband."

Sis tried to smooth things over, "Well I'm sure that Elizabeth feels the same way, but, as Regina's mother, it's a little different if she feels that her child has been hurt, even though she may support the decision to forgive and forget or simply to accept a set of circumstances." Elizabeth was still annoyed with Dan, but, grateful to her sister-in-law for her understanding. "I am angry with Regina for not being honest with me, and with you, Dan, for enabling her nasty little secrets."

Dan raised his eyebrows and replied softly, "Elizabeth, you are too wise to talk the way you are right now. I am not enabling anyone, but I am respecting other people's privacy. The terms 'nasty little secrets,' and 'Cuban scum,' are simply uncalled for."

From that point, the four rode home quietly. After dropping Bub and Sis off and arriving at their own home, Elizabeth yelled at Dan, "How dare you reprimand me like that! You ought to apologize to me, you bastard."

Dan took a deep breath before answering, "I ought to take you over my knee, Elizabeth. You are so consumed with your own disappointment that you are oblivious to Regina's feelings and consequently unable to be there for her as you should be. Did it ever occur to you that that may be why she doesn't confide in you?"

Fighting tears of anger, Elizabeth raised her hand to slap his face. Dan blocked her and sat her down firmly on her bed. "There'll be none of that dramatic nonsense. You are angry with yourself, not with me or with your daughter."

Elizabeth put her head in her hands and cried. Dan sat next to her and held her gently. "There, there now, honey, no harm has been done. It's perfectly normal for all of us to find this situation awkward. Nobody is trying to hide anything from you. Do you think this has been a cake walk for Regina?"

Elizabeth wrapped her arms around her husband, "She loves

you more than me. She trusts you more than she trusts me. I bet Frances and Lamar know the whole story."

Dan tried to sooth his shaking wife. "There is only One who knows the whole story, Elizabeth, and we must all trust Him. Regina does."

A few moments of silence went by before Elizabeth answered, drying her eyes, "And how could God allow something like this to happen to Regina?"

Laughing softly, Dan answered, "I would think that He sees Regina in a very special light, as a special messenger. Everything happens for a purpose, Elizabeth. The great I Am doesn't have to explain to us. He knows why, and has His reasons for everything. We just need to trust Him."

Elizabeth mocked, "Regina does."

Dan raised his eyebrows again, "Don't be smart," he laughed, "I admire our daughter and her husband. This can't be easy for him either."

Without thinking, Elizabeth snapped, "Oh, tough. That's just tough. I don't think this is any 'surrogate-mother-gone- bad' deal; I think the Great Frank Solberg was simply unfaithful."

Elizabeth started crying again, as Dan quietly prayed, "Father, please help us through this. Please help her to understand and to leave judgment to You." Dan answered his wife calmly, "Honey, we just don't know the details. We have to accept that and deal with this the best way that we can. We don't have to be around Eva and her mother; in fact, we don't even have to see Gabriella if we choose not to. There are plenty of ways to resolve this so that you feel comfortable, sweetheart."

Nodding in exhaustion, Elizabeth started, "and Regina ....."
Dan finished, "will be fine with any arrangement." Elizabeth
leaned against her tall, handsome husband. Dan was an angel.
Regina had always been his favorite, and maybe the fact that she
trusted and confided in her dad wasn't so bad after all. Even Bub
and Sis were on Regina's side. Dan smiled and hugged his wife
closely, as though he could read her mind. "There are no sides,
Elizabeth; we're all on the same team."

Dorothy and Raymond also rode home in a very pensive state.
"I can't seem to come to grips with this whole sordid thing,"
Dorothy finally broke the silence. "Me neither. I don't think we
should be subjected to this dark secret any longer. I would be
willing to bet that Frank did this for Regina, so she could have
another baby, and the deal went sour. I wish he had never met
that piece of slime," Raymond grumbled bitterly, and continued,
"Little miss prayer maker!"

"I wonder if I should call Elizabeth and try to have lunch with
her. I may be able to find something out, woman-to-woman, so
to speak."

"I don't know, Dorothy, she's not likely to give up any information, even if she does have the whole true story."

"Sure she won't, especially since it would be admitting to
her own precious daughter's screw up. It may still be worth a try.
Why should they know the truth and we are left in the dark?"

"We don't know that they do know the truth, Dorothy, or
what the truth even is. I just wish our son would come back to

us. Regina causes so many problems in his life. Gabriella is a little troll, and her mother is a low-life swine. You can see that Elizabeth can't stand them either."

"That's why they were only included in the pizza part of the day. Eva wanted Frank and Regina to see Gabriella in her hideous ballerina get-up. Raymond, it's time Elizabeth and I take these matters into our own hands. Saint Dan works during the week, and I will plan the lunch for then. I want the truth, and I want some rules put into place, whether little Miss Regina likes it or not!"

"Little Mrs. Regina, Dorothy, and how do you think our son will feel about this?"

"I really don't care. Frank is a spineless fool to allow Regina to continue this nonsense. If she can't carry a baby on her own, then they need to adopt through an attorney or be happy with Frank Jr."

Early the next morning, Dorothy telephoned Elizabeth. While Elizabeth wasn't especially fond of Dorothy, she accepted a lunch invitation in case Dorothy had some information to share. The two ladies met at the Lobster Trap in the Palm Beach Mall for lunch that afternoon. The conversation started easily, and finally Dorothy stated calmly, "Elizabeth, I'm not alright with this Gabriella situation. I am so angry about it, that I can't even function normally."

"Join the club," Elizabeth nodded.

"I hope Regina didn't humiliate my son into an artificial insemination procedure in an effort to get a second baby."

"I hope your son wasn't unfaithful and Regina is simply covering for him."

"Honestly, Elizabeth! Have you seen Eva?"

"Oh, yes I have. She has all the vital parts that it takes, Dorothy, just like any other woman."

"Frank would never stray from Regina."

"There is a DNA test that would beg to differ." The two ladies were now shouting.

"Yes, one that reflects your daughter's selfishness! The deal just went bad."

"Regina is trying to get pregnant again, Dorothy. Why would she now, but not before?"

"Because she sees what happened by messing around with low-life money seekers! I wonder how much they paid. They better not have sold our family diamond!"

"Well why don't you have your big shot lawyer go to Miami and find the paperwork on this case? It will say how this happened, and it's public record, because I called the courthouse before coming here."

"Well, why don't we ride down ourselves and look?" Dorothy growled.

"Because whoever's child is at fault will not be comfortable riding back, and we don't know how to look for the information we need." Elizabeth snapped.

"And I suppose this should be our expense?"

"It was your son's genetic material that made Gabriella, not Regina's."

Looking up, both ladies noticed a stylish Jamaican lady with a group of people at the next table. They recognized Sylvia and her mother seconds later. They came over to them, announcing that Sylvia had a continuing education class in Palm Beach to keep her court reporting up to speed in case she ever wanted to use it. Hyacinth spoke up, "Not dat it's my bis-ness, but court records don't necessarily tell what hoppen. Dey tell what people say hoppen. You two have two fine kids. Why not leave dem alone?"

"Oh butt out, Hyacinth!" Dorothy snarled. "And why is it that you were at the big Halloween bash at Daphne's and Raymond and I were not?"

"Because you weren't in-Vi-ted, my dear."

"My son is a doctor at Jackson Memorial!"

"Yes, girl, but you are not!"

"And why were you there then?"

"Because I am the head of the committee dat planned the event."

Elizabeth just listened quietly. What Hyacinth had said about the court records was true. Regina and Frank would stick to their story regardless. She could not restrain herself any longer. "Hyacinth, do you know the story behind Gabriella?"

"Elizabeth, we know what you know, and dat is what Regina and Frank wish us to know."

"Was she inseminated?" Dorothy asked through her teeth.

"I wasn't dere. You were not dere either, but Gabriella is here and she Frank's – so yes, Doroty, she was definitely inseminated."

"You know what I mean! Now answer me."

"I don't answer nobody's bis-Ness. Goodbye."

Hyacinth walked calmly away from the table and a stunned Sylvia followed.

Dorothy and Elizabeth decided that they would really never know what happened, but each woman left, believing that their child had been slighted in a big way.

The Nugents and the Solbergs had both been planning their second pregnancies, while Wyatt and Sylvia decided to be content with the three babies they had. Frank was concerned about Regina conceiving again, and had called Dr. Andrew Kingsley, who jokingly told him that if she did get pregnant again, he would move to the Middle East. He laughed and added, "Let me be one of the first to know, will you Frank, so we can start her on an early care plan? Oh, and don't tell her that she is my favorite patient in the entire history of my practice! Good luck." Frank had also been concerned that he and Regina had used no form of birth control since Frank Jr. was born and she was not pregnant, even though they both felt that she already should be.

Chapter Ten

Dorothy Giveth and Dorothy Taketh Away

Dan came home from work to find a troubled and frustrated wife sitting in the den, and sat down on the couch beside her, "Well, what in the world has you so sad?" Elizabeth told him all about the luncheon and the run-in between Dorothy and Hyacinth. Dan shook his head and laughed, "Dorothy is not going to be happy until somebody decks her." Elizabeth, surprised that Dan didn't appear to be angry with her, lamented, "I haven't even started supper, and Andrea left a note that she asked Brian to join us tonight." Dan put his arm around his wife and laughed again, "Well we're not exactly on the bread line, Elizabeth, and I'm sure the two love birds won't mind roughing it at the Gorgonzola Steakhouse tonight. Andrea loves the cheesecake there, and I know Brian enjoys the place as well."

Watching his wife for a reaction, he spread his hands apart and added, "problem solved." Elizabeth looked at her husband

and reminded herself again that she was very lucky to have him. Dan was everything any woman would want in a husband; he was very handsome, intelligent, understanding, financially set, gentle, and hilarious, among other qualities, and she vowed on the spot to take better care of him.

Andrea and Brian came in moments later and confirmed Dan's assessment about dinner. They made an adorable couple, and Dan was delighted to see it happen.

Andrea opened her shopping bag and pulled out six small bean bag animals from the Hallmark store that had been marked half price.

"Look what we picked up for the babies in Miami," she beamed, "I got Frank and Gabriella puppies, Charlie a kitten, and Sylvia's three little monster babies, mice!"

Elizabeth cringed at the thought that Gabriella was automatically included in the count. "Why did you get one for Gabriella?" She asked as calmly as possible.

"Oh, I just figured her in – why; is that a problem?" Andrea waited for an answer, but none came. Brian saw the problem and spoke up, "Yeah, those two Latin ladies sure look up to you, Elizabeth. Both of them were talking about how elegant you are, and how sweet Regina is."

After taking a minute to evaluate the comment, Elizabeth just nodded, "Oh?" Andrea caught her Dad's wink and picked it up from there, "Yes, Mercedes thinks you hung the moon, Mom, and Eva really likes you too. They sure hate Dorothy, though; but then, who doesn't?" Remembering the small plush ghost that she bought for Frank Jr. and nothing for the little girl, Elizabeth felt small.

"I should have picked something up for Gabriella, too, when I gave Frankie his toy on Halloween."

Andrea smiled brightly, "So you will next time; besides, you didn't give it to him in front of her or anything." Brian smiled at his boss and senior partner, "I really admire your wisdom in handling this, Elizabeth. I can see where Regina and Andrea get their excellent judgment from."

For the first time since they left Miami, Elizabeth smiled. She hadn't thought of the opportunity to set an example and to be seen as a leader. Dan was right - she had been completely wrapped up in her own disappointment to the point of side-stepping her own daughter's needs. She decided that she would make a sincere effort to correct the problem, and try to turn things around.

Dorothy Solberg sipped her wine cooler and stretched out on a patio lounge. She, too, was assessing her family's position, and decided to make some radical changes of her own. Frank and Regina had caused her plenty of trouble and they were going to be held accountable for it! At this point, it no longer mattered to her who was the cause of the mess. The two "kids" loved each other and stuck together – so they could suffer together. Feeling as though she had plenty of ammunition just in her "rights" to her grandchildren – or what she thought were her rights, the embittered matriarch pictured both young Latin mothers watching her load the grandchildren into her car for court-ordered grandparents' visitation. Furthermore, she would wallop the daylights out of the little darlings at the first sign of protest, as their mothers watched in horror. The very idea made her grin from ear to ear.

Stretching again in satisfaction, she called Stan Duncliff, their friend and attorney of nearly thirty years.

Raymond came out with a tray of cheese and crackers and listened intently to her plan. "Stan will meet us at the club for dinner at 7:30. I did not get into details."

Sighing, Raymond explained that Stan did not handle family law and would probably advise them against causing any upheaval. Dorothy was instantly infuriated, "How much are we supposed to let Regina and Frank get away with before we take action, Raymond?"

Wringing his hands, her worried husband replied, "It's not a question of letting them get away with anything, Dorothy; it's a matter of what rights they have and what rights we have. We must remember what happened the last time we presented ourselves as Plaintiffs. We damn nearly lost our son, and now we have a grandson to think about."

Standing to adjust her chair, Dorothy snapped, "Exactly, Genius! We now have what we call *ammunition*. Regina is not going to want us to take the two kids away from them for long periods of time and Eva will die at the thought. I will do whatever is necessary to get the information I want and the satisfactory agreements from both Frank and his goody-two-shoes wife. As far as Gabriella is concerned, that little girl is going to give up that bottle and Americanize!"

Raymond tried to reason with her once again. "Dorothy, I am not sure we will be allowed to simply take the kids. Their entire group will fight us together."

"We have what they call grandparents' visitation rights, Raymond. I have already called the courthouse to see what can be done. Let's see what Stan says. He may not do family law, but he must have some idea of what goes on in these situations."

"That's my point, Dorothy; this is not a typical situation. These people are all working together as a close-knit unit. I don't think you can simply seize children for spite. Unless you can prove that the mothers are incompetent or denying you access to the kids, I'd be willing to bet that we are just going to be spinning our wheels."

Dorothy stacked a few slices of cheddar on two crackers and handed one to Raymond. "Well it's worth a try," she garbled with her mouth full.

At the country club, the Solbergs learned that Raymond's information was, in fact, correct. "Grandparents' visitation is generally used in a divorce situation, and in this case, it will not serve you well. If you have 'walloped' the illegitimate child, and those Cubans did see you do it, they could sue you for that, and cause one gigantic mess, Dorothy."

"What about the court records?" asked Raymond.

"What about them?"

"Would they contain the facts of this matter?"

"They will contain what was stated in the proceedings. Not necessarily what you want to know."

"Can you get them for us?" Dorothy asked anxiously.

"Anyone can get what is in the public record, Dorothy, but that may be only what was alleged."

"Get it!" Dorothy snapped.

After thirty years, Stan had learned to simply accept Dorothy's rudeness, but he still cautioned them about the dangers of filing a frivolous law suit.

"First of all, no lawyer will take it, because it would be a risk to them in what is known as a Rule 11 Sanction, which is a penalty for filing a frivolous law suit. You cannot just sue somebody because you happen to be angry with them, guys. There must be just cause, or you could come out looking foolish and get counter-sued. I must caution you to be careful. I will get the records, though, and you can start there."

"Will the record prove if there was an agreement with Eva to carry a child for Frank and Regina, and who started that agreement?" Dorothy was determined to get the facts.

"The record may or may not reflect that. The problem with gaining all of this information could be the fact that the parties settled the matter amicably."

Raymond puffed up, "Frank will do anything to protect Regina. It's enough to make you sick!"

Frank and Regina opened their door to a ringing telephone. "I get it," Frank Jr. ran toward the receiver. Jeannie was calling to ask if they had anything for the flu. "Hold on, Aunt Jeannie, I will get Mommy," the little boy put the palm of his hand up as though the party on the phone could see it.

"Hi Regina, I didn't want to give this to the babies at the childcare center, so I stayed home today and Sylvia covered for me, but I have to get rid of it and get back to work."

"Well, let me come and get Charlie, honey, and I have some chicken soup and Ginger Ale; I'll bring it over with me. Is Chuck on call tonight?"

"Oh, of course, doesn't that just figure?" She managed a weak laugh.

Frank went to collect his puppets for a play session with the two little boys, while Regina started over to Jeannie's with the remedies for the flu.

Taking one look at her friend, Regina grabbed the phone, "Frank, do you think we should call Chuck? Jeannie is as white as a sheet."

"Does she have any fever?"

"She says no, but she has been sick all day."

"Can you handle the two boys if I drive her to the ER? Chuck can see her there and then we should probably keep her here with us tonight."

"Absolutely."

The doctor in the emergency room started the work up while they waited for Chuck. When he arrived, he kissed his pale wife and took her hand, "Honey, I'm afraid that you have a long-term flu; one that could last about nine months!"

Frank hugged both his friends and called Regina. "Jeannie's pregnant!"

Regina was delighted and prepared the guest room for her friend. Jeannie was so excited about her pregnancy, that she ate beef stew with everyone else and did just fine! Word traveled fast that there would be a summer addition to the group. "You're next, Regina," Chuck laughed.

"'From your mouth to God's ears,'" Frank answered seriously.

Stan called the Solberg seniors from Miami. "There is little in the record that would prove or disprove whether or not this was a pre-arranged deal that went sour. There is no contract of record and no medical report reflecting an actual insemination process. However, the DNA results are high probability that Frank is the father. How that happened is stated in the original complaint by the biological mother as a one night stand. That may or may not be true, though."

"Are there any other comments of interest?" Raymond demanded.

"Just one that I find interesting, by the Honorable Marcus Leonard."

"Well?" Dorothy was ready to strangle the lawyer.

"He said, 'God bless the defendant's wife.'"

"Oh, sure, Mother Teresa sets her husband up and takes credit for cleaning up the mess she made," Dorothy was wailing.

"Well actually," Stan answered in a very annoyed tone, "Mother Teresa isn't married."

"I want those records destroyed, Stanley!"

"Knock yourself out, Dorothy, but I am not tampering with legal documents."

"I want Frank and Regina out of our home. I want both apartments back. I want our diamond ring back... .....Hello, Stan..... are you there? I think he hung up!" Dorothy still seemed shocked that anyone would dare to do such a thing.

"We need to talk to our son, Dorothy."

"Good luck getting past his fire-breathing wife."

"Well, we'll write to them then. We'll order them out of our home."

"They own half of both units, remember? I'm just glad we didn't sign them over when he accepted his residency, like we had agreed to!"

"Regina won't fight us; she'll sign them both back over. They can forfeit their hard work on Frank Jr.'s nursery. Especially the grand detailed mural that they are both so attached to!"

Stanley refused to draft the letter and advised Dorothy that Frank and Regina were in no way obligated to return the apartments. He was disgusted with his friends and felt sorry for Frank and Regina, regardless of what circumstances had taken place. Dorothy wrote the letter herself.

Dear Frank,

Your bizarre set of circumstances has us stressed to a point that we can no longer tolerate. The biggest issue is the fact that you have been dishonest with us and probably with each other. I had lunch with Elizabeth, who stated the true facts which she heard directly from Regina. The pain is too much for us to bear. Why should she have been allowed the detailed facts and not us?

Your wife is a hurtful imposter and will get what she deserves for upsetting our family the way she has, and your son will hate her someday. Gabriella is not your child, Frank. Regina has engineered this whole mess. Please come back to us and bring Frank Jr. Your wife is mentally ill, my son, but together we can help her. You must trust us, Frank, for we have never let you down.

Unless you accept our help and include us, we cannot and will not allow Regina to live in our home any longer. Sign both units over to us at once by executing the enclosed paperwork and have it notarized. If you wish to be honest with us, we will be glad to reconsider this course of action. We can meet you anywhere and Regina need not know about it. I suggest that you hear what we have found out.

Love,
Mom and Dad

Regina received the letter addressed to Frank only, with a bright red CONFIDENTIAL stamped on both sides of the envelope; which arrived at Jackson Memorial Hospital. After reading it, she quietly passed it to Frances. The silence was broken by a joyful screech from Frank Jr. who was riding into the clinic on Grandpa Leo's shoulders with a squawking toy stuffed turkey. The loud toy sang *I'm a Turkey not a Chicken, Can't You See?* Frank had already learned all of the words on the way over and was singing them with Leo.

Frances handed the letter to Leo with tears in her eyes. The Colonel was furious. "Has Frank seen this nonsense?" Both ladies shook their heads no. "This psychotic woman needs to be sued for slander, and she can't take back her homes if they have been signed over." Regina burst out laughing, "She's an Indian Giver. Perhaps we should send her one of the headdresses that Frank Jr. wore for Halloween."

"What do you think you'll do?" her worried second mother asked.

"Well, I will have to show the letter to Frank, since he has to sign too. I would simply ignore all of her comments and return the signed papers by themselves. After we have moved out, that is."

"Did Elizabeth tell her everything?" The Colonel was angry for the second time.

"Impossible. My mother doesn't know anything to tell. I think this is a trap to befuddle everyone involved and cause a huge misunderstanding. They are hoping to finally get the facts that she feels are due to them. This is an angry reaction to her failed, deranged efforts."

"Let me call Lamar," Frances suggested, "There are two families by Wyatt and Sylvia that are going to be vacating, and I think those units may be available to rent."

"I better go find Frank," Regina said as he entered the room holding clinic papers.

Regina handed him the letter and cringed as he tore it into pieces. Glad that she had withheld the real estate papers, she asked him how he wanted her to respond. "We own the two apartments, Regina. I took my Residency here and that was the deal. We're suing them."

"We actually only own half of each, as they were never signed over, honey."

Frank was beside himself. He didn't know which was worse,

the anger or the hurt that he felt. He found relief watching his son play with his new toy, but he was instantly crushed again, realizing how much Frank Jr. loved his nursery, and remembering the hours of work he and Regina had put into it. Leo put his arm around his choice resident and suggested that they go for coffee. Frank looked at Regina, who nodded, and left the clinic with his attending.

"I am so furious with them, that I don't even want to speak to them," Frank said firmly.

"That's completely understandable. Those comments were unkind, untrue and uncalled for. Elizabeth didn't know anything to tell your mother, according to Regina."

"I know that. This is typical of my parents. They have exhausted all of their other resources to find 'the truth.'"

"Well, Regina was laughing and called them Indian Givers. She said she would like to move and give them back their apartments."

Frank shook his head sadly, "Why do they attack Regina? It had nothing to do with her!"

"They are in the dark and they don't like it, son. Regina is obviously never going to be controlled, and that is very hard for someone like Dorothy to accept."

Frank was flattered, but then asked sadly, "What will we do about Frank's room? He loves his Big Top. I'm thinking that we should fight this. We spent weeks decorating that place, and the mural of the crowd can't be moved. Frank talks to all of those people as though they are real."

"Before we dig in the battle ground, we better check back with your feisty little wife. She and Frances probably have the whole solution by now!"

"I just came from Andrew's office. I had myself checked because Regina has not gotten pregnant yet. The tests for men are much less complicated than they are for women, so Andrew suggested that we start with me."

"And?"

"I have a varicocele. My count is considered infertile at the present point."

"That can be surgically repaired, Frank; it's a simple outpatient procedure."

"Yes, but how will this effect Regina? Eva got pregnant with the odds like they are. It's next to impossible."

"Let's recheck the genetics."

"We did. Gabriella is my daughter. Regina will be destroyed."

"Don't be too sure about that, my son, it would take a hell of a lot more than that to bring Regina down."

"Should we go and talk to her and Frances now?"

"Are you comfortable doing that, Frank? I'm sure they will be fine with it."

Returning to clinic, the two "white coats" found Frank Jr. wrapping an ace bandage around his turkey's leg. "He broke his leg, Dad," the little boy smiled, "Yep, he fell and broke his patella." In spite of everything, the four adults laughed as Frank Sr. scooped his son up and hugged him.

"And where is his patella?" Grandpa Leo asked.

"Oh, Grandpa, you should already know that. It's right here on his knee; it's his knee bone."

Regina was not upset in the least about the fertility report, but concerned that Frank did not tell her that he was going for the testing. "If we can't have more kids, so be it. I don't want you to have surgery."

"Regina, I want more kids, and this is a simple outpatient procedure."

"He's absolutely right, honey," Frances reassured, wondering just how much more this young couple would be saddled with today.

"What are the risks?" Regina was still not convinced.

"None," the Colonel answered authoritatively.

Leo carried Frank Jr. and his turkey to X-Ray for a make-believe film, while Frank and Regina talked with Frances.

"Regina, it is against all odds that Gabriella could be mine, yet she is. We rechecked the DNA tests."

"So, we did good then! Perhaps it _was_ against all odds, Frank, but then it was even more clearly God's will that she be here. Who are we to question? Mercedes brought these pictures by from Halloween. Gabriella looks even more like your mother now that she is older. Whatever His reasons were and are, I feel honored to be a part of the outstanding solution!"

Frank grabbed Regina and lifting her from the floor, swung her around, "Part of the solution? You are the solution! I love you madly, girl!"

"Does this mean that you are not going to help your mother commit me?"

Frank and Frances burst out laughing, "Do you ever take anything seriously, Pollyanna?" Frances asked.

"Here's something we need to take seriously," Frank spoke quietly, "Our little son's room." Frances nodded sadly in agreement.

"What about it?" Regina seemed confused.

"It will be difficult to move a lot of it, and the folks at the Doral don't allow painting, except in neutral colors," Frances added.

"So we will create a whole new room! We don't present it to him as a loss, but as an exciting new adventure."

"What could compete with his Big Top, Regina?"

"'Elementary, my dear Watson,' I have already thought about that. Your son adores stuffed animals, especially monkeys. Grants had a barrel of adorable white monkeys on sale for $1.00 apiece two months ago. I bought all thirty-two of them just for the bargain. They will now be part of his new room – a jungle!"

Frank picked up the telephone on the desk, as Frances and Regina looked at him questioningly. Without explanation, he booked his surgery for the upcoming Friday.

The Colonel and his apprentice returned from X-Ray with a report that the turkey would be perfect again due to Frank Jr.'s excellent work.

"This day calls for an impromptu dinner at Shorty's," Leo smiled. Short notice or not, the entire twelve pack and all five babies were eating barbeque chicken and chatting busily about the impending relocation of the Solbergs.

Jeannie's eyes filled with tears. She and Regina had lived next door to each other since medical school started.

Hyacinth spoke quietly, but everyone grew silent and heard her. "Dare are going to be two empty spaces. Everybody needs to come to the Doral. Chuck, when is your lease up?"

"We rent month to month, and I have no problem moving by

Frank. We don't want to miss anything," he said laughing.

Hyacinth continued by sharing the information about the luncheon that Dorothy and Elizabeth had. "Knee-der laydee know any details and dey are floundering in the dark."

Frank was shocked and asked Regina, "Don't you think your mother has a right to see that letter?"

The answer was preceded by a sheepish smile, "The one you ripped into a million pieces? I would say that was Divine Intervention. There is nothing to be gained by showing my mother that nonsense, and less than nothing to be gained by acknowledging any of the other garbage contained in that vicious letter."

"The best reaction is no reaction," Hazel joined in the fight.

"You better believe it," Frances added crossly, "I would make your arrangements to leave Isla Del Mar as soon as possible and return the signed papers as requested with no comments. Your parents can churn themselves into a stupor guessing what your reaction was; and I am astounded that Elizabeth would engage in a luncheon with Dorothy over this."

The next day Regina and Jeannie were at the Doral. There were two large, two- bedroom apartments opening up, one building over from Wyatt and Sylvia. The girls each put a deposit down and planned their move for the following week. After being told that no paint other than off-white was to be used, Jeannie was concerned about both of their little boys' rooms, "The nurseries," she was almost in tears. "Not to worry," reassured Regina, "I've got this covered." Jeannie smiled and didn't give the problem another thought.

Chapter Eleven

Dan to the Rescue

Lamar called Dan and told him what was going on. Although he was usually a very laid-back person, he was furious, to say the least. "Where is this letter?" he asked his friend and former partner. "Frank ripped it to pieces in anger, but not before Frances and Leo read it."

Dan set the blue print on his desk aside, and put his feet up in its place. Lighting a cigarette, he took a long drag and exhaled. "I don't think Elizabeth could have told her anything, but she will be outraged at the accusation."

Lamar laughed, "Well Regina doesn't want her mother to know anything about the letter. She thinks they should ignore it, move out to the Doral, and sign the both places at Isla Del Mar back over to the Solbergs."

"Is Regina okay?"

"Strong as a stone wall, and running the whole show, as usual. She and Frances are 'large and in charge' - laughing all the way! I was afraid Frances was going to blast Dorothy at first, though."

"How is Frank taking all of this?"

"Hard. He is also having surgery tomorrow to repair a minor vein that is keeping Regina from getting pregnant again. You didn't hear that from me, of course."

"What about the spectacular mural on Frank Jr.'s wall? Have they voiced any concerns about that?"

"Yes, Frank Sr. is very upset about it and so is Frances. Regina said to present the opportunity of a whole new room to Frank Jr. rather than losing the one he has."

"That's fine, my friend, but that mural is coming down. We can probably cut the sheet rock in large pieces – like a puzzle, and store it. When Regina wants it again, it's just a matter of touch-up."

"You got my help, Dan, and Brian's too. I'm sure the three of us can make that happen. We'll just replace the sheet rock so we don't hear any garbage from Goliath!"

"Okay, I'll come down next week with the love birds. I may bring Elizabeth too. I just won't tell her about the letter."

Regina went to the Child Enrichment Center and sat on the floor with Frank and Charlie. "Boys, we have a chance to move so that we live by Uncle Wyatt, Aunt Sylvia, and Hyacinth, Harper, and Holly, (who had all joined the meeting). Not only that, but you two get new rooms! We could put away the Big Top and the farm for later, and have a monkey jungle room for you Frank, and Space Pets for you Charlie (his favorite T.V. show). Unless of course, you want your same old room in the new place."

Frank Jr. was delighted but did have one concern, "What about my el-phant? He can't be put away, Mommy, because I love him."

"Why, a jungle without an elephant? Unthinkable! Of course

he must come. Your other animals will come too! Your pop-corn wagon will be dressed up like a jungle jeep, and used in the new room as well!"

"All of my farm animals have to be Space Pets, Aunt Gina," Charlie looked worried.

"Why, of course, and your farm house must be dressed up like a shiny silver rocket, or how will you travel through space?!" Both boys and the triplets were cheering when Leo came into the room grinning. Frances and Hazel were teary- eyed in the observation room. Jeannie, both relieved and delighted, called Chuck.

"We can paint our new walls bright colors," Frank suggested to his friends.

"Yeah, and I need to paint my room with the crops like I have now."

Regina smiled calmly, and answered, "Well now, we can't paint at the Doral. We can only have white walls ----- Sooo, we need to put on our thinking caps and see what other things we could use besides paint." The five kids were mimicking putting on thinking caps and Hyacinth and Holly closed their eyes for extra concentration. Harper laughed and observed with the other two boys. Regina was in her glory, "What if we use another kind of color, like cloth?" The kids looked at her for more detail. "We can all go to Diamonds and get blue cloth for the sky, green and brown for the jungle trees and for the crops in space, silver for the stars, and yellow for the sun!"

"We will paint the walls with cloth?" Frank confirmed.

"Well, we will cover the walls with cloth! Why not? We will do what we're going to call soft-sculpture."

"Can we help too?" asked a very excited Hyacinth and Holly?

"Absolutely! We will need all the help we can get," Aunt Gina reassured.

"And mee too! Added Harper. " I want to help too!"

"No gurls," said Charlie, quickly gaining Frank's and Harper's support.

"Oh, Yes," Hyacinth was on her feet, moving in Charlie's direction, before being tackled in a hug by Regina.

"Now boys, there are girls' jobs and boys' jobs. Where would we be without both?"

"Okay," Charlie solemnly nodded, but they do the gurls' jobs, not the boys' jobs."

"Exactly," Regina had the whole group agreeing – for the moment anyway!

Regina returned to the clinic to find a message that Dan and her mother, Andrea and Brian, and Bub and Sis were coming down on Saturday. "Aunt Sis is bringing a ton of Lasagna and garlic bread, Andrea and Brian are making a big Caesar Salad. The whole twelve pack is invited, and we hope to see Gabriella too, since you have her this weekend." Frances added below – *all other food has been taken care of – you just supply the house.* Regina was delighted.

When Eva dropped Gabriella off for visitation, the party was just beginning. Elizabeth told her about the move and invited her to stay! "Mom is in the car," Eva answered.

"Well, bring her in, sweetie," Aunt Sis added.

Mercedes came in and hugged Elizabeth. In broken English,

she said, "Many avocados for all of you. Such a bod thing Dorothy does to these kids. Such a bod, bod thing!" Gabriella ran to join Hyacinth and Holly, and evened out the score!

Dan went up to Regina and gave her a huge hug. He escorted her to the nursery and explained that they were taking the mural down in pieces so that it could be used again. Regina wept for joy. She loved the wall and loved the fact that her husband had spent so many hours on it for their son. The detailed crowd of circus spectators held beautiful memories for all of them, and she had silently dreaded leaving it. Dan and Lamar worked diligently, removing the art while Brian and Frank replaced it with plain white sheetrock to be painted white.

Roger and Hyacinth laughed as they imitated the reaction Raymond and Dorothy would have when they saw it. Each piece was wrapped carefully like a giant puzzle, and carefully packed for storage. Frank Jr. was delighted to see that his very wall was moving too! While they were at it, Elizabeth and Mercedes carefully packed up the entire Big Top, and speculated how the pop-corn cart would look as a jungle jeep. The monkeys would "naturally" be selling the plaster-cast candy apples, so to Frank Jr.'s delight, they were also packed with the elephant for the Doral. "My monkeys are going to be just like real!" the little boy screeched for joy.

Dan took Regina by the hand and led her to his truck, where there were fifty-seven bolts of gorgeous fabrics in every color and texture imaginable! Long artificial grass in large boxes, were in good company with other assorted silk plants and berries. "We are rebuilding a craft center and these things were up for grabs," Dan explained, delighted to see his step-daughter's face. "I love you, little tower of strength," he hugged her again. On the way back in, they saw Brian and Andrea on the patio kissing. Dan winked at Regina, "There may be another wedding soon. Brian has a ring for her, but I don't know when he is intending to pop the big question." Regina was delighted, as she and Andrea had always been very close.

Elizabeth was sitting on the floor with all six children reading a book, and Gabriella was in her lap playing with her necklace. Mercedes and Eva were delighted and flattered to be included in the food preparation. Frances closed her eyes and whispered, "I love you, Abba! You truly are sensational - the Greatest!"

Everyone got ready to eat and Dan asked Brian to say the blessing. Blushing, the quiet young man began, "Father, we thank You for this wonderful day that has brought us all together. We thank You for this wonderful food and for the love that we all share here. Father, will You help me ask Andrea if she will marry me? Amen."

He walked to Andrea and got down on one knee, "Will you have me as your husband, young lady?" Too choked up to answer, Andrea nodded with tears in her eyes. Everyone applauded as Brian placed the ring on her left hand.

Dan and Elizabeth rushed to the couple for big hugs, followed by Frances and Lamar and Frank and Regina. "Regina, will you be my maid of honor?" Regina hugged her sister and answered, "Beyond the shadow of a doubt!" The excitement and fun continued until dark.

"What's 'marry me?'" Charlie asked Frank Jr.

"I think it means somebody is going to die," Frank Jr. answered solemnly.

The crowd laughed and needed several minutes to clarify the meaning of marry for all of the children. "Hey, leave him alone, he's got the right idea," Bub teased.

Elizabeth finally approached Regina, "I am so sorry, sweetheart. I should have been here for you earlier. That's not a nice thing to have to say."

"You were always here, Mom, but you were hurting because you thought I was. You were hurting for me – and that is a pretty nice thing to be able to say."

Dan smiled at his favorite daughter and hugged his wife. "Complicated creatures - women," he laughed. "That's why you die when you get married, Grandpa," his grandson reasoned, clearly not convinced by the previous correction.

"And exactly who taught you this?" Regina laughed.

"Grandpa Leo," the bright-blue- eyed young Solberg answered. Finishing his lasagna, Leo laughed, "Bury. Bury! I said you bury someone when they die. He asked me what it means when somebody gets buried." Frances and Hazel looked at each other and laughed, "Oh, sure!" they teased together.

"Oh yeah, 'buried', like the dead horse on telabision," Frankie saved the Colonel's neck!

The days passed quickly as the move drew near. Frank and Regina went to Chuck and Jeannie's to help pack up the house. They were wrapping glasses when there was a knock on the door. The UPS man had a brown box for Jeannie, from her parents. Opening it, she discovered new door signs for both Charlie and Frank Jr. Frank's was a monkey swinging from a palm tree, eating a coconut that said, *Welcome to the Jungle*, and Charlie's was a spaceship that said, *Welcome to Space Camp*. Both little boys were thrilled, and carried their new signs around until bedtime.

"It's a good thing we have great patios at the Doral too," Chuck said, opening a soda and watching Monique and Dodger survey the moving boxes with no real interest.

"I'll second that," Frank Sr. added. "The pool there is nicer than ours too. I'd be downhearted leaving this place if you and Jeannie weren't moving too, though."

"Same here, Brother, and I'm very glad that mural of yours is going out of here as well."

"So we're really only leaving our memories," Jeannie brightened.

"Who's leaving memories? We'll take them right with us too," Pollyanna reassured the group that there was nowhere to go but up.

"Will we miss the river, Pollyanna?" Jeannie asked.

"Nope! Not with the two boys getting older. Living right beside the river has concerned me on many occasions, but they were only babies. They are getting older now, and I cringe when I see all the young kids playing by the docks. It's just too dangerous."

"You know, I never thought of that," Frank and Chuck said almost at the same time.

"It's been wonderful since the boys were too young to be around it. That goes in the box with the memories," Jeannie laughed.

"Not to mention how great it will be to have everybody on one big turf, and Leo and Hazel two blocks away!" Chuck added.

The packing and laughing continued until it got too late to do anymore. While moving was usually a chore, the four decided that it was definitely fun in this case.

"I am so relieved to be free at last from any material ties with my parents!" Frank threw his arms up. "I wonder if they got the paperwork yet?"

"Did you guys say anything to them about all of this?"

"Nope. Regina just had the real estate transferred and included that they could take possession Sunday at 5:00 pm."

"Wait until they see that you've removed their wall!" Jeannie couldn't help an outburst of laughter.

"Well, they will probably think that we simply painted over it," Frank answered disappointedly.

"Don't worry, darling," Regina reassured, "Your little name-sake will clue them in soon enough!"

"When?" Frank wanted to be sure there were no solid plans to visit with either of his parents.

"Well they certainly won't go forever without seeing their grandson, or at least talking to him."

"Don't be so sure, Regina. If they gave a damn about their grandson, they wouldn't have done what they did!"

"I'll settle this problem," Chuck laughed, "just have Dan send them a bill for the construction of the new wall!"

Now Frank was laughing too, "I'm not usually one for spite, but I would like to see them find out that their little power struggle has back-fired as usual."

Regina was laughing quietly as her husband looked over at her. "What's so funny, Pollyanna?"

"Oh, nothing, just that the tenants in our old one bedroom called me the day you were taking down the wall to ask if it was alright that they had adopted four cats a couple of weeks ago. I advised them that they were supposed to pay a pet deposit and get approval first, but that we no longer owned either apartment, and gave them the number to your parents' home. They said that they were just going to keep them, and when Dad and I were coming in from the truck, they were carrying the shredded drapes from the master bedroom to the trash chute."

"I hope they know how dirty cats can be if they are not properly cared for," Jeannie grinned, "they obviously realized too late that cat claws can be hazardous to drapes."

"I hope they don't give a hoot, and let the cats stink the whole place up. It isn't ours anymore; not our asset and therefore not our responsibility!" Frank laughed as the others joined him.

Frank Jr. looked over and asked the adults if they were all playing nicely. The four just smiled and reassured him that they were.

Charlie put his little hands on his hips and addressed the adults, "I don't think you guys are playing nicely at all. We need to have a circle time about telling stories."

Regina and Jeannie simultaneously said, "'Out of the mouths of babes!'"

Dorothy was livid when she received the paperwork. "Not even a letter! Nothing but the deeds, the both sets of keys, and the time we can take possession! Who does that girl think she is? Where are they going to live now? If they move in with Frances, there will eventually be trouble. Raymond, don't just stand there like a jackass stuck in mud, – say something."

"Well, I don't know what to say. They have conveniently sent these papers back so that it is too late for us to talk things over. We had possession as of yesterday at 5:00 pm. They are gone and we don't know where they are. I wonder if they have the same phone number!"

"I hope they cried their heads off, and I hope that Frank Jr. was devastated saying goodbye to his little circus room. His idiotic parents spent all of those hours on that whole scene, and especially on the mural!" Dorothy laughed in satisfaction.

Raymond shrugged his shoulders, "Maybe there is a note in the apartment. We need to go to Miami to inspect the unit and get a tenant in there."

"Frank and Regina can be responsible for that part of it. We are not running back and forth!"

"I doubt that they will cooperate in any way with that, Dorothy, and we cannot legally make them."

"We can make Frank, as his parents!"

Raymond cringed as Dorothy dialed the clinic number. "Yes, I would like to speak with Dr. Frank Solberg or at least Regina Solberg, please."

Unfortunately for the caller, Frances had answered the phone. "And just who is calling?"

"None of your damn business, Frances," Dorothy screamed. Dial tone.

Arriving in Miami a few days later, the senior Solbergs were out-raged that the mural had been removed. They were instantly clued in by the tags that had been pulled off of the new sheetrock and "accidentally" left on the window sill by Dan and Lamar! Dorothy ranted and raved and called Stan Duncliff. "There isn't a single thing you can do about that, Dorothy. First of all, the place was theirs too. Secondly, they replaced the sheetrock and left no damage."

"So they destroyed the art work in front of my grandson! That's spiteful, mental cruelty. I will have their son taken away from them."

"Grow up, Dorothy! You don't have any idea what they did, and whether or not Frank Jr. was even there. You are making a fool of yourself, and that's exactly what they would tell you in court."

"Listen here, Stan, I... ....Stan, Staaan! He hung up on me again!" After slamming the kitchen phone back on the receiver with such force that it pulled free from the wall, Dorothy kicked it across the room.

Raymond noticed an envelope appearing under the door, motioned to Dorothy, and whispered, "They must not know that we're in here."

The irate matriarch motioned silence and mumbled, "Let them suffer and think about what they did. We will call down to them from the patio as they are leaving. They can walk their butts back up here and apologize. We'll have the truth now, my dear; it took less time than I thought!"

Quietly picking the letter up and opening it, Raymond looked at his wife in alarm, "It's not from Frank and Regina; it's from the tenants in the one bedroom," he rushed to open the door, just in time to hear exit door at the end of the hall slam shut. The note was scribbled in packing marker, and read:

> Sorry we had to move, but we got new jobs far away from here. We can't pay the rent because we used the money for the moving expenses. We also left the four cats because we can't take them with us. Sorry. Taped to the bottom of the letter were the keys to the rental unit.

"We must go after them," Dorothy shouted.

"We have never met them; we don't know who we are looking for."

"RE-GI-NAAAAAAH!" Dorothy shrieked as her face shook with rage.

The Solberg seniors rushed to the rental apartment to find it vacant. Inside, they discovered three very large cats walking around and no litter boxes! The carpets were matted with cat feces, and the smell of urine burned their nostrils. Turning in response to a cry in the kitchen, the outraged couple saw the detached oven door propped against the sink behind the racks and elements, to oblige another huge cat who had claimed the inside of the appliance to house her seven newborn kittens.

Chapter Twelve
Paint by the Yard

The move went very smoothly, and Regina directed the production of both of the boys' bedrooms. The jungle background was placed wall-to-wall in sapphire blue for the sky, while tiny artificial birds flashed their vibrant colors among gracefully floating Polly-fill clouds. Greens and browns for the ground areas were enhanced by velvet moss, sprayed with special sealant to prevent dust collection. Sewing machines were running, making 3-D ceiling-to-floor burlap palm trees with layered ridges going up the trunks that made them look real. Long, fingered, green felt leaves, housing bent coat hangers to add form, extended from them with clusters of round stuffed coconuts bulging from their bases. Large banana trees with wide, flapping leaves, hung in two corners. Bunches of felt bananas sewn with black thread were attached to a dangling stalk, for realistic appearance. Tall artificial grass lined the bottoms of the walls with thick colorful berry bushes among them. Groups of plush monkeys came to life in the display – two were in opposite trees, wearing raincoats (from Regina's doll collection) each aiming a water gun at the other. Two others were engaged in (a caulk- painted- pink) bubble gum adventure, blowing huge pink bubbles; while a third had "accidentally" stretched his share of the gum, entwining his whole body! Another small group was perched in a tree with small Chinese take-out containers. The monkey with glasses, who led this gang, was reading the messages in the fortune-cookies, and attaching them to a kite tail. Three other monkeys manned the candy apple stand from the Big Top, saluting two more who were riding the elephant.

Last but not least, three primates wearing sunglasses were engaged in a yoyo contest; two juggling the yoyos successfully while the third's wrapped around him in a comical tangle. Other various stuffed animals contributed to the scene as the old popcorn cart that was now transformed into a jeep, housed a large stuffed chimp in a safari outfit, reading a book to two small monkeys on the hood.

All six children were surprised with tent beds, with bases that essentially fit right over their mattress to form an adventure in itself! Frank's was placed under "mosquito netting," by Grandpa Leo, to prevent any risk of malaria!

Charlie's room was bedecked in one wall of navy blue sky to depict space at night, with tiny silver stars glistening merrily. 3-D planets were created from sprayed Styrofoam balls enhanced with glitter. Saturn's magnificent rings were florescent, but the other planets rivaled it with glamour of their own. The tent bed was a space camp and the old farm house successfully became a rocket, covered in silver fabric and positioned for blast-off, on one wall, as Aunt Gina had promised.

All of the farm animals were incorporated by riding shooting stars, hitching a ride on the rocket ship, or simply walking around the huge paper Mache' moon. A small family of stuffed rabbits slept soundly in a crater, with a bunch of paper Mache' carrots, from Charlie's former farm, nestled right next to them. It was amazing to everyone that Regina could make toys come to life simply by positioning them with other props!

Mercedes and Eva came by to bring pizzas to all of the help, and couldn't believe their eyes. When Regina presented Gabriella's tent bed, they were touched beyond words. "There is tons of fabric left, for a 'My Little Pony scene'," she added.

"No, no," Eva shook her head, "Your dad brought that stuff for you."

"He brought it for all of the children," Regina corrected, "and Gabriella is just as included as the other five hoodlums!"

"I don't know how to hang those rooms," Eva answered quietly.

"Well, so we'll all come over and do her room too," Jeannie beamed, happy to be part of the solution.

Mercedes clapped her small hands together and smiled. "You would do thees for Gabriella? You peoples are fontostic!"

The triplets were also delighted with their tent beds, but now campaigned for a "big kid room" too. "Thanks a lot guys!" Wyatt laughed.

"What kind of room do they want?" Frank and Chuck asked at the same time.

"I don't know," Wyatt looked surprised.

"Berenstain Bears?" Aunt Regina suggested.

"Yeah! The Berenstain Bears," The chants came from all six kids.

"Simple, there's plenty of burlap and felt for the tree house. Dad and Lamar could make the wooden, box windows, and you guys could paint them," Regina indicated Frank, Chuck, and Wyatt; "and Cracker Barrel has plush Berenstain Bears for the sculpture," the 'director' added. The scene outside of the tree house would be a burlap log campfire ablaze by orange, red, yellow, and blue felt flames. The bear family would naturally be roasting cotton ball marshmellows on sticks. The background wall would be a night sky, similar to Charlie's, while the other walls would sport the day-time settings in Bear Country! The triplets were delighted!

Once Gabriella's purple and pink mountains and streams were in place, with the little ponies happily residing among them, Frances had the newspaper come out and do a story on all four rooms. The news about this new way of decorating was traveling faster than anybody realized. Offers suddenly came rolling in!

The group decided not to bury themselves in work, but to take one project at the time and make extra money as a team. Regina immediately opened a savings account for all of her in-come from their new *Soft Sculpture Company, 'Stories in Cloth,'* to be used for a down payment on their first house. Jeannie and Sylvia followed suit. They would just sort of play with prospective orders for extra money and the sheer fun of creating the rooms.

Their husbands were proud, to say the least, and unintention-ally contributed to the flow of demands with their bragging. The ladies even had schools calling for orders!

Eva and Mercedes were both cleaning houses in addition to their regular jobs, to make ends meet. Regina learned about this, and felt that this was far too much extra work, especially for Mercedes. She appealed to Frank one night at dinner. "What if we put Gabby with the other five monsters and employ Mercedes as a teacher assistant? We have an opening, and Eva would save the daycare money that she pays her mother. Mercedes would draw a better check, and they could stop cleaning houses on weekends."

"Pollyanna, Pollyanna, Pollyanna," Frank hugged his wife, "you are determined to make this whole scenario into a fairy tale!"

"It already is a fairy tale, darling, but that's not really my doing."

"Well, okay, I will agree if you really want to. Both Mercedes and Eva love you very much, not to mention the fact that Gabriella adores you."

"Us, Frank; they love us."

The telephone rang and the tired couple decided to let the answering machine pick it up. Following the Florida Gator fight song and the recorded message, Dorothy's voice blared, "You two are making fools of yourselves. Fabric on walls! Who do you think you are? You need to stay out of the newspapers and grow up! Both of you need to grow the hell up! I know that you are there, Frank, and you better pick up this phone! You are to call me back at once and make arrangements to get tenants in both of those apartments. I can have you two arrested for damages to our one bedroom unit from all of those disgusting cats. I will have Frank Jr. picked up by Social Services. You call me now, Buster. I know you are home."

Regina and Frank looked at each other and laughed hysterically. Neither of them were the least bit concerned about Dorothy's idle threats, and neither had any intention of acknowledging the message. Exhausted from laughter, Frank finally spoke, "Well, the answering machine just paid for itself one hundred times over."

"I cannot understand why she harbors such anger and ill will," Regina looked puzzled. "You'd think that she would know by now that the antics she pulls will not be effective."

"My mother has always had full control of our family, Regina. She is having a terrible time letting go of that."

"Adam and Marge are still her subjects," Regina noted factually.

"Only because they have no choice," Frank added, "if they dared to take a stand against them, they would be out of an office and out of their home."

"It still wouldn't be worth it to me," Regina sighed. "I would rather have nothing and start from scratch than be controlled by someone."

"Well that's where they made their mistake. We began by taking a stand back in the beginning of medical school. Adam waited and waited, and now they don't own a thing without strings attached. They are told when and where they can go on vacation, and if they're ordered to the queen's home for a conference; they go. Period. I never realized any of this until after I was married to you."

"I hope that we never make Frank Jr. feel as though he is being controlled," Regina looked thoughtful. "Setting safety boundaries and healthy limits to teach children values are fine, but we also must allow and encourage them to be independent thinkers and problem solvers," she added.

"Well, that's where my folks won't bend. We are not allowed to deviate in any way from their opinions, even as adults. I always just went along with them to keep the peace. One day, I was going to date a girl that my mother didn't like. She told me over and over that she was upset by the plans, and finally, as I went to leave, she ripped a Pierre Cardin dress shirt off of my back. I still resent my reaction to that incident more than you will ever know."

"How did you react to such a thing, Frank?"

"I cancelled my date."

"And that's how you got stuck with me?"

"Very funny, Pollyanna!"

Their conversation was interrupted by five youngsters racing into the kitchen. Frank Jr. explained, "Listen guys, we need a lot of cereal and marshmallows to trap a wild and crazy dog that is very dangerous." As he spoke, Charlie and the triplets nodded along earnestly.

"You don't say," Frank laughed. "That's right Dad; that dog will eat everyone in this building if we don't trap him. He took all of Hyacinth's and Holly's cookies right out of their playhouse, and tipped over their tea set," the exasperated little boy paused to take a deep breath.

"Where is this dog, Frankie," a concerned Regina asked.

"He's hiding now," Charlie and Harper answered.

"That's why we have to trap him," Frank continued.

"How and where do you intend to trap him?" Frank Sr. asked.

"Dad, I know how to do this from the discovery channel. Charlie and I have the whole thing set up. We just need the food."

"Okay, well let's go see the set-up we'll bring the cereal and marshmallows."

"No pearlents!" Holly interrupted, holding up a 'STOP' hand. "No grown-ups can be near our trap, Hyacinth confirmed, "too dangerous."

"Well, I'm afraid that we need our parents to oversee some things, guys," Frank was struggling to keep a straight face.

"The whole add-bencher will be wrecked," Charlie fretted.

The "add-bencher" wreckers promised to stay back and follow instructions as the five crusaders carried their bait and walked ahead.

Outside of Chuck and Jeannie's glass doors, a trap had been built that was six inches wide and three inches deep, covered by a paper towel and multiple twigs. Upon further questioning, the nine-week-old lab puppy from the next building stood accused!

"What will you do with the dog once you trap him?" Frank Sr. asked.

"We will all lift him out of the hole," Frank Jr. seemed shocked at his father's ignorance.

"Then we will put him in my doll carriage and take him to the police," Holly answered seriously.

"How will you know where the police are?" Regina wondered.

"Aunt Geeeena, Harper and Charlie and Frankie will turn into the police!"

"Yeah," Hyacinth chimed in, "they will take the wild and crazy dog to his house and give him a ticket."

"Well I guess we should get out of the way then," Regina smiled.

"Independent thinking class 101," Frank Sr. mumbled, laughing.

"Just be sure they don't make it to the newspaper – you're parents will have heart attacks!"

Chapter Thirteen
The Makeover

Once the old friends had settled in effortlessly as new neighbors, Mercedes was employed at the Child Enrichment Center. Gabby joined right in with the other children, was in wonderful spirits, and advanced considerably on a social level. While Eva was sincerely grateful for all that had been done for her and her family, she began to feel isolated from the group. Since Mercedes transported Gabby back and forth to daycare and consequently to her visits with her father; Eva was no longer in the routine close contact with the others that she had been prior to the new arrangement. Reminding herself that she was entitled to nothing from the Solbergs or any their friends, she firmly forced herself to appear cheerful whenever she did see Frank and Regina. One evening, when they were bringing Gabby home, Regina sensed a deep sadness in Eva, and invited her to lunch the next day.

Delighted but concerned, Eva accepted the invitation. Regina was typically straight to the point, and Eva was deeply touched by her candor. "Eva, it is pointless to be troubled when you have an entire team of friends who want to help you. What is making you sad?"

"I already owe you too much, Regina, I cannot accept anymore."

"You owe bill collectors, Eva; but you never owe your friends."

"Friends don't do what I did, Regina," Eva was now crying softly.

"'Did!' Past tense, Eva; that's all water under the bridge."

"Oh, how I wish we had met before all of this happened. We could have been such beautiful friends," she shook with sadness as she tried to muffle her tears.

"Eva, we still have a beautiful friendship. Let the past go, will you?"

"I want so much to be one of you, and now with Mama working there, I am all alone. You three ladies are so beautiful, and you all have Frances and Hazel, and Mama adores you too!"

"Ah, but you have Mercedes as your own mother, and all of us as friends. Oh, and by the way, you have plenty of great looks yourself, Eva. You just need to steal the same tips that we all use!"

"Oh right!" Eva was laughing softly, "I am a beast."

"Not hardly, Eva. Why don't we have a makeover night at my house next week when Frank and Chuck are on call?"

"What is a makeover night?"

"It's when we give each other perms, facials, manicures, color touch-ups, et cetera."

"I don't know; maybe in many months from now."

"Maybe next Friday," Regina insisted.

"I don't even know where to start!"

"You start by showing up. The grandmothers will babysit all of the monsters, and the mommies will play beauty parlor!"

After some coaxing, Eva reluctantly agreed. Jeannie and Sylvia also agreed to "play," for Regina's sake. One of the neighbors at the Doral was a hairdresser on maternity leave, and was looking for extra work. Seeing the advertisement in the laundry room, Sylvia had used her before. She was hired to do a full gypsy cut, which would flatter the shape of Eva's face.

When Eva arrived, drinks were poured, a hot olive oil treatment was placed on her hair, and the scalp area was wrapped in plastic. Next an avocado mask prepared by Sylvia, was applied followed by a manicure by Jeannie.

The girls munched on chips, dips, party sandwiches, tea cakes, cocktail franks and mini pizzas, as they chatted and joked about men. Jeannie's baby began to kick inside of her. "It must be another boy," she laughed.

After the mask was removed and moisturizing crème applied, Regina started the shampoo while Jeannie called the hairdresser in. Chunks of dead hair fell to the floor as a new style emerged.

Regina applied a rich sable brown permanent color and set the timer. Once the color was rinsed, the hairdresser started the blow dryer, and Eva's new hairstyle fell in soft layers above her shoulders. The bangs framed her face but cleared her eyes so as not to aggravate the muscle imbalance. Jeannie applied subtle makeup and Eva already looked like a different person. The final step was style, which was Sylvia's area of expertise.

Approaching the full length mirror in the bedroom, Eva was shocked! She was on the verge of tears, but did not want to spoil her makeup. Finally, she could hold out no longer and placed her head in her hands. Sobbing, she told the three ladies and the hair-dresser that she did not deserve to look so good. Each of the girls reassured her, as Jeannie touched up her makeup.

"Past is past," Regina reminded.

"Come on, Eva, give yourself a break," Jeannie followed the lead.

"Oh yes," Sylvia added, "who doesn't ever make a mistake?"

The friends were interrupted by the telephone. Wyatt was calling Sylvia to report the results of her lab work taken that morning. "You're pregnant, my angel!"

The girls were all laughing and hugging Sylvia. "I can only hope that we are having one this time! I wouldn't mind another litter, though," she beamed.

When the four girls walked over to Frances and Lamar's house to collect the babies, the three older ladies were amazed. Roger and Lamar whistled, simultaneously. Eva was delighted with the complements, but continued to hang her head. It was the Colonel's wife who took over. "Eva, hold that pretty head up and walk like the striking lady that you are!"

Eva started to cry again, and Mercedes looked concerned. Moving toward her daughter, she reached out for her. The two began to speak in Spanish, but they were interrupted by Grandpa Leo, who came in the front door to pick Hazel up, and raised his eyebrows. "Wow!" he said, smiling. "I trust these are tears of joy."

Mercedes looked up and sadly shook her head.

"What then?" the Colonel didn't know what to think.

Eva looked shyly at him. "Sir, these are tears of regret; sorrow for all that I have done to this beautiful group of people. I don't deserve to be treated nicely by any of you."

"Outside on the patio, young lady," the no-nonsense Colonel commanded.

Eva quivered, but obeyed the order. Leo smiled gently, "Listen, Eva, there's nothing wrong with realizing your mistake and taking your share of the blame, but you certainly don't deserve to assign yourself a life sentence."

"Regina," she sobbed, "How could I have done such a thing to Regina?"

"Regina is a missionary, Eva, a messenger from God. What's done is over with. I think it's a miracle that things turned out the way they did. Your mother is doing a remarkable job at the Child Enrichment Center; Gabby is much more socially advanced than she was; and you look like a new woman. I can't see any way things could be better!"

"Things could have been better if I had a baby in an honorable way," Eva sobbed again.

"Everything happens for a reason, Eva. When we fall, we must pick ourselves up, right what we can right, and move on."

"How much time does it all take, Sir?"

"That depends on your ability to let go of the past and move forward."

"Frank and I don't even like each other now," Eva was correct.

"Well, at least you are able to be civil to each other." Leo could never bring himself to warm up to Eva either, but he was willing to forgive and forget on a workable level.

"I may try to go for some counseling," Eva answered slowly.

"Are you aware that there is free counseling at Jackson Memorial that is completely confidential?"

"I wasn't. Who can qualify?"

"Any resident of this county qualifies. Call the Crisis Line number in the yellow pages and they will put you in touch with someone who can schedule you."

Going inside, they saw Frank, Chuck, and Wyatt, who had all stopped by to congratulate Sylvia on her new upcoming arrival! Grandma Hyacinth was also glowing.

Chuck and Wyatt both commented on Eva's new look, but Frank barely spoke to her. It was apparent that the two each harbored a deep resentment for the other, as well as for their own actions of the past, regardless of the successful outcome.

While nobody addressed the obvious, they all knew that the scars would take time to heal over; time that Frank and Eva must be willing to spend on the problem.

Frank Jr. came out of the den and ran to Grandpa Leo. "Gabby needs a doctor, Grandpa; she picked herself, and now she's beeding! I told her not to, but she wouldn't listen. Now she will deflate like a pool toy!"

"Shut up, Frankie," little Holly came in behind him. "Gabby's arm is broken!" she addressed Frank Sr.

"Well now, we better have a look," Frank started for the den. Realizing that Eva was behind him, he motioned her back, "I think I can handle it."

One Tinkerbelle band-aid later, the crisis was over, but Gabby still wanted to go home with her mother and grandmother, and Frank was furious. "No honey, it is your weekend with daddy." Eva tried to stand firm in spite of what she really wanted.

Gabby ran to Regina, "Sati, I want to go with Mommy," she cried.

Looking at Frank for approval, she answered, "Okay sweetheart, you can come over and play tomorrow."

On the walk home, Frank Sr. voiced his feelings loud and clear, "Listen Regina, I think you need to understand that I detest Eva and I am not in the market for making her life any easier! Oh, and by the way, she is still a beast, make-up or not."

"She looks much nicer, Frank, and I was not necessarily trying to make her life easier, but rather your daughter's. We certainly don't want to force visits on her and make her uncomfortable. She hurt her arm and needed her mother's comfort."

"She picked a scab, which is disgusting, and she has another mother here!"

Frank Jr., believed to be asleep until now, started laughing. "She picked a scab," he giggled, "Yes she did, Dad, and I told her not to."

"Gabby has a Sati here, not another mother, and whether she picked a scab or not, she was upset."

Frank Jr. was now walking alongside his parents and continued, "I hope you two know that Grandpa Leo doesn't like Aunt Eva."

"Why do you say such a thing?" Regina asked with a slight tone of distress.

"He never said he didn't like her," the little boy continued, "but I can just tell."

Frank Sr. was about to goad him on, but took one look at his wife and thought better of it, "Grandpa Leo likes Aunt Eva, son, he's just serious sometimes."

"Okay, but I don't think so."

Changing the subject, Regina brought up the expected babies. Arriving home, both Frank and Regina put their son to bed.

"I would like to see you have another baby, sweetheart," Frank said as he raided the fridge.

"When the time is right, I probably will."

"I hope we have a girl this time to take the spotlight off Gabby, and give you your own daughter to dote over."

"I love Gabby, Frank, but I love her as a godmother-type figure. I will love my own daughter, if I am ever blessed with one, as well. I am very fortunate to be able to experience both of our children, especially if we don't have a girl of our own."

"But... ...you wish I would be nicer to Eva."

"Frank, you and Eva must find your own resolve; and the sooner the better, for all concerned."

"I just don't want her to become close friends with you."

"Why?"

"Because."

"Well, I don't think she will ever be as close as our long time friends are, Frank, but there are many different ways to love people."

"Not to change this uplifting subject, but Leo is going to retire next year and may be moving to Tennessee!"

Regina's eyes filled with tears, as Frank held up his hand. "Before you panic, he has found a position for me there as well, and Frances and Lamar are talking about moving too, if we leave."

"Where in Tennessee?"

"Memphis area, but we would be in Bradington. It's about a half-hour away."

"Is this definite? Does anyone else know? What about..."

"Hold on, little worry wart! It's only on the drawing board!" Frank suddenly realized that he could have picked a better time to spill the news.

"Frances and Lamar may not be willing to move after all, Frank, and what about the rest of our beloved twelve pack? What will everyone else do?"

"Frances and Hazel are like sisters; they definitely won't go far from each other or from us."

Sweetheart, we all must realize that we may not always live in walking distance from each other, but that doesn't change the fact that we love each other and will see each other a few times a year."

Regina felt a deep sadness, and sat down quietly. Frank continued, "You know, it may be better with this entire situation, if Eva and Gabby didn't live ten minutes away."

"How, Frank? How could it possibly be better?"

"Because Eva and I despise each other, and we are uncomfortable around each other."

"I understand that, Frank, but you will not be able to see your daughter nearly as much."

"Yeah, well that may be a good thing too. She's not really my daughter anyway; she's a trap."

"Frank!"

"I'm sorry, sweetheart, but that's how I feel. Tonight when she pulled that 'I want mommy' crap, I was completely disgusted with the whole set-up."

"Frank, she is still a baby. Little children usually want mommy when something is amiss."

"It's still very awkward for me, even when we are here and Eva is not. I just don't feel the same way about her as I do about our son."

"Well, we need to carefully consider our future plans then, honey."

"Do you honestly love Gabby the way you love Frank Jr., Regina?"

"I don't love any two people the exact same way, Frank. There are boundless ways to love people, all different, but not necessarily more than each other."

"I don't understand how that is possible."

"It works for me, Frank. You must find the way that works for you. Please understand the difficulty that Gabby could have with long visits and no contact with her mother and grandmother. Remember that she is still very young."

"She will adjust, and I don't give a damn about her mother. I'm not crazy about her grandmother either. They both march around like everything is okay. Well it's not okay! They're sickening."

Regina did not answer. She bowed her head and closed her eyes, fighting back tears. "Abba, they're all Yours. Please guide me, as I am now lost."

Frank went over to Regina and sat down. "Sweetheart, I love you and Frank Jr. more than anything in the world. I just don't know if I can ever love Gabby the same way. I don't know that I want to."

"It is not unusual to feel that way, honey. We have a very unique situation and not only the baby, but her mother and grandmother must be considered. Cuban families are very close, Frank. I think that you are a wonderful father, and that in time, you will find your own feelings for Gabby."

"Regina, I have prayed about this for a long time and I think a separation from Miami will help all of us. I don't want to be reminded of the incident that brought Eva into to our lives, or Gabby either, for that matter."

"Is that the main reason we would be contemplating a move?"

"Yes. We also have a great opportunity in Tennessee. It would be a branch office for me to run. By the way, Chuck has a fantastic offer in North Carolina that he may be considering as well. Don't tell Jeannie, though. He will do that when he has all of the information."

Regina was now crying, "I guess I just thought we would all live together forever. You know Wyatt and Sylvia won't move. He has a new practice here."

Frank held his wife close to him and whispered, "Darling, this is no place to raise children. Miami is very dangerous unless you're damn careful where you go. As the kids get older, we will have to be even more cautious. Chuck and I were talking about it at lunch today."

"North Carolina is so far away," Regina whispered.

"Only a few hours from where we are looking, honey. Let's get some rest now. Nothing is going to happen right away."

Chapter Fourteen
New "State of Mind"

The next Saturday, the twelve-pack met at the Gerehauzers' for dinner to discuss the possible relocation of some of the friends, and the impact that it would have on all of them as a group. After a brief settling-in, the five children moved to the den to play while the adults all positioned themselves in the living room with drinks and tasty snacks of chips, dips, pigs-in-the-blanket, pinwheel sandwiches, sausage puffs, and bacon-wrapped water chestnuts. Leo opened the conversation in his usual no-nonsense way. "We are all as close as any <u>extremely</u> close family is. We also know that life holds new adventures and opportunities that could easily separate us geographically. We can embark on these in a positive way or in a negative way. It's not like the times of covered wagons, ladies. Modern travel is such that we can and will see each other on a regular basis. Jump in any time, Pollyanna!"

"The Colonel is right," Regina added quietly. "Frank brought up a very important point last night as well. Miami is really not the best place to raise children. I will just miss everyone so much," she could no longer withhold the tears.

Wyatt stood up and captured a pinwheel sandwich, "Miami is definitely not the best place to raise children, and I have considered that as well, as we contemplate buying our first house; since four children in the same small apartment is not going to work."

Sylvia reached for the chips and quietly added, "Five."

Wyatt continued, "One of the nicest neighborhoods that we have investigated here had a burglary last week. The elderly woman who was robbed spoke on the news explaining why she shot the intruder! I was – what did you just say, honey?"

Sylvia took a sip of her soda and laughed, "Oh, I just said 'five.' The twins will make five."

Wyatt was momentarily as stunned as the rest of the group. Everyone laughed and stood up for hugs.

"As I was saying," he raised his eyebrows at his wife, "I was contacted today by a group in Hilton Head Island, who happen to be looking for a partner. I will definitely need more time off call with the new baby – babies- coming and three small children already here, so we may also be leaving."

Chuck grinned and put his arm around his very pregnant wife, "See, Jeannie, I told you we would not be the only ones!"

"What about you two?" Regina looked at Roger and Hyacinth.

"We goin right wit dem, dahlin," Hyacinth smiled. "We moved all de way from Jamaica to be near de babies. Our friend just got mugged at the grocery store two weeks ago. At our ages, Miami is far too risky."

Roger, still looking puzzled, addressed his daughter, "Sylvia, how long have you known about the twins?"

"Just found out today, but I was thinking of the right time to tell Wyatt."

Everyone laughed again and turned as Frank Jr. and Holly burst into the room. "Daddy," Frank Jr. spoke matter-of-factly, "What is twins?"

"What *are* twins," Frank corrected, "Twins are two babies born at the same time."

"I told you, Holly, and I also told you that your mother is not going to name one of them K-Mart!"

Holly put her little hands on her hips and answered, "Frankie, you are not in the club anymore."

"Oh yes he is," Charlie had come into the room with Hyacinth and Harper, to join the fight, "You and Hyacinth are not in the club, because you are cootified girls."

Hyacinth moved to shove Charlie, but was intercepted by her father. "Okay, that's enough. Everyone plays nicely and nobody has cooties."

The five small children nodded obediently and turned to leave the room as Holly said, "And we are so naming one of our babies K-Mart, Frankie. You're not the boss of us!"

The adults didn't know whether to laugh or cry, so they did both. "Okay," Chuck took the floor, "so we are all probably moving - but all within a couple hours of each other!"

"Exactly," Lamar added, "Frances and I, and Leo and Hazel may be in Memphis, Tennessee, Regina and Frank may be in Bradington, Tennessee, Chuck and Jeannie will be exploring Castle Rock, North Carolina; and Wyatt and Sylvia, and Roger and Hyacinth are looking in Hilton Head Island, South Carolina. Let's think of all the fun we will have visiting each other and taking turns hosting the holidays!"

"I wonder how my parents will feel about this," Regina looked thoughtful.

"They'll probably be delighted," Frances hugged her. "They hate Miami and would love to see you move."

Frank laughed as he talked, "And lest we forget the biggest bonus – we won't be near my charming parents!"

"I wouldn't laugh too hard, Frank," Regina smiled and added, "they will eventually visit, and for long periods of time, fully expecting to stay with us!"

"We have had a significant enough history with them to place them in a hotel!"

"Okay," the Colonel's voice boomed, "so is it a fair statement to say that we are at least a little happier about all of this, now that we learned that we will all most likely be leaving?"

The group agreed and hugged each other again. Nobody brought up Gabby, out of respect for Frank and Regina. The ladies talked about it in the kitchen, though, as they prepared the dinner.

Hyacinth prepared a wonderful array of Jamaican kabobs with rum sauce and wild grain rice, Frances was tossing a fantastic gorgonzola cheese salad, and Hazel checked on her corn pudding and sesame seed rolls, while the three younger women arranged the desserts! Regina made a huge chocolate trifle, Jeannie brought turtle cheesecake, and Sylvia made butterscotch brownies. The ladies looked at the spread of food and wondered who was going to eat it all!

Typically, everyone enjoyed the evening immensely, and left feeling a whole lot better than they had earlier in the week.

Frances and Regina talked about the move in detail at work, and the need to train new folks for their positions once the plans materialized. Regina's worries about Gabby occupied her thoughts day and night. Frances noticed the distraction and asked if she could help. "I am concerned about Gabby and Eva; Mercedes too, for that matter."

"What about them?" Frances asked without feeling.

"How difficult will all of this be for them?"

"They will adjust, as many other families do. Frank will need to do a Consent Order for new visitation arrangements and file it with the Court."

"Eva will be beside herself, Frances, especially if plane travel is part of the equation."

"Well, now, that's a given, honey. The distance is too great for regular visits to be done by car. Let's see if the issue doesn't work itself out."

"The holidays will be here before we know it, and now we need to visit Bradington for an interview," Regina reached for the counter to steady herself.

Frances looked concerned, "Honey, are you alright?"

"Sure, I just felt a little dizzy; I think that all of this talk about moving has upset me."

"Have you considered that you may be pregnant?"

Regina looked stunned. "No, I never thought of that. Maybe I'll get a test run, but I don't want to get my hopes up either."

"Why? Frank's surgery was a success. You shouldn't have any problem getting pregnant now, sweetheart."

Frank and Leo came into the clinic for lunch, talking about Tennessee as though it was a done deal. "We have an interview in Bradington in two weeks, Pollyanna," Frank beamed. "The pictures of that place look great."

"We can all fly out together," Leo added, "Hazel is making the reservations."

"So Lamar just telephoned and said," Frances seemed as excited as the others, as she stirred her coffee.

"Okay," Regina added, "But when do we tell our parents?"

"Yours now – mine never," Frank laughed and Leo joined in.

"Hazel and I have already got toys and games for the plane for Frank Jr.," Leo stated matter-of-factly.

"We do too," Frances added, "Maybe we should keep our stuff for the interview time."

Regina listened quietly. She could not get caught up in the excitement of leaving her work in the clinics, being separated from her close friends, and leaving Gabby, to whom she had grown very close. Nobody else seemed to be even considering this little girl, and that also made her uneasy.

Frances took one look at her and knew just what to do. "I have been thinking about whether or not we should bring Gabby along on the trip. It would be your weekend to have her."

"I think that would be a great idea," Frank added, "Eva can just find out at the last minute."

"No way," Regina intercepted, "Eva and Mercedes must be told in advance so that they can prepare themselves for the changes to come if this works out."

"Fair enough," Leo winked at Frank, "the less drama, the better."

"May I tell them at lunch time?" Regina looked at all three of the others.

"Sure," Frank answered.

The lunch did not go well. Both Eva and her mother were in tears, but understood that they would have to cooperate. "I just don't want Gabby on a plane without me, Sati," Eva cried. "May I come too and leave on the next flight and then return and come back? I will not bother you guys in any way. You will not even know that I am there. I won't even let Gabby see me; I will hide ..."

"Why would you do that?" Regina interrupted.

"Because if the plane crashes, I wish to die too," the protective Cuban mother sobbed. "I will work two jobs to pay for my airfare every time she comes to visitation."

"Okay, honey, I'm sure that will be fine, at least until you feel secure letting us take her back and forth."

"Thanks so much!" Eva seemed partially relieved.

"Sati, what about my yob?" Mercedes was worried about the fact that the Solbergs would be leaving.

"There should be no problem with your job, sweetheart; in fact, I should think you could advance in the absence of Sylvia and Jeannie."

"Sylvia and Jeannie are going too?!" Eva was panic-stricken.

"They are not moving with us, but they may be relocating to the Carolinas to start their own new lives."

As Regina had expected, everyone left the cafeteria heavy hearted. When she returned to the clinic, Frances reminded her that they were waiting for the results from her pregnancy test. Regina walked over to the lab and was greeted with, "Congratulations, Mrs. Solberg."

Frances burst out in tears and asked her when she would tell Frank. "Where is he?" Regina asked.

"He and Leo are in surgery," Frances answered dabbing her eyes with a Kleenex.

The lab tech had been listening and made a suggestion. "Mrs. Solberg, on weekends I do singing telegrams. I would be glad to do one for free to the surgeons' lounge."

Frances and Regina looked at each other and laughed. Both at once, they asked, "What will you sing?"

"Well how about, 'Doctor, have a peachy day – our new baby's on the way!'"

Regina and Frances went to the gift shop for some balloons to accompany the singer. They both waited for the elevator to open and when it did, the two surgeons still in scrubs rushed to Regina for huge hugs. The rest of the twelve-pack was called along with Dan and Elizabeth and Bub and Sis. Frank refused to tell his parents on the grounds that they had been viciously unkind to Regina and his son, as well as to him. Eva and Mercedes were the next on the scene to join in the excitement.

"You don't need to be here, ladies," Frank could not have been ruder.

Frances and Leo were stunned, but Regina made a joke of

it and everyone laughed to smooth things over. Leo announced, "This calls for a celebration at Shorty's!"

"We will be delighted to watch all of the kids," Mercedes offered.

Regina smiled and answered, "You and Eva will be joining us with Gabby."

"Of course," Leo, Frances, and Frank added.

The impromptu dinner was a blast and Dan, Elizabeth, Andrea, Brian, Bub and Sis all came down to be a part of the festivities. After a long and late night, everyone hugged good-bye and left to go home.

Regina hugged Dan and cried, "I don't want to be so far away from you, Dad."

Dan held her close and reassured her. "Sweetheart, Tennessee is not that far away. I will be retiring in a few years, and we will be pestering you more than you know!"

Regina dried her eyes and smiled, "Promise?"

"Promise," Dan reassured.

Without realizing that Regina had not yet told Frank about the lunch meeting, Eva turned to him at the car and politely thanked him for their understanding and the opportunity to fly with them to break into the new routine easily. Frank blasted her in the parking lot, fortunately far enough away so that the entire party couldn't hear him.

"Go to hell, Eva. I don't care how hard any of this is for you. You are not my concern and you are not coming! You are not even going to have the flight information. You'll see Gabby when we return. Got it?"

Eva did not want to spoil Regina's evening, so she got into her car quivering and left for home in tears.

Mercedes shook her head, "Frank will never agree to have you on the plane, but Sati will find a way to call us and tell us they are safe. You wait and see."

Frank and Regina put Frank Jr. to bed and sat out on the patio to wind down from the exciting day. "Eva wants to fly to Memphis with us in two weeks – OUT OF THE QUESTION!" Frank was angry, in spite of the wonderful news of their new pregnancy.

"Well, I wonder if we couldn't just take Frankie this time and Gabby at a later date. You will be thinking about the interview and talking with Leo and Lamar, so perhaps we should take it easy on this first trip."

"Yeah, but what will my new prospective partners think when they don't see Gabby and then they do on visitations?"

"They will think no differently either way. They'll certainly know that she doesn't live with us full time. I would not go into detail at all. Gabby is simply a child from another relationship."

"In between Frank and the new one? Oh sure, that will sound great."

"Many couples marry and separate and remarry. Some couples marry and each of the partners, have their own kids. Others have shared custody with foster children being reunited with their parents, among other scenarios, Frank. You don't have to explain our personal business to anyone; especially in this profession!"

Frank smiled and took a deep breath. "Well maybe you're right, as usual."

He walked over to Regina and hugged her. "We can leave Gabby with Chuck and Jeannie for the weekend then."

"Why not leave her with Eva and Mercedes?"

"Because I'm still entitled to the time."

"Then why not switch weekends? I'm sure they would be delighted for us to do that, rather than see her go to Memphis."

"That's just it! They won't know that she isn't going."

"Frank, that's not a game I want to be a part of. Why in the world would you deliberately inflict worry on the mother of your baby?"

"Because the mother of my baby trapped me and screwed up my life!"

"How, honey? How did she screw up your life?"

"Child support, visitation, anger; I could go on all night."

"There is definitely child support, but visitation is a choice you get to make, and so is anger."

"She knew I was married, Regina."

"That's all in the past, sweetheart; can you let it go or not?"

"That's what the move could accomplish for us, honey. When I heard that Chuck was looking and that Leo was retiring, I thought of the big picture."

"Okay, well it may help, but please try to evaluate how you feel about Gabby, Frank. It is far better for her to have a long distance relationship with you, than an antagonistic drama with her mother resulting in mutual resentment; especially if the reason is strictly to get even."

"Alright, Pollyanna, I will make a sincere effort to be nicer to Eva and overlook her faults and her past."

"Do you want me to trade weekends with them, or just give her the extra time?"

"TRADE!" Frank caught his own tone of voice and softened. "We also need to go to court for new visitation."

"We don't need to go to court; we need only to get a new consent order."

"Fine, I want Gabby's birthday, Halloween, Thanksgiving, Christmas, Easter, and the entire summer."

"Not Martin Luther King's birthday as well?" the feisty redhead's sarcasm typically surfaced, "Great! Good job, Solberg. You definitely do want to return to court, and the court will not give you all of those. They will also demand production of your new salary and rip you a new one for child support."

"Fine, I'll take whatever is customary in these cases."

Eva was delighted to side-step the plane trip to Memphis in exchange for a trade in weekends. She and Mercedes were also happy to agree to visitation changes coordinated by Regina, rather than by the Court. "Okay, let's say you trade the different holidays each year, and that Christmas is always with you, Eva. The second week can be with her father, and how about half of the summer?"

"Can we split that up two weeks each month, Sati?" Eva was crying. "I can't be without her for six weeks straight. Not at first."

"She is too young for six weeks straight as well, now that you mention it, Eva."

"I will work until I die if I can pay my plane fare and transport her there and back myself."

"Her father will be responsible for the plane fares, as they need to be paid either way. If you don't bring her, one of us would have to fly back and forth."

"No, Sati! Unless I pay, he will never allow me to do it. He will make me suffer."

"He most certainly will allow it, Eva. Leave that to me."

When presenting the new visitation agreement, Regina said, "Look, Frank, I do not want you on a plane without me, or in Eva's company without me. So we will need to allow for both of us and Frank Jr. to fly back and forth with Gabby."

"Well she can split the airfares."

"Negative, 'Ghost Rider' – the courts will make you pay for the airfare. On the other hand, it would be to our benefit and clearly considered part of the child support, if an issue should ever arise," Regina faked a small snicker, "if perhaps you should let Eva sink in her own swell, and be our gopher and fly her back and forth!"

"What?"

"Let Eva run her butt off while we save money."

"Would I have to pay Eva's airfare too?"

"Hers, or all three of ours; four when the new baby arrives."

"So I would definitely come out ahead!"

"Yes, you definitely would, and let us pray that doesn't dawn on them!"

Frank smiled at his wife. He was relieved to see the upcoming distance from this 'chink in the chain.' He loved Regina and his son, and hoped that the next baby would be a girl!

"I just want Eva as miserable as I can possibly make her. In fact, I may just have us fly there and get Gabby."

"Either way is fine with me, honey, but remember that you will be taking a lot of call and when you finally do get time off, it would be spent all day traveling back and forth and messing around at the Miami International Airport. Delays are a pain in the rear as well, and that time could be spent playing golf with Leo and Lamar. In addition, we will eventually be traveling with three kids, but it's up to you. Just let me know so we can generate the Consent Order. A Consent Order cannot be changed, even by a judge, unless both parties agree to change it."

"It would still make Eva suffer if we do the traveling and she does the worrying the entire time."

"True, until she adjusts to it. Then we would be the idiots who are running back and forth, once the Consent Order is in place."

"Pollyanna, your evil intentions pleasantly surprise me! Okay, fine. Let Eva fly her up and back, but I am not paying for Mercedes to come along."

"Hell no! No way!" Regina laughed to herself, wondering if she should have been an actress!

Chapter Fifteen

That Cotton Picking State!

The flight to Memphis was wonderful, and Frank Jr. behaved like an angel. Grandpa Leo showed him off to every passenger and flight attendant, as though he were the only reason for the trip. When the pilot asked him where he was going, he answered, "We have to find a job for my daddy. We got kicked out of our apartment, but I have a new room in a jungle now. My tent is in mosquito netting so I don't catch malaria; it's a very bad disease."

The Tennessee Orthopedic Associates housed four surgeons in Memphis and one in Bradington, to draw business from there. Frances and Lamar were planning a wonderful weekend of house-hunting with Hazel and Leo. Frank, Regina, and Frank Jr. were to be escorted; complements of the hospital, to Bradington, to see the branch practice that Frank would possibly take over. The visit was for the entire day, and included appointments all over the town with bankers, realtors, school personnel, and the hospital administrator. Following the meetings, the four partners and their wives were scheduled to have dinner that evening with the Solbergs and the two older couples back in Memphis.

Bradington was a charming town with field after field of cotton growing along the highway. The escort pulled over to allow Frank Jr. and his mother to pick some, before informing them that they could be arrested, depending on whose cotton they were picking! The children ran around carefree and basically unsupervised, which was foreign to the Miami residents. Everyone seemed to be very calm and happy, and the surroundings were immaculate. The neighborhood yards were as well-kept as the town itself, and Regina did not see a speck of trash on the ground anywhere. The air was clear and cool, and the sky was a gorgeous shade of bright blue.

Regina had made prior arrangements to rent a car later in the day. The escort was wonderful, but she felt as though it might be better to be able to talk privately as they explored their prospective relocation. The hospital was state of the art and the practice was of the same caliber. Frank immediately fell in love with the whole package and was ready to jump in with both feet before even discussing his contract with the group of orthopedic surgeons that were obviously begging him to join them.

Regina asked him if he wouldn't want to look at some other opportunities before making his decision. Frank smiled at her and answered, "Why? This is perfect, and we will be close to everyone else here."

"Yes darling, but we would be close in any of the other locations in the Carolinas as well."

"Don't you want to be close to Frances and Hazel?"

"Of course I do, but I also don't want to make a quick decision based on a four hour visit."

"Well Michael Dougherty, the head of the practice, is hoping for an answer by Sunday, so I don't know if we should take a chance on losing this offer."

"Dr. Dougherty has three children of his own, Frank, and I'm sure he would allow you time to think their offer over, once you have it."

"That will be Sunday morning over breakfast."

"And you intend to answer right then and there?"

"I don't know; I thought about it."

"Let's finish looking around, and perhaps you could ask Leo before you commit."

"Of course, but how do you like it here, sweetheart? Are you as impressed as I am?"

"I'm not ready to commit yet," Regina smiled, "but I will go wherever you feel is the best place to set up your practice. Please keep in mind that we have been in Miami for years, so any decent city will be attractive."

The people in the town appeared to know each other, and every visitor, all too well for Regina's taste, but the schools were lovely and the people all seemed friendly. They were introduced to a realtor, Doug Stanley, and looked at several huge, elegant, historical houses, none of which impressed Regina. At last he chose to introduce a smaller neighborhood with a dead-end street. There was a large two-story brick house with an extra lot that came with it. There were six bedrooms, four bathrooms, a formal living room, a large family room, a formal dining room, a large eat-in kitchen with a gorgeous bay window, a large built in swimming pool, and a large finished basement as an added bonus. The homes on the block were well-spaced and well-kept. The over-zealous realtor was quite the salesman, "I'm sure there would be no trouble getting one hundred percent financing, Dr. Solberg. The local banks cross over all the lines for doctors, especially surgeons."

Frank was flattered and enjoyed every minute of the regal treatment that the interview promised. Regina was bored and totally unimpressed, as the pitch continued, "The price of the house is $159,900.00, and we could contact the owner and get the deal papered before supper. Just say the word," Doug smiled, already spending his commission.

"Well, sweetie, what do you think?" Frank couldn't believe that his wife was not already reaching into her purse for a pen.

"I think we should take a short break and discuss things before we sign anything."

"Why?"

"Because we need to," Regina answered in a firm but pleasant tone.

"The Mrs. is right, Doctor. Why don't I take Frankie to my house for a while and give you two a little privacy? While I'm there I will contact the owners."

"We appreciate all that you have done for us, Doug, and we would be delighted to allow you some office time to contact the owner of this lovely home; but we will keep Frank with us."

"As you wish, ma'am," he smiled.

Walking to the car, Frank was disappointed and a little confused.

"Regina, why didn't you let him take Frank Jr.? He is trying to accept us, and we need to be more cordial."

"First of all, we don't even know him or anything about where he lives; so Frank Jr. stays with us. Secondly, we do not just buy a house at the asking price without making an offer."

"Oh. Did you see the formal living room, the dining room, the den, the family room, the huge deck, and patio?"

"Yes I did, and they are all wonderful."

"What about that gigantic basement? Did you see that?"

"Yes, dear, of course I did; it's also wonderful."

"But?"

"We need to know the appraisal of the property and the values of the other houses on the street. I would start there. If you are certain that you like it here without question, we will make an offer. The seller will either accept it or he will make a counter offer."

"How do you know all of this, Pollyanna?" Frank was pleasantly surprised.

"While we have been saving all of the soft sculpture money, I have been researching the subject of real estate investing."

"Wow!"

"It will not surprise you to hear that your parents have made a fortune doing just that."

"What's the next step?"

"Let's take Frank Jr. to Dairy Queen for lunch and to play on the playground there. He's been an angel, but there is a limit to how much can be expected from any child his age. We also have a dinner party to attend tonight."

"Frank Jr. has been invited to stay with Mike Dougherty's kids and their baby sitter."

"Frank Jr., is coming with us."

During lunch, Regina called the realtor to ask if there had been an appraisal done on the property and for some comparisons on the street. She added that they would like to make an offer of $135,000.00. "That's low," Doug answered and waited.

Regina waited too. "Well I guess I could present it and see what happens. Did I mention that Mr. Jefferson at First Financial would definitely finance the full cost at a fair market interest rate?"

"You did, Doug."

"Make the lower offer anyway?" The realtor was not sure quite sure of how to deal with Regina.

"Please."

"Pollyanna are you sure that it is wise to try to get the house for less, when we can get the whole cost financed?"

"Frank, we don't want to finance all of that."

"Why?" Frank looked confused.

"Because we still pay interest on the amount that we finance," Regina was recalling a joke that she had heard about orthopedic surgeons 'they're strong as an ox and twice as smart.'

"So in the long run, would it matter that much?"

"Sure. The first thing is the price of the house; then negotiations for a rate of interest and closing points. If we have a good down payment, which we do, we can make a very good deal and save a good bit of money."

"How much of a down payment do we have?"

"We have $18,000.00, not touching allowances for moving expenses."

"Wow! How?"

"Frank, you continually amaze me. I have told you numerous times about the soft sculpture account and we have certainly been carrying a household savings account. You may wish to pay attention, darling; if anything ever happened to me, you don't even know what we own!"

The ride back to Memphis was scenic but Frank Jr. slept. Regina was tired herself and thought about lying down for awhile before dinner. Frank looked over at her and squeezed her hand. "Honey, I really want you to be happy with our move too, and if you're not, please tell me."

Regina smiled back and answered, "Honey, I am happy. I just don't want to move too fast. I will also be changing obstetricians and that's another concern. I love Andrew Kingsley, and we understand each other."

"I understand, sweetheart. Jeannie is much farther along than you are and she will need to start over too. Sylvia as well, with twins on the way!"

When they arrived at their hotel there was a message waiting. The realtor had a counter offer and relayed it to Frank. "Regina, the seller dropped the price! We can get the house for $148,000.00. Should Doug go ahead and write the contract?"

"No, Doug should counter back with a split of the difference."

"Soooo, it would be …."

"$141,500.00," *So-oxen could be quite lovable after all; scary though, since they could take humans apart and put them back together again;* Regina shook her head in amazement.

Frank hung up the phone and hugged Regina. "I am the luckiest man on Earth!"

On the way to dinner, the Solbergs stopped at a Piggly Wiggly grocery store to get some snacks for Frank Jr. Regina was not sure that he would find what he was used to eating at the Petite Marme, a very elite restaurant. When they went to pay, the cashier noticed that Regina was pregnant. "Yins must be the new town doctor," she gazed at Frank in awe. "We hope ya like it here. Do ya like it, Mrs. Solberg? We would sure love to have yins in our garden club! I hope that yins will trade with us. Ma sister and I both babysit too. I'll write ya down ma number."

"Have you ever seen such friendly people?" Frank asked on the way to the car.

"Have you ever seen Green Acres?" A very tired Regina answered, as Frank Jr. laughed.

Frank laughed too, and then he addressed his son, "What do you think of this place, Frankie?"

"I love it. Let's move here, but I hope we buy the big yellow house. It's not haunted and it has a tire swing."

"Is that the only reason you would like to live here, honey?" Regina asked.

"I also like the Dairy Queen."

"Like father, like son," Regina shook her head.

The four partners could not have been more pleasant and Frances and Hazel were having a wonderful time in this new "state of opportunity."

Michael Dougherty was a middle-aged man with steel gray hair and blue eyes. He was well over six feet tall and in excellent shape for his sixty years. His fourth and current wife, Marilyn, was very well dressed and extremely attractive.

The second partner, Phillip Talato, was a dark-haired and dark eyed man in his early fifties. His third wife, Beatrice, was also attractive and very assertive.

The third partner, Edward Monahan was a good bit shorter than the others and had more of a stocky build. He was in his mid-thirties and had a sandy colored hair and blue eyes. His second wife, Jessica, was taller than he, but very quiet.

Last but not least was the youngest partner, Bruce Beattie, a red- headed, fellow with dark brown eyes. Although he was barely thirty, he was already on his third wife, Joanne, and had kids from each marriage.

The entire group was impressed with the Solbergs, and could not believe how self-entertaining and well-mannered their young son was. While the ladies welcomed Hazel, Frances, and Regina, they made it very clear that their group was exclusive to themselves. Hazel and Frances exchanged several glances during dinner, undiscovered by their husbands. Regina was tired and just went with the flow.

Hazel and Frances had seen two very promising homes on the golf course, and were seriously considering making offers on them.

"So, Frank, can we convince you and your delightful family to move to the Volunteer State?" Phillip Talato held up his glass.

"I must say that I love it here, and I have placed an offer on a house, followed by a counter and then for a split of the difference. We'll see what happens."

"A businessman," Michael announced.

"A bull #*@+ artist," Regina thought to herself as she nodded along lovingly.

"Regina, how's your dinner, honey?" Michael addressed the prospective new partner's wife.

"Delightful, Michael, thank you."

"How did you like Bradington, my dear?"

"It is a lovely town and the people seem very sweet; I'm also amazed at the cleanliness."

"Did you have a chance to see the Charms Factory?"

"No, but I believe that we are scheduled to do that tomorrow."

"Bradington has the only Charms Factory in the world."

"Young Frank," Michael glanced fondly at the child drawing quietly in his chair, "What do you think of the Charms Factory?"

"I don't know, Sir. What kind of charms do they produce?"

Thoroughly amused, the senior partner explained. "Charms candy – lollipops, blow pops, tootsie roll pops, small charms candy squares in tins, and sour balls."

"Oh, I see; I love blow pops, and I would love to see how they are made!"

"Well," Michael moved his chair closer to the table to lean in Frank Jr.'s direction, "I heard that they send you home with samples!"

"Wow!" Frank's eyes were as big as saucers.

Michael's beeper went off, so he excused himself to return the call. Returning to the table, he announced, "Frank that was Doug Stanley, calling to say that the seller has accepted your return offer. He is willing to meet you after dinner to reduce the terms to writing and pick up an earnest check, which we will of course be delighted to front."

"I love this guy," Phillip raised his glass again, "a real no-nonsense business man!"

"Well," Michael continued, "Do you want to call him back and set the meeting for tonight?"

Frank glanced at his wife for a signal. "Honey, perhaps we can set the meeting for tomorrow," Regina was far more irritated than she sounded.

"Sure, I'll just tell him that it's getting late and the day has been a long one!"

Marilyn glanced in her direction and added, "Ray-gina, darlin, we are hoping that you will be the one to start a whaves club in Bradington. The staff at that hospital needs one, and the whaves in Memphis don't have time to spoon-feed the process."

"I am not familiar with that club," Regina looked confused.

"Wives of the doctors," Leo smiled.

"Oh, joy," the redhead thought as she hoped that she didn't look as bored as she was, "Well I'm not much with clubs and organizations of that nature, but I'm certainly flattered by your thought."

"Well, it is our duty as doctor's whaves to form support clubs, dearie" Beatrice jumped in to support the idea.

"We love our club here," Joanne added sharply, while raising her perfectly manicured eyebrows and glancing at Frances and Hazel, "but we would certainly look to you to form one at your own hospital. You see, we don't allow out-sahders from other cities."

"Oh, I don't have a hospital, and I don't join or start clubs," Regina smiled and added pleasantly, "I am a lay-missionary and I have my own work to do."

"I see," Joanne answered and looked toward the three other partners' wives.

"I'm glad, because it would just be too bad if you didn't see," Regina thought to herself as she saw the Colonel wink at her and smile.

After dinner, Leo shook hands with Michael and quietly mentioned that Regina was not the type to be pushed. Michael looked concerned, "I hope to hell we didn't blow this, Leo. We were being very pushy and our wives can be very snobby."

"I doubt it. Frank seems to be very satisfied with the whole set-up."

On the way to the car, Frank whispered to Regina, "Hey, what is an earnest check?"

"Earnest money is placed on the contract to ensure the seller that we are serious, since the house is now basically off the market. In the next 60-90 days, we will get inspections, title searches, et cetera. When we close the deal, the earnest money is credited toward the price of the house."

"Oh. How much will we pay?"

"One thousand dollars."

"Oh."

Frank Jr. was so excited about the Charms Factory that he talked about it all the way back to the hotel. He was even more delighted to learn that the both sets of adopted grandparents were to join them for the tour, and to see the new house that they were looking at. Looking directly at Leo, he whispered, "Grandpa Leo, I need your help. The big yellow house is better than the brick one, because it has a tire swing."

The next morning, the Miami crew hailed to Bradington to see the glorious Charms Factory. The tour was spectacular! Long ropes of cherry and grape candy moved along the belts for stuffing with bubblegum, as multicolored tootsie pops competed next door to be joined with their chocolate insides. The machines then cooled the confections and sent them along. The tour guide handed each of the guests a warm sucker which was still so soft that it could be stretched! They were delicious.

They next witnessed sour pop packaging production and the creation of small Charms squares and sour balls. These were canned by other vast machines. The entire group was amazed and left with a huge bag of samples from each creation. Lunch was a blast and Regina was finally able to relax and enjoy herself a little.

Hazel and Frances raved about the inside of the house that the young Solbergs were buying, while Lamar and Leo checked out the attic and the outside of the structure. Both older couples agreed that they were getting a steal of a deal!

The sellers, Eugene and Jimmie McDaniel, wanted to meet the Solbergs, but the realtor refused to allow it.

"That could blow the deal!" Doug shouted, "You should have no contact with each other!" They finally told him that they would get in touch with Frank either way, so he may as well cooperate.

"Look, Doug, we are under contract so your precious commission is safe," Eugene assured, "and we can certainly find Dr. Solberg through the hospital." Although Doug was very annoyed, he saw no choice and relayed the message.

"They are in their seventies and want to downsize to the house on the corner, which will not be vacant until the early spring. They wanted to discuss the possibility of staying in their house after the closing, and renting it back from you, until you guys are actually ready to move in when May rolls around."

Regina was delighted to meet with the sellers, who fell in love with her right away. I do not need my dining room set anymore, Mrs. Solberg, and I will be willing to leave it in addition to the rent if you would let us stay here, instead of moving twice."

The hand-carved cherrywood set was exquisite, housing fourteen chairs, each one boasting cherub carvings to match the table legs. It was in mint condition and beautifully polished.

"Please call me Regina" she smiled, "and we will be delighted to either buy the set or trade it for the rent."

Eugene was relieved and insisted that they still pay rent. "No, Sir, one or the other," Regina smiled. Leo invited the Mc Daniels to join their group for dinner, and they accepted. They talked about Bradington and the history of the town. Eugene and

Leo ordered two glasses of ice water to enable Frank Jr.'s GI Joes to submerge and ascertain that they would in fact change color. Jimmie looked over and addressed the men, "I declare! The little boy behaves better than the grown men."

"I'm getting some of these GI Joes on my way home, Jimmie," Eugene smiled.

Regina was delighted to know that these people were to be her neighbors if the contract presentation went well, since she already loved them.

The Miami visitors were mortified to learn that "colored people," were not welcome at the Bradington Country Club, even though the Chief of Staff at the hospital, Dr. Thomas Alfred, happened to be black. He and his wife, Sharon, just graciously accepted the "way" of the people and avoided the annual hospital ball, or any other functions that the community hosted there. The local skating rink had the same policy. The three couples inquired further in an interested manner, except for Regina. She said nothing, but turned ashen white with anger. "God help us," Leo noticed her reaction and laughed to himself. "Bradington may never be the same."

The partner contract was offered for $150,000.00 annually, plus quarterly bonuses, full health and dental insurance coverage for the entire family, malpractice insurance coverage, life insurance, a wonderful retirement plan, all moving expenses, and continuing education courses. The partners were practically begging Frank to sign before leaving to return to Miami. He called Leo, spoke briefly with Regina, hugged her for her approval, and signed the contract.

The plane ride home was filled with interesting conversation. The three men talked golf, but Regina, Frances and Hazel talked about the wives of physicians and what utter snobs they could be. "Notice that none of the partners has his original wife," Regina addressed both older women. "I know that, honey," Frances consoled, "but that doesn't mean a thing. Look at Hazel and Leo."

"You bet," Hazel supported, "We were among the few and far between, and so will you be, sweetheart. Many wives cannot handle the profession and leave their husbands. Those wives' clubs weren't for me either," she laughed.

Regina felt much better after learning that she was not the only one who was uncomfortable with the group of wives. Glad that she would see them only on occasion, she sighed in relief. "I'm not having anything to do with that nonsense either; I can't stand pity parties or gossip," the little redhead was feeling more and more like herself. Leo and Lamar had also put up earnest money on their homes and both couples were very excited about the upcoming move.

Regina couldn't wait to see the others in the twelve-pack and compare notes. Chuck and Jeannie were leaving next weekend to investigate a new location, and Wyatt and Sylvia were already away on an interview and would return home from it in two days.

Chapter Sixteen
Dr. Kingsley, To The Er –

The girls always loved to gather for lunch, and they couldn't wait to talk about their new upcoming relocations. The week after Jeannie returned, she, Regina, and Sylvia took a trip the Sandwich Shack on the beach. Comparing notes, the three younger women all had similar experiences with the prospective partners' wives, and all three girls attributed them to the same fact, which Regina pointed out. "We are also, a very unique and close group of friends; but we are loyal to each other and have deliberately chosen to stay unaffiliated with any of the typical hospital drama." The twelve-pack had always kept to themselves, engaged in no outside gossip, and never spoke a syllable behind each other's backs unless it was for a surprise party.

"Well, I'm going to bury myself in my own activities and stay away from all of them," Jeannie decided, rearranging the bacon on her club sandwich. "Those women in Castle Rock wouldn't hesitate to draw their claws on each other, much less a newcomer. I was in the ladies room, and the senior partner's wife came in to 'warn' me about the other two wives. I knew right then and there that I was already homesick for you guys and that I was going to have to steer clear of any un-necessary contact."

Sylvia smiled, spreading mustard on her Reuben, "Wyatt's three partners are nice enough, but they also gossip. None of them is on his first or even second marriages! I won't have too much time to be involved either, with five young kids, two of them newborns!"

Regina laughed and reached for the salt, "None of Frank's partners live in our town, thank heavens! None of those couples are on their first marriages either. I already told them that I will be busy with my missionary work and will not be available for any wives' club nonsense. Even Frances and Hazel commented on the 'snake pit,'" she laughed as she shook her head.

"What's with all of these multiple marriages?" Jeannie looked worried.

"No telling," Sylvia stirred her iced tea, "but most of them probably didn't make it through medical school or residency, and we all have."

Regina stood up to visit the ladies room, and collapsed back into her chair in excruciating pain. "My legs are shaking and sharp pain is shooting through them."

"I'm calling Frances," Sylvia was on the phone in an instant.

"Call an ambulance, Jeannie," she said after hanging up with Frances, "We are going to the ER, and Dr. Kingsley will meet us there.

Regina closed her eyes and called for Help, "Abba, please stay right by my side; I'm frightened. I want this baby to be safe. I

love You above anything else, though, and 'Thy will be done.'"
The ambulance pulled up to the emergency room, and was not only met by Andrew Kingsley, but by Frank, Leo, and George Easterlin as well. Regina's legs were both in spasms and the pain was horrible. Leo spoke first, "With all due respect, Andrew, this is a case for Orthopedics."

Andrew nodded and answered in his usual crisp British accent. "Be that as it may, but Regina is my patient and a high risk pregnancy. We will work side by side on this one with all final decisions being mine."

"Hold it, Andrew," George Easterlin was concerned, "you can't make decisions for our department."

Regina sat up on her elbows, "You can all tell me what you <u>think</u> you are going to do, and I will be the final decision," she added in her usual can-do voice.

The three physicians exchanged surprised glances, laughed, and proceeded quietly.

The tests ordered to tract the tibial nerves in Regina's legs were too painful, which was indicative of a bilateral nerve injury. Leo demanded partial sedation to allow the test to continue, Regina refused, and Andrew agreed with her. George was clearly irritated, and sided with Leo. Regina asked Leo to do an exploratory surgery under spinal anesthesia to rule out bilateral tarsal tunnel syndrome, a painful compression of the nerves in both feet.

"What is going on here?!" the worried Colonel vented, doing his best to keep from smiling; "you are the patient, young lady!"

"I am the mother of this unborn child," Regina added, "and therefore the Chief of Staff in my case."

"You don't say," Andrew rubbed his eyebrows.

"We're wasting time," Frances was now in tears, "your parents are on their way, sweetheart."

"Please tell me that you were talking to Regina," Andrew caused everyone to laugh in spite of the current crisis.

Eric Hernandez was the fourth-year anesthesia resident on call, and the only one available. He introduced himself to Regina and reassured her that he would protect her baby at all costs. Regina liked him right away and consented to a spinal block. Leo and George turned to Frank and simultaneously said, "Out!"

Frank kissed his wife and headed for the surgeons' lounge, where he buried his head in his hands. Frances came in behind him and put her arms around him. "She'll be fine, Frank; the hospital policy does not allow you to be in the operating room."

"Why must she suffer like this, Frances? Where is God?"

"Right by her side; honey; He's right by her side."

The nurses prepped Regina's ankles with iodine scrub, but were so busy talking about their upcoming dates with medical students, that they did not hear her say that she could feel the washing procedure. Dr. Hernandez was gentle and kind, and stood by Regina as Leo and George each prepared to open the inside of an ankle to rule out tarsal tunnel syndrome. Regina felt the sharp slice of the blades, similar to a kitchen cut – quick and then burning. Leo and George felt her twitch and exchanged panicked glances and Leo shouted through his mask, "The spinal did not take!"

"Mask the patient!" George followed with his order.

"Negative!" Regina tried to sit up but couldn't, "you <u>will not mask me.</u> I am pregnant!"

"Local!" Leo was fighting to keep his composure.

Once they injected the local anesthetic, Regina felt no more pain. The surgery was completed and she was taken to Recovery.

"We need to keep her overnight," George paced the floor in the surgeons' lounge and wiped the sweat from his forehead.

"Surgery without anesthesia – how great!" Leo bellowed. "What the hell went wrong, Hernandez?"

"I don't know, Sir," the resident stuttered, "I used the smallest needle that I could. I cannot mask a patient who is lucid and refuses to let us, especially if she's pregnant."

Both surgeons shook their heads as Leo's pager went off.

"Mrs. Solberg says she is not spending the night, Sir," the nurse explained.

"Why not?" George asked from the coffee pot, seeing the look on Leo's face.

"She will not leave her son overnight," the nurse continued, "Dr. Solberg does not want to upset her."

"Lord help us," Leo prayed. "Please do something with Your headstrong little missionary!"

Leo entered the Recovery Room with Frank Jr. which was

against hospital policy. The nurse explained this policy, but Leo shouted, "Surgery without anesthesia is also against hospital policy. Get Mrs. Solberg a semi private room and tell them that both Dr. Solberg and his son will be staying here with her."

"Yeah!" Frank Jr. Hugged the Colonel.

Frances appeared at the door with overnight supplies and Dan and Elizabeth, as Regina raised her hands in defeat. "I'm hungry," she said, "and he must be too," she nodded, indicating Frank Jr. "I don't need to spend the night. We would all be better off at home."

"Well don't just stand there," Frances winked at Frank Sr. "Order pizza!"

Frank Jr. watched the door with his bright blue eyes set on alert, "when will they bring in the baby?" he asked.

Leo picked him up and explained that the baby was still inside mommy.

"Well what were you guys doing in there then? We need to get the baby and take him home," he added firmly.

"The baby is not ready to come out yet, honey, he's not finished growing," Frances explained, "he will be born in your new house."

Frank Jr. accepted the fact that he would have to wait, but still didn't understand why. He walked over to his mother's bed, asked for confirmation, and climbed up next to her. Regina hugged her little son and whispered a prayer to thank Abba for everything. Dan was shaken and Elizabeth was desperately trying to hold back her own tears of worry. They spent the night with Frances and Lamar and planned to see Regina the next morning. They would decide from that point when they would return to Wellington.

Regina woke up to Andrew Kingsley and George Easterlin arguing loudly in the hallway. "Damn you, Andrew, she must have pain medication!"

"Listen, George, I know her better than all of you, and the medication that you are suggesting is harmful to the development of the baby's skeleton."

"We have to treat the mother first!"

"Naught that mother," the crisp British accent caused the nurses to stop their morning report and listen.

"Doctors," the head nurse interrupted, "Mrs. Solberg has refused all meds during the night. Dr. Solberg just smiled and motioned us out of the room."

Leo and George entered the room and asked Regina what she wanted to do.

"I really don't want any medication," she sighed, then continued, "we have waited a long time for this baby, and I don't want to take any chances."

"You will be in excruciating pain until those incisions heal, honey," George tried to reason. "There is no solid proof that the medication would hurt the baby."

"Is there solid proof that it would not hurt the baby?" When neither Orthopedist answered, she added, "That's what I thought."

"Constant agony won't exactly help the baby either," Leo answered firmly.

"Let's take it one day at the time, okay?" Regina smiled weakly. "May I please go home now?"

"Can you walk?"

"Yes, I think so."

Frank helped her out of the bed but she quickly fell back against it. "My head hurts," she said without any apparent distress, "it feels very heavy."

"Uh-oh!" Both attending physicians (doctors who are part of the faculty in a medical school) answered.

"I can try again," Regina suggested, afraid to frighten Frank Jr.

She rose slowly and took a few steps. "These casts hurt; can they come off?"

"No," Both attendings answered in unison again.

George motioned to Leo to step outside. "We need to observe her for a spine fluid leak, she's as white as a ghost."

"Agreed," Leo was beside himself.

After explaining the possible dilemma to Regina, Leo called Andrew back into the room. Regina still insisted on going home, and promised to return if the headaches continued. Once she got home and in her bed, she felt that she would relax and be alright. The three doctors consented under the condition that both Frank and Leo would be available and permitted to keep a close watch on her.

Dan and Elizabeth stayed until she was settled in then left for Wellington asking Frances to call them if anything else went wrong. "We'll see you this weekend, sweetheart," Dan kissed her, trying desperately to hold back the tears that were welling up in his deep blue eyes. Elizabeth was not as successful, and cried when she hugged her daughter. "Don't worry, Mom, I'll be fine," Regina smiled.

Midnight revealed otherwise as her headaches continued to pound and she was able to keep nothing in her stomach. Frank called Frances and then called the hospital. Andrew was called, as well as Leo and George, and all three insisted that she come in by ambulance. Regina had asked to wait until morning and was not in agreement with the method of transportation, but cooperated anyway.

"We didn't need to wake people up at this hour, sweetheart," she clutched Frank's hand, and then pleaded with Frances not to call her parents back there unless things got serious. "Things are serious, Regina, and your parents would want to be told. How about if I call them and tell them not to come back down unless it becomes more serious? I'll explain that you are worried about them traveling all the way back here at this hour."

"Okay."

Once at the hospital, a blood patch was ordered to rule out a spine fluid leak. The Anesthesia attending explained, "We are going to draw blood from your arm and inject it into your spine to stop the fluid leak. If there is indeed a leak, it will be as though someone has flicked a switch and the headaches and nausea will vanish like magic."

"Sounds good to me," Regina answered with a slight smile.

Andrew supervised the procedure whether anybody liked it or not, and it was in fact a spine fluid leak. Regina was delighted to be over it, and Andrew was relieved, but thoroughly disgusted.

"Leave it to those 'carpenters' to screw things up," he did not bother to exclude Frank from the insult. "Someone ought to seal those orthopedic guys up in a lovely garage and let them play with their tools there."

"I'm very hungry and I am ready to go back home," Regina laughed.

"I would like for you to stay here until tomorrow," Andrew answered firmly.

"No thanks, but I appreciate the offer," Regina was ready to leave right then and there.

"It wasn't an offer, Regina, it is an order."

"Please let me leave, Andrew. Frank will be there with me and so will Frances. If anything else goes wrong, I will return and stay as long as you want."

Andrew slowly took a deep breath, "You continually amaze me! Frank, I trust that you will call me at home with the slightest change. Remember your promise, young lady."

"Rye-toe," Regina mocked, while her British doctor laughed and rolled his eyes in frustration.

Dr. Hernandez walked into the emergency room and apologized to Regina. I am so sorry, Mrs. Solberg; I used the smallest needle possible, and we still had complications." Regina reached for his hand, "Sometimes things are out of our hands for reasons we cannot possibly understand, Dr. Hernandez. The fact that you wear scrubs and are excellent in your profession does not ensure automatic immunity from any complications. The baby is safe, and that's all I care about. I have no concerns of negligence, and I will be calling Risk Management to send me a full release of liability to sign, on behalf of the hospital and the entire surgical team. ”

Returning home, Regina was able to eat and drink freely, but had strict orders not to move around unless it was absolutely necessary. Although in the excruciating pain that the orthopedists promised, she was restless to start packing for the move in the summer.

The boxes from storage that were needed to decorate for the holidays were already set aside, and she hoped to place some of their bulk possessions in storage among them after the season.

Dan and Elizabeth returned with Bub and Sis, and Andrea and Brian came over in their own car. Regina tried to reassure everyone that she would be alright, but Leo had already clued them in about the agony that this healing carried with it.

“We usually prescribe pain medications to carry patients through this, but Andrew has foolishly advised against them. We should make him come over and watch her lay there in pain,” the Colonel was more than a little upset. “He can also keep his remarks about orthopods to himself in the future,” he snapped explaining the garage suggestion that Frank had shared with him the day of the blood patch.

As weeks went by, close friends were in and out and watched over her while Frank was at the hospital. Frank Jr. was a gem to care for and Regina loved his visits to her room with his GI Joes. The bulk of the neuropathy pain was at night, but she still refused to take medication for it. Instead, she focused on the tiny life inside of her and continually prayed. Mercedes came over with some flowers and a bag of avocados, but wept when she saw Regina.

In spite of Regina's gallant efforts to be cheerful, the agonizing pain was obvious, and everyone continually begged her to use pain killers.

"The baby may not even be affected by them," Elizabeth was at her wits' end.

"What about something very mild?" Dan pleaded.

Frank Jr. came in and opened his Fisher Price doctor's kit. "I will make this pain go away now, Mommy. I cawn't believe that I wasn't cawled in on this case ehrlier," he added, in his best British accent.

"Who are you," Elizabeth asked able to laugh for the first time since the onset of pain started.

"I'm Doughtor Kingsley, Grandma!" Cawn't you tell by how funny I tawlk? Here are some magic baby pills for the pain, Mommy." Regina took the candy pills and laughed.

"Is the pain gone?" the somber little "physician" asked.

"Yes! It is all gone, Sweetheart," his patient answered laughing and wiping a tear that slipped down her cheek.

"Grandpa, we need to get these for Jackson Memorial Hospital! They cured Mommy," he called as he ran from the room to find Leo. "Get them before they seal you and Daddy up in the garage!"

Regina laid awake all night every night, watching the skies for morning and wondering why the pain was so much worse after dark. Each day at the break of dawn, she saw a gorgeous cloud in the shape of an exotic angel. "My Abba, I love You! Thanks so much for the beautiful cloud and thanks even more for sending it every day. Please keep this baby safe, Father, and don't worry about me. I'll gladly take the pain as long as I can keep the baby. Please just keep my baby safe."

For the first time since her pregnancy, Regina felt the baby move as the sun burst through her window. She wept and tried to tell God just how much she loved Him. Unable to find the words, she realized that she needed only to think them. From that morning forward, the pain subsided enough to allow her to move about a little. Although Regina did not see her angel cloud again, she made a secret promise to God. "Abba," she whispered, "If You've sent us a baby girl, I would love to name her Angela Dawn. What do You think?"

Chapter Seventeen

Watch Out For The Gentrys!

While holidays came and went in a flash, they still managed to hold fantastic memories. Regina moved slowly but surely to pack the house, and honored Frank Jr.'s wishes to transfer his jungle to his new room in Bradington. The pregnancy proceeded without further problems, and Regina was radiant.

The three girls spent every moment possible together, quietly dreading their last day in Miami. Although they would still talk every day and see each other often, they all knew that things would never be the same, and tried to be strong for each other.

Dan and Elizabeth were taking two weeks off to go to Bradington with Regina and help with the move. Bub and Sis wanted to join them, but they were afraid that the extra house guests would be too much for Regina. Frances got wind of the issue and decided to once again make use of her *license to meddle*. Regina was delighted that she did, and called her aunt and uncle.

"Please come, Aunt Sis, it won't be too much work; it will be too much fun – and I don't want to miss out!"

And so on the big day, everyone said "happy-sad" goodbyes and left for their new homes. Regina was heartbroken as they crossed the bridge, but kept her feelings to herself. Dan was fully aware that his daughter was anything but happy about this move, and shared his knowledge with Leo. "Could it be caused by leftover anxiety from the surgery or maybe the ongoing pregnancy, Leo?"

"No, I don't think it's either one of those two factors, but I have also sensed this deep sadness in her, and I'm concerned about it too."

"Maybe we can take turns talking to her and try to resolve whatever the problem is if we can."

"Hey, I'll do anything at all to help. I wonder if she's upset that Hazel, Frances, Lamar, and I will be forty-five minutes away."

"That shouldn't be that hard on her; Regina is usually a stone wall."

"Agreed, Dan, but I noticed when we operated on her that she actually bled."

"Meaning?"

"That we sometimes forget that she's as human as we are and even though she's tough as hell, she still has the same feelings and emotions as the rest of us."

Dan lit a cigarette and took a deep drag as he continued to evaluate the situation. "Okay, let's just take turns asking her; then we'll compare notes and meet with Frank, though he most likely knows if there's a problem."

When the whole gang stopped to rest for the night, Leo nodded to Dan and pulled Regina aside. "A penny for your thoughts," he smiled, taking the overnight bag from her.

"I want to go home," she uncharacteristically burst into tears. "I had all my work there in Miami, and all of my friends; I was sent there by Abba. I'll miss my family terribly, Frank's parents don't even know that we are gone, and what about Gabby? We'll hardly ever see her and it will be very difficult for both her and Eva when we do."

Leo hugged her and spoke very gently, "Regina, you will have new work in your new home. Abba already has that set out for you. We are all leaving Miami, but we are all still bonded together. Gabby will be fine, honey, and Eva will too."

"I'll miss the clinic, Leo. I'll miss my patients," she sobbed as though she would never stop. "I'll miss Eva and Mercedes too."

"You will find new people to help, sweetheart, you'll see. Eva and Mercedes, will cross paths more often than you think. Your parents will have longer visits, and they will also be more often than you think, since your dad is the senior partner. He told me just this morning that Brian can run the place as well as he can in his absence. Blueprints travel easily, and your mother loves to take long car trips. They'll probably pester the hell out of you!" Regina laughed and nodded along as the Colonel continued, "Since Frank's parents are a pain in the butt; we don't mind losing them for a while, do we?"

"No," she laughed again, counting her blessings.

"If you want to work in the hospital, we can certainly arrange that, even if you only wanted to do it part time."

"No, I think that would be a problem. These are a whole different kind of people and I need to stay with the kids and find another niche to fit into. I'm sure that Abba already has one for me, so I just have to wait to get my new orders, Sir!"

"That's more like it, soldier," the Colonel boomed his military voice, accompanied by a smile of relief. "And you will let me know if I can be of any assistance- UNDERSTOOD?!"

"UNDERSTOOD, SIR!" The little missionary laughed and dried her eyes, deciding to wait patiently for Abba to assign her new position.

The next day the group met for breakfast at The Pancake Factory, a famous restaurant nestled among gorgeous trees and a rushing brook. Brilliantly colored birds flew overhead, causing patrons to look forward to the waiting list. In addition, a huge attached playground kept Frank Jr. busy and the ten adults in his personal fan club thoroughly entertained.

Dan went to the gift shop and bought two adorable pandas – one for Regina and another for Frank Jr. to ensure that she would keep it for herself! The large stuffed animals had adorable faces and wore sun suits embroidered with bright green letters that said *Pandemonium*, which was his nickname for the little redhead who could set the world on its' ear if given half the chance to do so. Handing Frank's panda to his father, he took Regina out by the brook and gave her the other one. She hugged her father and cried. "Dad, I am going to miss you so much."

"No way; you won't have a chance. We have already set time

aside to come every other month. We may even be able to bring Gabby down the line."

Regina was relieved and clutched her panda as though she were five years old again. She and Dan talked about the new house and he confirmed the same points that Leo made regarding new work for the baffled missionary.

"I hope that He has something for me to do here too, in addition to our wonderful children. I want to serve Him too, Dad; I want to help other people."

"Regina, there's not a doubt in my mind that you will be called to do more of Abba's work. Everything happens for a purpose, honey. He assigned you work on the cruise lines, did He not?"

The small missionary, who looked even smaller pregnant, smiled as though the light had just come on. Glancing up at the gorgeous sky, she noticed the dawn greeting angel cloud of months before. It had suddenly reappeared as though a wink from Abba, Himself!

"Look, Dad! Do you see that cloud? It's shaped like an angel, and Abba sent it every morning during my recovery."

"See? How many of us get our own greeting clouds from the great I Am? And you were worried about getting canned!"

They walked into the restaurant to find Aunt Sis on her way out to call them.

Dan winked at Leo and picked up a menu.

The group of four headed for Memphis and the other seven to Bradington, all marveling at the new scenery. Bradington was a charming town, and the people there gave the impression that one was on a TV set filming *The Andy Griffith Show*.

As they pulled into the driveway of the new home, neighbors came pouring in with cakes, pies, cookies, casseroles, bottles of salad dressing, a basket of vegetable seeds for a garden, and plants. They introduced themselves and came right in as though they were expecting a party of some kind. Jimmie and Eugene McDaniel, the former owners of the house, came over too, but allowed the overzealous visitors to stay for about an hour before they shooed them off good-naturedly, and left themselves.

The moving men had dropped all of the furniture off the day prior and set it exactly as Regina requested. Boxes piled in neat stacks stood in every room, and the house had been left immaculately clean. Regina and Frank laughed as they tried to gather their thoughts after the unexpected reception.

Dan and Bub inspected the house while Elizabeth and Sis stocked the fridge with drinks and snacks left over from the trip. Frank Jr. and thirteen children came in asking for permission to swim in the pool. Regina lined all of them up and asked their names, although she knew she wouldn't remember all of them for awhile. "Okay, troops," she said in a no-nonsense but fun tone, "pools are fun as long as they are safe, yes?"

"Yes ma'am," the group answered."

"So the first thing we need to do is to establish some rules to be sure that we are safe, and I will need your help, one person talking at the time, so we keep the information straight."

Dan and Bub could not believe the undivided attention

that she had and the excellent conduct of the "troops." Frank Sr. laughed, "Are you kidding? Thirteen kids are a joke to her. This place will be the hit of the block and as organized as a country club swimming class," he smiled at his wife with pride.

The next morning the troops were back to swim and their parents eventually came over for coffee. The neighbors were all friendly but a little too friendly for Regina's taste. She liked her privacy and could clearly see that some tactful boundaries were in order, and must be placed immediately. They arrived in two's, and the first were Gayle Jenkins and Nyla Caldwell. Oblivious to the fact that the Solbergs had just arrived yesterday, had four house guests, and needed to settle in; they asked for a tour of the house, "while the coffee's a-perkin." Sis and Elizabeth were laughing as they set out cake plates, but shared Regina's concerns.

Gayle was married to Bob Jenkins, the town manager, and had two young sons, Peter, 4 and Paul, 2. She stirred her coffee, helped herself to a huge piece of cake and three cookies, and immediately advised "Gina" which Regina corrected, to "Regina," to "Watch out for the Gentrys! They are Vernon and Marge, and they live yonder three houses down on the rahght. They have seven boys and they are dangerous, honey, and ah mean dangerous! He's in the military and his wahf is near a nervous breakdown. You don't want Frankie over there and you definitely don't want them over here. Those boys have been in trouble up to their ears, but because their daddy is a Navy officer, they stay out of juvenile delinquent holdings. They have, and will, harm animals and small children. Keep a very close ahye on that baby when it's born too," she added, indicating Regina's stomach.

Nyla and Darren Caldwell lived down the block next door to the Jenkins,' and had three sons, Duncan, age 7; Danny age 5; and Dodge, age 4. She also stressed the dangers of the Gentry boys. "The oldest boy, Gerald, keeps to himself, the next one, Jonathan, molested our son Danny. Their kindergartener, Shawn Mah-cal, cut the head off the barber's cat and put it over their doorknob last Hal-a-ween! He's five years old, mind you!" Regina was concerned, but made no comments as Sis and Elizabeth gasped. "Ah don't know if you know it or not, but Darren is the manager of the Charms Factory," Nyla continued, "He cain't stand those boys and he refused a field trip to a class that had one of them in it. Finally, the teacher asked Marge Gentry to keep her son out of school for the day, so the rest of the kids could enjoy the trip!"

The visit was pleasant enough, but Regina ended it by saying, "Thanks ever so much for stopping by. Let me give you my number in case you would like to visit again. I am a lay-missionary and I must take all guests by previous arrangement. I have thoroughly enjoyed meeting both of you, and your children are delightful." The two ladies left gushing, and not yet realizing that they had just been firmly curbed from future drop-in visits. Elizabeth and Sis exchanged glances as Frank, Dan, and Bub shrugged and giggled.

"Their kids seem very polite, honey; are you happy with the mothers?" Frank asked, thoroughly enjoying the grand reception that they had received so far. He felt that it was due to the fact that he was the new town surgeon, and wanted to be sure that they were well-liked, and stayed that way. "Yes, they are very pleasant, sweetheart, but I want to be sure that we set limits so that we don't offend anyone down the line. Drop-in visits can be disruptive, especially when the new baby arrives."

"We also need to steer clear of those Gentry people. They sound like they can be a nightmare. I heard the kids warning Frank Jr. about them yesterday. He's scared to death of them already."

"Daddy, Shawn Mah-cal is riding his bike down the street in front of our house! He is a Gentry and he will kill Monique! Keep her inside and away from the window!" Frank Jr. was near hysterics, as he tried to draw the blinds.

"Frank, the young man's name is Shawn Michael. Some of the people here just have southern accents, honey," Regina laughed and hugged her young son.

"I don't see anyone riding a bike out there," Dan reported.

"That's because Miss Nyla told him to get home or she will call the police, but he was out there, Grandpa, and he knows we're here!"

"Frankie, have you actually seen Shawn Michael?" Dan asked calmly.

"No, but Danny said he was out there! He saw him from the tree on the front lawn, so I ran straight in here," Frank Jr. gasped for another breath.

"Well, I wouldn't worry too much about him, Frank; he probably knows not to come over here."

"Duncan said that he will damage our house and that his brothers could easily kill us. Their father works in the White House and so they can't be punished. The White House is where the President lives, Grandpa. They are friends with the President!"

"Well then why aren't they all in Washington? How can their father work at the White House when he lives here, and do you think that the President would allow any child to behave like that and not take action?"

Frank looked thoughtful and answered slowly, "I'm not sure."

"Well I think that sometimes stories accidentally get blown out of proportion and people get all shook up about nothing," Dan smiled, taking a box of ice pops out of the freezer. "How about this, let's all go out to the picnic table and have a nice ice pop. If the Gentry boy comes about, I'll be right there too."

"Okay, but are you armed?"

"I believe so," Dan laughed and waved both of his arms.

Frank Sr. settled into his new clinic and the hospital staff loved him. He seemed very content, and Regina was happy for him. The unpacking and decorating went well, and Frances and Lamar were riding over that evening with the Gerehauzers for a cook out by the pool. Regina came in with a bag of groceries and walked over to Dan. "Dad, I passed the Gentry house twice this morning, and those kids look like anything but trouble. They were all in their own yard eating a plate of cookies that their mother, or I guess it was their mother, brought out."

"Well, be careful, honey. We don't know anything but what we have heard about them, which is all bad."

The Solberg's yard was full of the neighbors' children, cookout or not; and their parents did not call them home. Frank and Regina showed off the house, which was really starting to take shape. Everybody sat around the pool and laughed until they cried. The phone and the doorbell rang simultaneously and Frank laughed, calling over his shoulder, "I got the phone." Dan motioned Regina to remain seated, and headed for the door.

"Jeannie had a little girl, Robin Renee Nugent! Another Cesarean Section, but they are thrilled. Charlie asked the nurse for a cooty shot," Frank shared the news from the telephone conversation.

"Frank Jr.," he called, "Aunt Jeannie had her baby."

"What's his name, Dad?"

"<u>Her</u> name is Robin Renee."

"Yuck, a sister; I hope I don't get a sister! Does Charlie want to move in here?"

"No, but he wanted a cooty shot."

"When is our baby coming home, Dad?"

"In a few more months, son."

"I wondered why your mother looked so blown up," Danny Caldwell mentioned, wide-eyed. "So you're getting a brother soon?"

"Yep," Frank Jr. nodded, leading the gang to the watermelon bowl.

Dan came in from the door and motioned to Frank and Regina. "The police are here to see you. It appears that they have had a call complaining about the Gentry boys peeping through the privacy fence."

"A complaint from who?" Regina was puzzled.

"I don't know, but the officer is in the living room."

The officer introduced himself to the Solbergs and apologized for interrupting their party. "We had a complaint about the Gentry boys peeping through your fence."

"A complaint from who, Sir?" Regina asked calmly.

"I assumed that it came from here, ma'am."

"No, Sir, I don't think so. I did not see anybody peeping through the fence."

"Well, I'll go over and question the boys and see if I can get to the bottom of this."

"Officer, perhaps you can tell us since we are new here, exactly what the problem with the Gentrys' is."

"Well, it's hard to say, ma'am, but I'm inclined to think it's more of a clique situation."

"Do you know anything about the barber's cat?"

"Yes, ma'am," the officer laughed, turning a little red. "Sid, the barber, cut the little youngster's hair far shorter than he was told to, and then laughed at him, saying that he could be a peeled onion for Halloween. Well, that young man, Shawn Michael, was humiliated and pulled the black cat decoration off of Sid's lawn that night. Thomas Henry, his twelve-year-old brother, cut the head off it and put it over the doorknob with a note from Shawn Michael that said, *You are a fat fink, mister.* Now, Vernon Gentry, is a Navy Chief and didn't take kindly to either of his sons' reactions. He made them do chores to earn the $5.75 and took them to Wal-Mart to buy another cat. Then he and Marge drove them over to Sid's to apologize and put the new cat back on the lawn's all."

"So this was a fake cat?" Regina asked laughing.

"Oh, sure! Plastic, I think."

"And what about the son named Jonathan allegedly molesting another neighborhood boy? Are you privy to that?"

"You must be talking about Danny Caldwell, that feller has quite a mouth on him! He called Vernon Gentry a punk and the "punk's" son washed his face with a jella donut in front of God and everybody."

"May we walk over to the Gentrys' with you, Sir?" Regina asked, unable to keep a straight face.

"Regina, that might not be wise at all," Frank spoke up for the first time since the officer arrived.

"Why?" Regina asked calmly.

"Well, honey, because everybody else on the block hates them."

"Well I don't hate anybody, and I'm going over there."

The Gentrys were finishing their supper when the three visitors arrived. Marge answered the door and turned pale. "Good heavens, officer, what have we done now?"

"These are the new neighbors, Marge, Frank and Regina Solberg."

"How do you do Mr. and Mrs. Solberg."

"Doctor," Frank responded coldly.

"Regina, if you please, and did I understand correctly that your name is Marge?"

"Yes ma'am."

The officer continued, "We got a complaint that the boys were peeping through the privacy fence, but the Solbergs here didn't know anything about it. The complaint, that is."

"We looked once!" Shawn Michael cried, "Once! Then Miss Nyla drove by and said that she was calling a complaint to the law."

"We meant no harm, officer," the next boy in line, Anthony, said in his brother's defense. "We just wanted to see what the new neighbors looked like."

"Miss Nyla sent Shawn Michael home a few days ago just because he was riding his bike by the new neighbor's house. I saw him, Mom and Dad, he was in the street," the oldest boy, Gerald added politely.

Vernon Gentry, who had been standing quietly, was a good looking man, well over six feet tall. He had dark hair, big blue eyes and a definite military appearance. His wife was considerably shorter with blonde hair and lighter blue eyes, which were filling with tears. He spoke softly but sternly, "I would like to introduce my sons, Dr. and Mrs. Solberg. Then those who were trespassing on your property will apologize to you and they will never repeat that behavior again. Is that understood, gentlemen?"

Seven adorable boys answered, "Yes, Sir."

"Gerald is 15, Jonathan is 13, Thomas Henry is 12, Gregory is 10, Justin is 8, Anthony is 7, and Shawn Michael is 5."

"I feel like I am on *The Sound of Music*," Regina laughed and clasped her small hands. "Your children are handsome and very well-mannered, Sir."

"Vernon, if you please ma'am."

"Regina, if you please."

Frank stepped forward and extended his hand, "Frank."

"Now who was trespassing?" Vernon looked at the seven serious faces.

"If I may, Sir, ah Vernon, nobody was trespassing, as there are no such signs and we have made no such complaint," Regina casually bit her lower lip to keep from laughing.

Marge smiled gratefully at Regina, and was shocked when she said, "Please come over and see what the new neighbors look like. We have plenty of dessert, and my 'second father,' a retired army colonel, is visiting. In the future, there is no need to peep through the fence since we have a door that reveals much more."

One by one, the boys walked over to Regina and kissed her on the cheek as their father raised his eyebrows. The missionary gushed with pleasure as she led the group of nine over to their new house to meet the gang. Leo walked over to Regina and whispered, "Reporting for duty?"

"Sir! Yes Sir!" she answered, smiling at Dan, who knew exactly what they were talking about.

Marge was delighted to meet Elizabeth, Sis, Hazel, and Frances and loved Regina the minute she saw her. She thought she was dreaming, but warned, "you may have to keep our acquaintance a secret, Regina, and don't let on that you have been kind to us, or you will be black-listed."

"I've always loved black, and I will keep nothing a secret. You are welcome here."

Vernon already had a deep respect for this pregnant little fire-ball. He sensed that she could cordially hold her own without any real effort. The Gentrys played with all of the other neighborhood kids, and Frank Jr. was delighted that nobody killed Monique. After the party he said to Dan, Leo, and Lamar, "They are very much like real people, those Gentrys."

Chapter Eighteen
Just Dessert!

Bright and early the next morning Gayle and Nyla were at the door. Elizabeth and Sis exchanged worried looks as Bub rolled his eyes. "Dan, those neighbors are here," Elizabeth whispered.

"Regina will handle it, honey," he put his arm around his wife.

"Good morning, ladies," Dan answered the door and showed them into the living room. "Is Regina expecting you?"

"No," Gayle answered suddenly remembering that they were to call prior to coming. "This is important though, and we need to see her."

Regina walked into the room, greeted the ladies, and took a seat.

"I'll go first," Gayle held her hand up toward her friend. "Gina..."

"Regina," Regina calmly corrected.

"Well then, Regina," the neighbor snapped before continuing, "Air boys will not be allowed to play here if the Gentrys are permitted to come over. Nahla called the police as a favor to you because they were peeping through your prahvacy fence. And what do you do? You ignore all that we told you and walk over there to meet those disturbed people and bring them back here among air children! We are very upset, Gi..Regina."

"I can see that you are very upset, Gayle, and that is why I hope you will relax. I must tell you, however, that this is our home and our decision who may visit and who we chose to meet. I hope that you reconsider banning your delightful boys from playing here, and I think that you will if you ever see how nicely everyone plays together."

"Well mahne won't be coming back," she stood to leave as Nyla shrugged and joined her.

"I'm sorry to hear that, Gayle, and I truly hope that you will reconsider. If you do, you have my phone number. Perhaps if you two ladies discuss it further, you may feel differently. I hope that will be the case."

Both ladies turned on their heels and left, chattering all the way home.

Regina joined the breakfast table and reassured Frank that all would be well.

"Regina, we can't afford this. Now— trouble, is what we have!"

"The only pool on "air street," is also what we have," the involuntary smart-aleck lurking in Regina's soul mischievously surfaced. "If their little darlings wish to come here and play; then everyone else should be able to join in too. I find the Gentrys to be lovely people, and they should not have to look through the fence or listen from the street, while everyone else on the block is jumping in and out of the pool. In addition, I will not be told who I may or may not talk to, Frank. By anyone!"

Frank walked over to his wife and hugged her. "I'm sorry, honey. I just want everything to work out well for us. We want to get along with everyone and not become the butt end of a feud."

"Exactly; it is not our feud and we are staying out of it. Did you hear any of the Gentrys utter one unpleasant syllable about anyone?"

"Well, no, now that you mention it, I didn't."

"Your visitors are back," Bub sang from the living room window and giggled.

"Regina, we want to try to explain something," Nyla spoke this time.

"I'm all ears," Regina smiled.

"This neighborhood will be one big tangled mess if you start socializing with the Gentrys. Caint you understand that?"

Frank cautiously walked into the room and Regina excused herself for "a moment."

"A tangled mess is what we'll have, Dr. Denoff," Nyla started to cry. "Caint you help us?"

Returning with a box, Regina set it down on the coffee table. By this point the other four adults wandered into the living room out of sheer curiosity. Regina opened the box to expose a pile of mosquito netting, the finishing touch for Frank's new room. "This appears to be a big tangled mess, and one that could easily be one heck of a problem. Is that what you are saying?"

"Yes!" Nyla smiled brightly.

"Now, we have a room full of capable adults who could each take a section," she added handing out the tabs, "and if we will all gently move back and look at the situation, we now have a safety net!"

Everyone just waited quietly for the next step.

"Now, Dad, if will you drop your tab, please," the net immediately puckered, as Regina continued, "Behold what happens when just one of us is left out.

If we all work together, and decide to have fun, we can provide each other with a very useful safety net. Nobody should hurt or feel uncomfortable about joining in, as long as there are thinking adults on the scene, ALL working together."

As the group laughed, Nyla hugged Regina. Sis invited the two ladies in for coffee, but both ladies looked at Regina for approval, realizing that they came over for the second time in one day without calling.

Walking over to Gayle, Regina asked, "Can you help us organize some pool games for some summertime fun? After all, you are the town manager's wife."

"Well Ah… Well if… Well, okay," Gayle threw in her towel and joined in the laughter.

The Solbergs took their little son to the school to enroll him in Kindergarten. Frank seemed comfortable but asked very few questions. He saw the classrooms, the library, the playground and the cafeteria. The lady in the office smiled at him and gave him a list of supplies and a school handbook, and told him that they would see him after the summer vacation.

"Well?" His father asked as they walked to the car.

"Well what?" Frank Jr.'s big blue eyes searched for the rest of the question.

"How do you like your new school?"

"I think it will be fine, but I wish Charlie and Harper, were going here with me."

"Your new friends will go to school here too, honey," Regina smiled.

"Are you sure, Mommy?"

"Why, yes, I'm sure."

"Well then why aren't they here?"

"Because they are already registered, and you just moved here."

"Oh, well then it might be kind of fun. Can we all swim when we get home?"

"Absolutely," both parents answered at once. Frank Sr. added, "In fact, I think we need to order pizza!"

Frank Jr. high-fived his father but mumbled a warning that there could be a serious problem down the line for both of them. "What kind of a problem, son," his father stopped walking to listen.

"Mom could have a girl baby, like Aunt Jeannie did," he whispered to his father, "and if she does, we're doomed."

Over the summer neighbors came and went, and although they did not like the Solberg's "no gossip rule," and said so behind their backs, they certainly respected them for it. The Gentrys were gradually accepted as neighbors, especially since Frank and Regina had grown very fond of them. There was to be a huge "back-to-school" pool party at the Solbergs,' and Marge and

Regina were decorating cigar boxes for favors, and filling them with pencils, erasers, glue, scissors, bubble gum, M&M's, and stickers. The kids ran in and out bursting with excitement and introducing the arrival of different neighbors bringing goodies to store in the fridge for the big bash. Gayle came in with a seven-layer- shortcake and Marge jumped up to help make room for it on the top shelf. "Thanks so much, honey," Gayle was startled to hear herself being kind to the lady she had spread so many lies about. Both women, momentarily taken back, smiled at each other and returned to their work.

During the party Vernon Gentry stopped talking to Frank Sr. midsentence, and shot into the pool like a torpedo. Everyone turned to see him taking Dodge Caldwell out of the deep end, gasping for breath. Frank took over from there, and fortunately the child had not lost consciousness. "Where is his life jacket?" Regina asked firmly and slightly shaken. "I let him walk around for awhile without it, Regina," his father confessed, "I didn't real-ize that I was violating a pool rule. It will never happen again," Darren Caldwell said as he went over to shake Vernon's hand and thank him for saving his son. Nyla walked over to Vernon sob-bing and kissed him on the cheek. With tears still flooding her face, she proceeded to the bin of back zippered life jackets, to re-turn to "compliance" with the Solberg's Rules of Safety.

The school principal had called Gayle asking her to round up some mothers for lunch room duty; so she made her announce-ment as dessert was being served. "Regina, you're excused since you are very pregnant."

"Nonsense, I will take my share of the job until the baby arrives. Then I'll need a few days off, and I will return."

"Okay," she laughed and passed out the schedules.

Regina and Marge Gentry would start out as a team as would Nyla and Gayle. The teams would change partners each quarter, giving everyone an opportunity to work with each other.

Frank Jr., Shawn Michael, and Danny Caldwell all wound up in the same kindergarten class with a wonderful teacher, Mrs. Houseman, who had just turned forty. She was pleasant and very dedicated to her work. Frank Jr. liked her right away and seemed relieved that Regina was going to be working in the lunchroom. "She has three boys of her own at home, Mom," he said as though surprised. "Does anyone in Bradington have any girls?" his father asked, just realizing that there were none on the entire street where they lived. "No," Frank Jr. laughed, "Girls are not allowed here."

Constructed at tremendous expense, Bradington Hills Elementary School, was housed in a tremendous, rambling, structure that encompassed grades K-6. Everything was first class right down to the water fountains. Impressed by the facility, Regina was equally shocked to learn that the school promoted corporal punishment, as it was forbidden in most states. The principal, Mr. Barry Walker, was a tall, thin man with straight brown hair which he wore slicked back. His cold, beady, black eyes were almost squinted, and he was feared by all of the students but two, who happened to be his own children. Nick and

Debbie, the Walker twins, were in the fourth grade. They had the same skeptical squint as their father and looked at everyone as though they were hired by a secret agency to find fault with them. Regina was uncomfortable, to say the least.

Walking into the school office one morning for cafeteria supplies, she heard the principal yelling at two boys, one black and one white. He then took a leather paddle and told the black boy to bend over. He wailed his backside with such force that Regina was sure the child would fall over. When the paddling was completed, he belittled the boy and gave him a detention slip. The white boy also received detention, but no paddling, and no degrading comments. The black boy was ordered to "keep his eyes down and return to class," while the white boy was simply told to "return to class." Regina felt as though she was going to be sick. She approached Mr. Walker and asked what year it was. When the stunned principal answered, she replied, "That's what I thought."

The next day, a certified letter was generated to the school board, warning them that under no circumstances was any member of the faculty or staff in general, authorized to use corporal punishment on Frank Solberg Jr. While cleaning tables, Regina looked up and saw Mr. Walker coming toward her. "Mrs. Solberg, what makes you think that anyone would ever lay a hand on your son?"

"Oh, perhaps the charming scene that I witnessed in your office the other day."

"Those boys were talking when the teacher was!"

"Both of them?"

"Yes, both of them."

"Well then why did only one of them get his butt beat off?"

"Because he was------"

"Black? Mr. Walker?"

"Well not only that, but because he seemed to be more apt to misbehave again."

"Let us hope that black children are not being oppressed in this school, Mr. Walker, as I am always looking for a new project."

"Isn't your baby due soon?"

"Never you worry, Sir; babies love projects too."

"You're from the north, aren't you?"

"Yes, I am from the Bronx."

"Oh, great," the ever so slightly shaken Mr. Walker muttered as he walked away.

Arriving home Frank Jr. ran to answer the telephone. "Mom, it's Uncle Wyatt!"

"Wyatt, what a lovely surprise! Two identical little boys! Well that evens out the score – in fact now you need another girl!"

"Sylvia's delighted, and sends her love. We named them Roger De Brett and Ryan Dominic."

Frank Jr. ran to tell his friends the great news, "My friends Harper, Hyacinth and Holly have two new baby brothers, Roger and Ryan. I don't remember their middle names, but Harper is one lucky duck! Charlie got stuck with a sister!"

Regina continued to work at the school and continued to see that the black children, especially those from lower income families, were clearly mistreated. While it broke her heart, it also made her angry. Not only was this "black and white" discrimination disgusting, but it was decades behind the times, and she could not believe that it was still happening. During lunch one day, an adorable little black boy named Darrell walked up to the lunch counter, and asked to go back to his classroom to retrieve his birthday card so he could buy an ice cream pop.

"My Aunt sent me two dollars," he explained, "and we came in here right from the fire drill, so I couldn't get my money." At six years of age, this child had a charm that would dazzle the Ku Klux Klan. Marge Gentry told him to go ahead and get the ice cream and that she would ask his teacher to walk him back to his room when she finished talking to another student.

"Okay, boy," a cross-looking line cook grabbed Darrell's arm and jerking it up toward his shoulder, shouted, "you're gonna git your little black keister blistered fer stealin," she motioned for Barry Walker to come in haste and assist in the apprehension of the thirty-five pound felon. Marge tried to explain, but the lunch lady hushed her.

Observing Regina in a fast walk toward them, and knowing that she wouldn't be hushed, Barry Walker, smacked the heel of his right palm against his forehead, "Great! Of course 'Rosa Parks' would have to be here today."

"Boy, what do you mean by taking that ice cream?" Barry tried to sound calm and reasonable.

"My Aunt sent me two dollars in my birthday card," the tiny boy shivered as he burst into tears.

"Well I doubt that," Barry snickered.

"Well I do not!" Regina answered loudly.

"Mrs. Solberg, it may be time you got your just dessert for butting into affairs that don't concern you."

"Perhaps it's time that you got your just dessert from the NAACP, Sir, and since I am a volunteer for a county school, this child and all of the others here, are in fact, my concern!"

"Okay, I'll make a deal with you. I'll just walk the boy back to his classroom. If he has such a birthday card, he'll go unpunished and can buy his ice cream."

"No dice! We will both walk Darrell back to his room and if he does have such a birthday card, we will negotiate his terms to drop an impending discrimination case against your school."

"Unheard of! There's no such card!"

"Then perhaps you wouldn't mind taking our little stroll."

Regina put her arm around the little boy's shoulder, and walked to his classroom with Barry shadowing them. Darrell reached into his desk, removed the card from his aunt, and showed them the two crisp dollar bills inside. "Well, how about that! Barry smiled at the child. Looks like you do git to buy you some ice cream!"

"Well how about this," Regina was furious and her voice reflected it, "You git to buy him some ice cream today and everyday for the entire school year, after you and the bouncer on the lunch line apologize to him in front of all the people that witnessed your despicable accusation. You hang on to your two dollars, Darrell," Regina placed the money in his pocket.

"You don't want to buck the system here, Mrs. Solberg."

"You don't want the newspaper here, Mr. Walker."

The three walked back to the cafeteria and Barry signaled the lunch lady who grabbed Darrell. "Hilda, we owe this youngster an apology. He does have a card from his aunt."

"Go on," little Darrell held Regina's hand tightly and smiled bravely.

"We're going to give him complementary ice cream for the entire school year to compensate for his humiliation."

"Damn," Hilda responded, mortified, "But whah?

"Oh it's called Just Dessert! Darrell, why don't you select which ice cream you would like and eat your lunch," Regina continued, noting the time. "He will probably need extra time to eat, Mr. Walker. With your permission I will wait with him and escort him back to his classroom when he has finished his lunch. He'll also need a new tray as that food is cold now."

"But of course, Mrs. Solberg, unless you would like all of us wait and walk ahead, dropping rose petals for the two of you to step on!"

"That will not be necessary, sir, but we appreciate the offer," Regina was anything but intimidated by the arrogant attitude. Frank Jr. and Shawn Michael were beaming at Regina, although both were too scared to say anything.

Thomas Alfred's kids came home from school and told the hospital's Chief-of-Staff what happened in the lunchroom. "Well

I'm not all that surprised," he answered, gently laughing with his children. "Mrs. Solberg is from the Bronx in New York. They are not prejudiced there." His children looked as though they didn't completely understand, so he continued. "In places like that, black people may do the very same things as the white people. They may skate at the skating rinks, go to the country clubs, and use public pools. It should be that way here in Bradington too, but they are a little behind the times here."

"Dr. Denoff is very kind too, their mother added. The Solbergs don't see the color of one's skin as a reason to treat him differently. One of your father's patients is seeing Dr. Solberg for a broken foot, and raves about him."

"Frank Solberg is the kind of doctor who puts his patients first and the town loves him for it. He is an excellent surgeon, but also a personable and caring physician. The hospital personnel were touched last week when he called Regina to come over and bring some candy to a child from a poor family who had multiple fractures from a fall. He's always bringing pumpkin bread or cookies or some other treat that Regina has baked to the lounge," Thomas recalled thoughtfully.

Everywhere the Solbergs went someone knew them and stopped them. Frank was in his glory; always flattered to be hailed a hero by his patients, while Regina and Frank Jr., were proud of the recognition. Regina loved her husband and would have gone anywhere to make him happy. Their new baby was due in a couple of weeks and the staff at Bradington General Hospital continued to voice their disappointment that the couple had chosen to use the facility in Memphis.

While Frank was concerned about the distance, he understood Regina's request for privacy. Recalling the incident that sparked her decision, Frank laughed to himself. Regina had come home with a bag of groceries and a very concerned expression. Frank, relieved to see that she had not caught him tossing a Frisbee with his son in the living room, asked why she seemed upset.

"Well perhaps you could ask Thelma at Piggly Wiggly," she sighed, "she seems to know everything else about the Solbergs!"

"Like what, honey?" Frank struggled to keep a straight face, but his young understudy, who had not yet mastered the same self-control, laughed out loud.

"Like I was checking out and she says, 'Mrs. Solberg, you just bought coffee ice cream two days ago; you surely haven't eaten it all by now.'"

Both Franks laughed at first, but tried to recover themselves when they saw that she was not joining them.

"I am not, N-O-T, having my baby here. These people are far too nosy for my taste and that's final!"

"Don't worry, Mom, we can all go to Memphis," Frank Jr. added gently.

"No, honey, all three sets of grandparents will be here before anything happens," Regina reassured, "they are all coming to wait here with you while Daddy and I go to the hospital to have the baby."

Placing the last of the groceries in the fridge, Regina called Frances to be sure she had just informed Frank Jr. correctly.

Now that the pregnancy was nearly at term, Regina asked Dr. Scott Montgomery, her new obstetrician, about the possibilities of an induced labor and delivery. "I see absolutely no problem at all, Regina, and we'll only have to keep you overnight."

"I am planning to leave the same day, Doctor."

"What?!"

"The Indians have their babies and miss only a row or two of corn," she smiled.

"Regina, that is unheard of. You will need to say just the one night beca…" he stopped just realizing what she had said, "because you're not an Indian!"

"I am leaving soon after the baby arrives, unless there are complications."

"Okay," the doctor did not want to distress his patient, "How about this; we will see if you are ready to leave and if you are, I will release you."

"Sounds fair to me," Regina smiled gratefully, reassured that once the baby was born, she would be leaving whether they liked it or not.

"I'll schedule you for the day after tomorrow."

"We'll be here bright and early," Frank beamed.

Dan and Elizabeth were already on standby along with the four from Memphis.

Frank Jr. was concerned about not being allowed to accompany his mother, and told Dan so. "What if something happens to Mom, and I never see her again," his blue eyes filled with tears?

"What's going to happen to her?"

"She could die, Grandpa."

"No way, women have babies all the time, Frankie. We'll be able to call her right up until the baby is delivered and if there is any danger, any at all, I will personally drive you to Memphis. Deal?"

"Deal."

On the morning they were going to Memphis, Regina made blueberry muffins for Frank Jr. and left them on the kitchen table with a note. The number for her room was on it, and she reassured him that she would be home later on. Elizabeth saw the platter and the note and asked Frances if they would really let her daughter leave that soon after giving birth. "Let? They'll need a team of Navy Seals to keep her there overnight. She already called Mindy in Miami to ask about AMA forms and just how to use them," the retired army nurse laughed pouring cream into her coffee.

"Who is Mindy and what are AMA forms?" Elizabeth looked concerned.

"Mindy is the hospital attorney who married the warden in Miami, remember?"

"Oh, yes," Elizabeth remembered meeting them one Christmas.

"AMA forms are documents stating that a patient is leaving Against Medical Advice."

"Who is leaving against medical advice?" Leo asked coming in from jogging.

"Nobody yet, but once Regina has the baby, she said she is leaving whether they like it or not," Elizabeth shared the news.

The Colonel laughed, as he reached for the orange juice, as though he wasn't the least bit surprised.

The labor was relatively short and the nurses in Memphis fell in love with the Solbergs. They were fun and Regina's laughter was contagious! They had given her an epidural, so she was feeling only pressure, and enjoying every minute of expectation.

Frank asked her if she wanted a girl or boy and got the answer he expected, "Either, preferably twins!"

Dr. Montgomery raised his eyebrows, "Madame, you are a high risk pregnancy, so let's carry one at the time, if you don't mind."

"Well if there are two, I am taking both home!"

"By the way, I spoke with Dr. Kingsley yesterday. He sends his regards and wants to be notified when the new little Solberg arrives."

Regina smiled remembering the last delivery, and still hearing the crisp British accent in her mind.

An hour later, Angela Dawn Solberg came into the world smiling. The doctor was concerned at first, as she didn't cry. She was the picture of Frank Jr., blonde hair and blue eyes, and unusually alert for a newborn. "Now where are you two getting these Scandinavian babies from?" Dr. Montgomery laughed.

"She looks like a doll," the nurse gushed.

Regina closed her eyes, "How do You like her name, my Abba?"

Frank was teary-eyed, and overjoyed when he held his new baby, "I am absolutely defenseless. 'The world is her pearl!'"

The calls were made as Regina rested, and to everyone's surprise Frank Jr. was delighted. "I have the only girl on the block! I'm saving her a muffin, and I'll get to hold her when she comes home! When are they coming home? Hey, Dad, is she black or white?"

Late afternoon, when Regina asked to be released from the hospital, Dr. Montgomery called Andrew Kingsley and asked for his opinion.

"Well I'll tell you, if you don't allow her to leave, she probably will anyway. I would let her go and make her promise to check in. After all, her husband is a surgeon."

"Okay, I will release her and ask her to return to Memphis as needed before the regular post-partum check up."

"We are on the way home," Frank announced to nobody's surprise.

Pulling into the driveway, everybody on the block came running over to the car, as Frances and Hazel handled crowd control. Frank Jr. was delighted and held his tiny, new baby sister, as his friends watched. Neighbors came right in with balloons, flowers, cakes, cookies, pies, cold cut platters, salads and gifts. Leo shook his head and laughed. "Don't these damn southern belles remember what it was like having their babies? I doubt they felt like hosting a party!"

Regina was up and about greeting everyone and winked at the Colonel. "At least I got to come home," she whispered and hugged him.

"Where is your genetic material, young lady," Dan asked admiring the adorable bundle he held.

Chapter Nineteen

Square Peg In A Round Hole!

Having everybody at the house had been like old times in Miami, and Regina was delighted! The best part was that the visitors would not go home for long, before returning with the rest of twelve-pack from Miami for the Christening. Angela was a little doll and smiled constantly. Watching her father gush over her, Regina asked him if he felt that he should call his parents, and waited patiently for his answer. "I would love to call my parents and let them know that I am in my own practice now, and that we have a gorgeous new baby," he looked very thoughtful and a little sad. "I miss them, Regina, but I can't allow them to disrespect us or control us." Regina waited for her husband to continue speaking, but he didn't.

"Well, I think we've made ourselves perfectly clear that we have no intention of tolerating either of your concerns. The only way to know their reaction though, would be to contact them."

"Do you want me to do that? Do you want me to call them?"

"I want you to do what makes you comfortable, sweetheart."

"Do you remember what they said about you, Regina?"

"I remember a very wise old saying, 'let bygones be bygones.'"

"Speaking of bygones, isn't it time, or rather way past time for Gabby to have visitation?" Frank added bitterly.

"Yes it is. Have you mentioned it to Eva, or would you like me to?"

"You can, if you would. I want her here, as the Consent Order requires her to be. Eva has very conveniently let the first visit slip by hoping we would forget," a cold dark bitter look crossed his face.

"I thought we all agreed to get settled in before pursuing the visitation," Regina answered gently.

"Well we are settled in, and Angela is light years more beautiful than Gabby!"

"Angela is light years different from Gabby, Frank," Regina answered in a loving but matter-of –fact tone.

Eva and Mercedes were understandably upset by the thought of Gabby's first visit, as they had silently hoped that Angela's arrival would eradicate the need for Gabby to be flown back and forth. Reservations were made and Eva and Gabby were to fly into Memphis two weeks later. Mercedes had saved some money in case visitation did materialize, so that she could accompany Eva on the first trip. The two ladies would then have dinner at the airport and return to Miami.

Regina was concerned about the over-all attitude of the upcoming visit and the real reason for it. She talked at length to Frances about it and agreed with her "second mother's" theory. "I think that once Frank has Gabby for visitation, one of two things will happen. He will enjoy the visits since Eva will not be close by, or he will reassess the entire situation, view it much differently, and send for her very rarely."

"I just don't want him to send for her to spite Eva," Regina said, fighting tears.

"No, I don't think that would benefit anybody either. Why don't you all come here for dinner after you leave the airport? I'll have Leo and Hazel over too."

They continued to chat about the upcoming Christening celebration for Angela until a fierce bolt of lightning disconnected the call to introduce crackling thunder that shook the house. Going to the door to call Frank Jr. inside, Regina started at the pitch black sky. The little boy was examining the mud bricks that he and his friends made in shoe boxes earlier, which were carefully lined up on the patio to allow sun but not rain.

Frank Sr. was in surgery and would be coming home late, so she continued to prepare dinner for Frank Jr., and gave Angela a bottle. Suddenly, a piercing siren went off followed by another loud noise like a freight train, both competing as they blared outside. Regina calmly directed Frank Jr. to take his plate and drink and come to the basement as she followed with the baby and Monique. The tornado went down the street uprooting two trees and setting them on cars along the way. Trash canisters blew by like soda cans and the distinct sound of broken glass antagonized the setting further. Regina prayed that her husband and all of the neighbors were safe. While she set out flashlights, the battery operated radio warned people to stay under cover. Frank Jr. remained calm but appeared to be concerned. "Is Dad alright, Mom?" He watched for any signs of panic in his mothers face, and found none.

"Dad is fine, honey. The hospital is one of the assigned shelters in Bradington, and he is well inside it." Angela sat quietly in her swing looking all around as she rocked back and forth. After the noise had stopped, Regina listened for the all clear signal and cautiously took the children and Monique back upstairs.

The telephone was still dead, but someone was pounding on the front door. A police officer asked if they were alright and explained that Dr. Solberg sent him over when he couldn't get through on the phone.

"Is everything at the hospital okay?" Regina's voice shook as she noted the Gentry's front door on her lawn.

"Yes, everything is fine, and it looks like nobody on your block got hurt. I'll help Vernon Gentry replace his door, and be on my way. They hope to have the phone service repaired quickly."

Frances called to report that they also had multiple tornadoes, one of which had uplifted an above ground pool causing damage and local flooding. Nobody there was injured either, but there was plenty of damage in the city. Regina and Frances simultaneously whispered a prayer of thanks. After putting the two children to bed, Regina continued making Frank Sr.'s dinner and a cherry pie.

The telephone rang constantly and Eva finally got through, in hysterics. "I am not bringing Gabriella there, Sati! There is no way. That is a very dangerous place to be, and she could get killed."

Regina tried to calm Eva down, explaining that tornadoes were not common there and that they had a full basement for shelter.

"I won't do it! I'll take her and run away, do you hear me?!" The loud cries clutched at Regina's heart as she let the lady vent. "Frank does not even care for Gabby," Eva continued between sobs, "he hasn't even called about her. When I talked to him yesterday he was rude and told me never to call him again. He said that Gabby will have a 'hell of a lot of adjusting to do when she sees how beautiful Angela is.'"

"Eva, you are too upset to discuss anything right now. Please go and have some tea and call me back when you have settled down. Just for the record, Gabby is gorgeous too, and looks entirely different than Angela. Those little girls won't be thinking along those lines at all. Gabby is a dark beauty and Angela a fair beauty. Both little girls are adorable and will hopefully be very close."

"Those remarks were cruel, Regina, and that mindset could harm Gabby."

"Those remark were hideous, Eva, and will not be made in the future. Both you and Frank will hopefully find a way to deal with your anger toward each other, and leave our innocent children out of it."

Eva contacted her lawyer at home, in spite of the hour. He advised her that any deviation of the Consent Order could result in her losing custody of her baby. Hanging up the phone, she sat in a chair and cried as though Gabriella was being removed from her home for good. Mercedes called Regina and begged for her help. "We must allow visitation to take place, sweetheart, and we must be very alert as to effect that it will have on all of us. If Gabby senses your fear and upset, she will be upset too. Let's give it a try and see what happens."

"He said that we no can call her, Regina. Frank said no calls."

"Well Sati says that you most certainly can call, and Frank is not home all day."

"When Frank sees how upset we are, it will bring him pleasure."

"Ah-ha! So what should one do if they feel that is the case, Mercedes?"

"No let him see us like that!"

"Exactly!"

"Will Frank's parents be around Gabby?"

"Nope, Gabby will be in my presence every second that she is here."

The Christening Gala was being planned at a restaurant called Master Chef's. Doctor Solberg had an unannounced visitor come to his office to complain about the plans. Luke Hanley, Chairman of the Board of Directors for the Bradington Country Club, apologized profusely for stopping by without an appointment, but stated that he had an important matter to discuss. Frank finished with his patients and welcomed him in.

"Dr. Solberg, when the town paper did an article on the birth of your new baby, they assumed that her Gala would be held at our country club. We were astounded to be told that it is not. This not only offends us; but it makes us look bad."

"Well Regina is planning the party and I'm sure that she didn't realize that you had hoped to have the celebration there."

"Let me set up a meeting for the three of us since nothing is set in stone yet."

"Mr. Hanley," Regina greeted the impromptu dinner guest with a warm handshake, "Please, do come in."

"Luke, please ma'am. I must say that you look wonderful and hardly like you just had a baby a couple of weeks ago!"

"Thank you," the small missionary blushed as her husband smiled with pride.

"Would you like to see the nursery?" Frank offered without thinking, as usual.

"Indeed! I read about it in the paper." Regina rolled her eyes, and hoped that their guest missed her reaction. Two newspaper reporters had come over when Regina was at the doctor for Angela's first visit, and she had not appreciated them bombarding her house guests with questions and flashes from their cameras.

The nursery, done in Elves and Angels, was a showplace. There were fairies by a little 3-D creek watching mischievous elves flying kites on the adjoining wall.

A paper Mache' apple tree, housing more elves and fairies reading books and blowing bubbles, brightened up another corner. Under the tree, a little plush caterpillar rubbed his hands and grinned as he approached a half eaten apple with the full intention to make it his dinner. Assorted sizes of glass bubbles traveled all the way across the room, some in mid air suspended by fishing line from the ceiling, before fading into a rainbow, which two colorful tiny fairies were sliding down. Over the door was an exquisite Christmas angel who had been transformed into a guardian angel. The colors and life like scenes were breath-taking and Luke was speechless. Over a small bookshelf, two elves were holding a wide ribbon that said, *"'These Little Elves Put the Books on Our Shelves – But They Say It's A Must That We Read Them Ourselves!'"*

"Regina does this as a hobby," Frank bragged, "She has been in the newspaper in Miami on many occasions."

"Why does she keep this a secret?" Luke asked puzzled. "Is your son's room like this?"

"He has a jungle," Frank explained, leading the way to Frank Jr.'s room.

The jungle scene stood in its' own glory just as it had in Miami. Regina promised to move it exactly as it was, and she was true to her word. Frank Jr. loved his room and so did the neighbors.

"I am so impressed!" Luke shook his head smiling. "Does she still do these outside of your home?"

"Not yet in Bradington, but Regina can look at a room and make it come to life."

"Where do you get the props?"

"We make some of them and Regina is an avid doll collector. She can take a lifeless toy and just by positioning correctly and adding props, it looks real."

Luke was equally impressed by a "typical" dinner at the

Solberg's house. They had thick pork chops, bulging with pecan corn bread stuffing and then topped with plum sauce, spinach artichoke casserole, fresh Italian garlic knots, Gorgonzola cheese salad, and a chocolate trifle for desert. "You just called her from your office to invite me here, Frank! Do you eat meals like this all the time?" The guest asked in shock. "All the time," Frank answered brimming with pride.

"My wife would kill me if I walked in with a last minute dinner guest," Luke could not even entertain the idea.

"Regina, if I may," Luke began, "we had hoped for the honor of hosting Angela's Christening party at our county club here in Bradington. It is our pride and joy, and we are wondering if you wouldn't be willing to change your mind. We use top notch caterers from Memphis and we would be willing to refund any deposit that you may have already put up at The Master Chefs."

Regina spoke slowly and calmly, but very clearly. "I'm afraid that we can't have our party at the country club, Luke, as I understand that you don't allow black people there. Thomas and Sharon Alfred, among many other black people, are our friends. We also have black friends from out of state."

"Oh, they understand that, and wouldn't take offense at all, Regina. It's the way here in Bradington. Could we have a separate party for them and the black folks from out of state? We would be paying for it in full."

"While that may seem to be a solution to some, Luke, and I certainly salute the Alfred family, it is I who would take offense, as that ignorant way of thinking doesn't fly with me."

"The newspaper has already committed, Regina, and the hospital will also want the party there."

"First of all, that kind of gall is out of place, sir. Your newspaper needs to set boundaries to respect the personal space of the citizens here. Moreover, let us pray that the reason for our decline does not get out among the public, shall we? It could be a huge issue given the date in time, and some of our neighboring cities would find the facts as appalling as we do."

"Do you think that it will get out, Regina?" Luke was shaken by the very idea.

"Not by us, it won't; but I think it was unwise for the press to make any commitments for us without first securing their information. They burst in here like gangbusters and started snapping pictures and collecting our private information when Frank and I weren't even home."

Luke put his elbows on the table to rest his chin on both closed hands. "What must we do to sway you, Regina?"

"I cannot be swayed. If black people are not permitted at your country club, we will not patronize it. More coffee?"

"Please," he smiled, once again impressed with the Solbergs, and comfortable enough to help himself to seconds on the dessert.

"Luke, can the club make an exception for a private party, say on a one time basis?" Frank wanted to keep peace at all costs.

"Don't know," he answered thoughtfully dropping sugar cubes into his coffee.

"Don't care," Regina smiled, "I still will not have any event there as long as that is your policy."

"Would you be willing to meet with that Board of Directors, Regina?" Luke avoided her direct line of vision as long as he could without being rude.

"Sure, but I am going to stand firm on my decision. I would also have to cater by Master Chefs, as we have already committed ourselves to them."

"That would be no problem at all," Luke tried to reassure himself more than Regina.

The following week Frank and Regina went to the Bradington Country Club conference room to find a lovely luncheon of club sandwiches, assorted chips, cold salads, soft drinks, and cookies and pastries from the town bakery. The meeting was started promptly to accommodate Frank's afternoon clinic schedule. Accidentally omitting introductions, Luke opened the meeting with a prayer. "Our Father in heaven, please help us to convey our community's needs to the Solbergs. We are all Your children, Father but we must have rules to protect ourselves. Please let our guests be open to these." One big 'amen', and he got right to the point.

"Dr. Solberg seems to understand our policy regarding the banning of black people here at the club, but Mrs. Solberg does not seem to, so we are here to help her understand it," Luke took a sip of his coke as his hand shook.

Board member, Earl Turnbull, a large-framed, car salesman with a smug expression that Regina would have loved to slap from his face, took over. "Now, the beautiful Mrs. Solberg here, appears to be one heck of a high class lady. I am sure that her standards are sky high; or at least they seem to be. You folks are well known in a humongous city like Miami, and we respect that."

Luke addressed Frank, "Do you support our rules, Doctor?"

"Well, I understand that you have had these in place long before we came here, and we are not in a position to ask you to change them."

The spineless group nodded smugly, and continued to gobble at their lunches.

"Nobody is saying otherwise," Regina spoke, out of turn or not, "nobody has asked you to change anything; it was you who approached us. Our standards are sky high, Mr. Turnbull," Regina looked steadily at him, "and they support our Constitution, and our country's values," she added indicating the American flag at the front of the room. "All men are created equal, sir, with no notation added that black people are beneath white, or allowance for special restrictions to be imposed on any race based on the color of their skin. Such thinking is asinine in my opinion."

"And we support your opinion, ma'am," Earl slapped the table and grinned a huge, toothy, bigoted smile, "I love all ma brothers and sisters in the Lord, but there are just a few places where folks have restrictions. Mrs. Solberg, you must know the importance of rules judging from all of your work in Miamah." Regina noted the sudden southern accent pouring into the bigot's conversation, and it sickened her. "Now Ah don't know if you all know this," he swept his large hand around the table, "But these people," indicating Frank and Regina, "worked in the prisons in Miamah! Got a grand recognition for it too! Mrs. Solberg, am Ah right?" He flashed another huge smile that made her cringe.

"Yes Sir," the small framed missionary answered, "We saw more "what" prisoners than black, by the way, and they all got the same treatment. While in Miami, we also witnessed a disgusting riot due to man's ignorance and narrow mindedness." The other members did not know how to respond to this bold ridicule of their accents and "rules." Noting the aggravated silence, she continued as Frank sank in his chair. "Let me reiterate once more that we are asking for nothing. We simply will not patronize bigotry and ignorance."

Earl's face turned red as he stood and circled the room, "Then you think we should let just anyone in here, Mrs. Solberg?"

Regina stood in place and answered, "I don't care who you let in here. I believe I made that clear, sir. We stand on no soap box, but we must do what we believe is right."

Luke motioned Earl to take his seat and Regina sat down after he did. "Mrs. Solberg, may I remind you that the Alfred family knows its place and is totally comfortable with it?"

Regina answered calmly, "This isn't about the Alfred family, Luke; it's about a race of people being oppressed in a city right here in the United States. This is about a handful of bigots breaking the law and clanking glasses as though they have won some prize for getting away with it. This is about our freedom to act and react the way that we believe is right; whether or not your club gets the recognition that you feel it deserves regarding the birth of our daughter."

Earl was on his feet again and banged the table, "Listen here you stinking Yankee, don't you buck the system here, or you'll be sorry. We'll run ya out of town!"

Luke stood in panic and apologized to Frank. "Don't apologize to me, Luke, apologize to my wife."

Standing, Frank pulled Regina's chair out and addressed the small group, "I believe that we will leave now. Thank you for lunch."

The group of men stood, open-mouthed as the Solbergs left the building. They were not used to women speaking their minds or taking the lead as Regina had. Mrs. Solberg did not strike them as the type who cared about what anybody thought, and they were at a loss, since Dr. Solberg obviously supported her.

On the way to the car Frank hugged his wife and apologized to her again.

"Did it ever dawn on these jackasses that you play golf and have not joined their little white club?"

Frank laughed as he looked into the solemn, deep brown eyes. Regina was beautiful and he loved her madly. That's all he could think of right now.

Luke called the Bradington Hospital Administrator, who called the group in Memphis. Michael Dougherty, the senior partner was furious. "How dare you threaten our surgeon and his wife. You will not run anybody out of town with your old, worn out traditions! You all better fairly hope that the press doesn't get a hold of this nonsense!"

Michael hung up the phone and immediately called Frank to apologize to him. "I hope they didn't cause you guys to have second thoughts about moving here. You have done an excellent job, Frank, and I happen to think that your wife is a doll! Good for her! Very damn good for her! Earl Turnbull is a jackass, and Luke has ruffles on his shorts."

Frank laughed as he leaned back in his chair and played with a paper clip. "Regina is going to proceed with her plans for the party, Michael. I asked her to evaluate what the board of directors will think of us, and her response was, 'I don't give a rashed rear end what anybody thinks of us, Frank. We did not come here to be evaluated by these people, and I will not be told who I may invite to a party that we are hosting.'"

Michael laughed so hard that he started coughing. "I liked your wife the moment I met her, Frank. She is very sweet, but nobody's fool. Regina gives me the impression that she makes no trouble, but takes no rubble!" the senior partner slapped his leg, and continued laughing at his own joke.

"I appreciate your kind words, Michael," Frank answered, realizing that he had a waiting room full of patients.

Luke called Bob Jenkins to discuss a possible alert, and the town manager was anything but pleased about the upset. "What were you thinking, Luke? What were any of you guys thinking? The Solbergs are our neighbors, and they are very staunch missionaries. While they're not trouble makers we have to worry about this getting into the hands of others who may be. Why in the hell did you guys call Memphis?"

Luke did not answer at first.

"Well?" Bob persisted, lighting a cigarette and turning his chair to stretch his legs out in front of him.

"We didn't call Memphis, Bob, the hospital here did."

"Why did you call the hospital, then? They can't force the Solbergs to have their party at the country club."

"I know, I know! I was at their home for dinner to discuss this last week. They are fine people, Bob."

"So you figured that threatening to run them out of town because they are from the north would enhance their decision to move here?"

"It was Earl Turnbull who made that statement, Bob, and we did apologize."

"Do you know how it could affect this town if that crap gets out among the citizens? Mrs. Solberg already had a go round at the school regarding a black child who was being mistreated."

"Have you been to their home?" Luke was trying to make a point rather than change the subject.

"Of course I have; we go over there all the time."

"Did you notice the huge picture of Abraham Lincoln sitting in the armchair, hanging in the living room over the fireplace?"

"Yeah! Did you?!"

"Sure, and I told the guys on the board about it before the meeting, hoping to alert them. The portrait is known as *Lincoln in Thought*, the saying underneath it reads:

> *'If I were try to read, much less answer all of the attacks made on me, this shop might as well be closed for any other business.*
>
> *I do the best I know how -*

The very best I can; and I mean to keep doing so until the end.

If the end brings me out all right, what is said against me won't amount to anything.

If the end brings me out wrong, ten angels swearing I was right, would make no difference.'

Abraham Lincoln

Luke drew a breath and continued, "The Solbergs make you feel right at home, Bob, and I am sorry that things went down like they did. I am at a real loss now."

"Well, I think we should meet at my office to discuss this issue and I am also inviting Noah Cadence from the skating rink. We better watch our actions here in Bradington. Mike Dougherty is right! We are carrying on 'old, worn out, traditions,' and this town is too much of a melting pot for that way of thinking. New folks moving in here <u>will</u> see us as bigots; especially those coming from big cities."

"Like Miami," Luke laughed.

"Like the Bronx!" Bob laughed, although he really didn't find the potential risk funny at all.

"Like Memphis," both added together, suddenly aware of Michael Dougherty's big mouth and realizing the new risks involved.

Regina and the two children were shopping when they passed a pet shop in the mall. Angela was in her stroller and full of smiles as soon as they entered and saw all of the exotic pets. Frank saw a baby guinea pig, and asked Regina if he could buy it with his hard earned allowance. Considering the responsibilities of owning the new pet, he solemnly nodded along as they listed the chores together. When they went to get the little guinea pig out of the glass tank, it ran over to the only other one there, and started nursing. Frank's blue eyes opened in surprise, and when the shop owner told him that the baby was ready to be taken from the mother, they filled with tears.

"Well, I don't see why we wouldn't just get both of them," Regina smiled and hugged her son. "Should we get a pet for Gabby, Mom, since she'll be here tomorrow?" Regina was touched by the thought but suggested an alternate surprise.

"Gabby is still a baby, sweetheart, so she is not ready for a pet. Perhaps a stuffed toy or a doll would be better." Frank checked his pockets and looked worried, "Will I be able to pay for all of that? I will need a stuffed toy for my baby Angela as well!"

"Well, I think that Daddy and I will treat each of you to a surprise. Yours will be the guinea pigs and the girls can get stuffed toys."

Frank put his small arms around his mother and whispered, "I'm glad that my guinea pig gets to stay with his mom; I would be very sad if someone took me away from you, and you would probably cry too."

"'That, is the understatement of the century,'" Regina hugged him tightly, and crouched down to the stroller to replace Angela's slipping sock.

Before leaving for Memphis, Frank Jr. fed his new pets, Andy and Candy, and changed their water bottle. The family of four looked like they had just come out of a magazine. Frank was striking in beige slacks and a navy blue golf shirt, while his understudy, dressed in the same colors matched him with exactly the same mannerisms, which always made Regina smile. Angela was dressed in a pale green jumpsuit with tiny light jade earrings and a matching bracelet. Regina made a little barrette for her from baby silk daisies. Together with the corn silk hair and bright blue eyes provided by Abba, the colors were gorgeous! Having lost all of the weight from her pregnancy, Regina wore a green and white flower print sun dress with a full flowing skirt. She had her thick auburn hair pulled to one side in a pony tail, and looked like an older sister rather than the mother of the children she accompanied.

Waiting for the plane to arrive was an easy task as the airport was entertaining to walk through. When they came to the gate Frank immediately spotted Aunt Eva and ran to her with open arms. The gesture caused both Cuban ladies to sob and Frank Sr. to squeeze his eyes shut to keep from vomiting. Regina hugged both ladies, genuinely delighted to see them, and then hugged Gabby. Mercedes and Eva both rushed over to see Angela. Frank was about to signal a stop, but catching Regina's eye, he decided to resist the urge. Eva clasped her hand to her mouth and raved – "Sati your children are gorgeous."

"Look who's talking," Regina picked Gabby up and hugged the little dark beauty again.

Gabby was dressed in a full petticoat dress of red, white and blue with white tights and red buckle shoes. She had small gold earrings on and a gold matching bracelet. She carried a dirty blanket and a small stuffed poodle named Gordo, and reeked of heavy perfume. The large dark eyes had a skeptical expression, which did not please Regina in the least. "Abba, she whispered, please stay with us and help us to act in Your love for the best interest of all of our children. Please help Eva and Mercedes through this difficult time. I love you, Great Father! No, scratch that- I adore You!"

"Well we better get to Frances and Lamar's house," Frank said coldly as he pried Gabby from Regina's arms, "they're expecting us." He had yet to say one word to either of the two ladies, or to his daughter who had come all the way from Miami. Gabby started to scream, and struggled to free herself, reaching for her mother.

"Why don't we grab a soda and let the children settle in for a few moments?" Regina's suggestion sounded sort of like an order, and was immediately agreed upon. Gabby hung back from her father's arms crying loudly, and reached for her mother again. Bitterly handing her over, Frank muttered, "Fine, enjoy her while you can!"

Eva fought back tears and out of shear desperation, Mercedes kept her mouth shut.

"So why are you here?" Frank nodded rudely toward Mercedes.

"Bee-couse, I weesh to be," the older Cuban woman smiled proudly, still carrying Angela.

At the restaurant Eva handed Regina a wrapped gift for the baby and a coloring set for both Frank Jr. and Gabby. The two older kids set right to work on the art, and Eva could have kissed Frank

Jr. for the attention he was giving his little sister. The beautifully presented gift for Angela, was wrapped in paper that was literally too pretty to tear. "My father painted it," Eva pointed to the paper proudly. "Well we must not tear it," Regina reached for a knife and cut the folds of the package carefully along the tape. "This paper will hang in her nursery." Inside the box was a lovely hand-made blanket with *Somebody Special* embroidered on it. Regina was deeply toughed and embraced both ladies.

Mercedes asked cautiously, "Do you have a sweeming pool at the house?"

"Yes," Regina answered calmly and continued in Spanish, "A swimming pool with a safety fence that is drilled into the patio and locked. There is also a disc that floats in the pool and sounds an alarm if the water surface is broken by so much as a pine cone." She answered laughing, and then went on describing the safety precautions to put the ladies at ease. "Anytime a small child is anywhere near the pool, an adult is with them and they wear a life jacket that zips up the back and cannot be removed."

Frank Jr. recognized the worry on the grandmother's face and came to the rescue, "Yeah and we can't even get to the patio area unless a door is unlocked for us!" Regina translated in Spanish, but Eva, now close to tears, put her sunglasses on. "We better get to our gate, Mama; they will be calling our flight soon."

Mercedes handed Angela back to Regina, who handed her to Frank. Gabby grabbed her mother and said good-bye to the Solbergs, adding "Come another day." Frank Jr. walked over to her and said, "Gabby, we are going to Grandma Frances' house to see her and Grandma Hazel and both grandpas. You don't want to miss that fun. We also have two guinea pigs and you can hold them! We'll call your mom as soon as we get home to Bradington, and I'll show you all around." Gabby smiled at her brother, but did not let go of Eva's leg.

Eva picked her up and handed her to Regina, as Frank smiled smugly. She quietly whispered in Spanish, "Please call me, Sati."

"You bet I will," Regina answered handing her Frances' new phone number.

"Drop dead, Frank, you pompous pig," Eva added as she started to cry.

"That was real smart, Eva," Frank answered, "You can just wonder if your child is at the bottom of the pool! There will be no phone calls!"

Eva lunged for him, but was intercepted by her mother. Mercedes nodded gently at Frank and in a sweet tone, let out a line in Spanish that would make a sailor blush, but made Regina laugh. Hugging Regina she added, "I love you, Sati." The two ladies turned away quickly as Gabby cried after them, "Abuela, Mama! No! - you no leave me. I want to go home," she sobbed, pulling in their direction. When the ladies were out of sight, the little girl buried her head in Regina's shoulder and sobbed so hard that she was shaking.

Regina whispered in Spanish, "It's alright sweetheart, we will talk to mommy as soon as we get home." When they reached the car Frank placed Angela in her car seat, checked Frank Jr.'s seat belt, and then took Gabby from Regina and firmly placed her in her car seat. Frank Jr. reached over to comfort her while

Angela watched, wide eyed and fully aware that something wasn't quite right. Frank turned to Regina and demanded to know what Mercedes said to him at the airport.

"She said that she knows that you will care for Gabby well, since you are a marvelous physician," Regina answered, hoping that the fate of Pinocchio was indeed limited to the fairy tale!

Frances, Lamar, Hazel and Leo rushed to the car. Frances grabbed Angela at the same time Leo grabbed Frank Jr. and Hazel grabbed Gabby. Lamar hugged Regina and Frank saying, "Okay, we need one more kid for me to capture!"

A wonderful cook out of chicken, burgers, and hot dogs followed, and one would have thought it was Christmas, for the toys that the three children raked in! Gabby would not leave Regina's lap and Regina allowed her to stay there. Frank showed off his other two children and paid no attention to Gabby, save the disgusted looks he shot over to her. Frances and Hazel both noticed and exchanged glances throughout the evening.

Leo hugged Regina and stated matter-of-factly, "I didn't think you could get any prettier! You're radiant, my dear!"

"Sir! I miss seeing you every day, Sir!" Regina answered in her best army voice, and hugged him again.

"Well, we're coming down next weekend for the whole weekend, whether you like it or not! Understood?" The Colonel boomed doing his best to conceal his large dimples.

"Sir, Yes Sir!" Regina answered, tears of joy welling up in her big brown eyes.

The both older couples had planned the weekend visit to Bradington to see their "stolen" daughter and grandchildren. They wanted to help the Solbergs through the first visit with Gabriella; who had just left Regina's side with Frances and Hazel, to try on her "high heels, like mommy wears!"

Frances bought her a carrying case of four pair of plastic slip-on heels, each with the picture of a Disney Princess on them that matched their colors. Gabby adored Cinderella and presently wore the blue ones. She also clutched her new Cinderella play figures and was delighted to have an old purse from Grandma Frances to cart them around in safely, accompanied by her video of the movie which had to be unpacked on the spot much to Frank's annoyance. Frank Jr. was intrigued with his Space Legos, while little Angela was jabbering to her wind-up toys.

Frances, Hazel and Regina were having seconds of dessert and coffee on the patio, while the guys planned a golf game for the next weekend. Because of the circumstances at the country club in Bradington, they decided to commute to Memphis and let the ladies shop with the kids. Hazel and Frances both noticed the way Gabby was being snubbed by her father, but kept their comments to themselves until Regina brought it up. "The scene at the airport was slightly shy of criminal, and I don't know how much more I will be able to tolerate before intervening on Gabby's behalf," she sighed, breaking a cookie to dip in her coffee.

"Well it certainly is criminal to take her just to spite her mother, and Gabby will sense that and later resent it," Frances answered in her own army "whether you like it or not" voice.

Hazel looked on sadly and finally added, "What are his plans for her during her visit?"

"That's just it," Regina answered shrugging, "There aren't any plans. I suggested the Memphis zoo and he just said, 'We'll see. Maybe we'll get a sitter for the girls and take Frank Jr.'"

Gabby came running out to the patio and pointed to a plane overhead, "Mommy came back for me," she squealed with delight, "We go to the airport, Sati?"

"Mommy will come back, sweetheart, but she is not on that plane," Regina's heart ached for the little Latin Cinderella.

"We wait at the airport, okay?" Gabby clapped her little hands together, "We will show Mommy my new shoes and toys."

"How about if we wait in Bradington, at Sati's house and then go to the airport when Mommy's plane comes in?" Regina suggested in vain.

"No! I want to go and get my Mommy," she cried and noticing her father in the doorway, climbed up to Regina to be held. "I don't like Daddy; I want to go home!"

Frank was furious, "You listen here, young lady, you knock it off right now. You are with us for visitation and that is that." He turned and went back inside.

"Boy! A regular Mister Rogers, that one," Hazel said, more than a little disappointed in the great Dr. Solberg.

Gabby cried all the way to Bradington, begging to be returned to her mother. Regina gave her and her Cinderella figures a bubble bath and some milk and cookies. Finally she fell asleep as Regina rocked her and she was transferred to her bed without waking. Moving on to tuck Frank Jr. in, she was taken back when she heard him talking to God. "Abba, can you please get Aunt Eva back here? My little sister can't understand what is going on, and I think she needs to go back to Miami." Frank saw his mother and burst into tears, motioning for her to close his door. "I can't let dad see me crying, because he hates Gabby."

"Your father doesn't hate Gabby, honey; he just doesn't always understand her."

"Well how did she get here anyway, and why is she his child when he has never been married to her mother?"

"There are many different circumstances in life, Frank, and we don't always understand them. You are too young to worry about those things right now, but when you are older you will understand."

"Is my father a good man?"

"Your father is a wonderful man," Regina hugged her son.

"Well somebody better teach that to Gabby, because she doesn't think so, and neither does her grandmother. I think that she said something mean in Spanish. She was very sweet about it, but I still think it was mean, and I'm going to learn Spanish tomorrow!"

"Sometimes grown up people can be very childish and mean to each other, but that doesn't last, honey. Sooner or later they come to their senses and behave the way they ought to."

Frank had two stories and fell asleep during the second one. Angela was all ready for bed before they left Memphis, so she was fast asleep among the elves and angels in her nursery. Joining Frank in the living room, Regina asked him if he would like a snack or something to drink before bed. "No thanks, sweetheart, I'm still full from the food Frances and Hazel prepared. I could have smacked Gabby's little butt off for her performance over there tonight."

"Gabby is a baby, Frank; a baby from a different culture than ours, and too young to handle what we are expecting of her."

"Look at Angela and look at her! Do you see a difference?"

"Sure."

"Gabby is going to straighten out! Pronto."

"Why did we bring her here, Frank? For what purpose did we send for Gabby?"

"Oh Regina, how many times must I go over this?"

"Until we are certain that we are doing the right thing!"

"I am entitled to my time with her! I am going to have it; and they are not to be called or to be permitted to call here."

"Your Court Order obligates us to call them, and allows them to call here."

"What do our neighbors know about her?"

"Only what you have told them."

"Well, that means nothing. I am going to tell them that she is a foster child."

"As you please."

The next morning Gabby woke up crying for her mother and Frank could not have been colder. He didn't hold her or tell her he loved her, but threatened to spank her if she needed something to cry about. "I don't like you, Frank," the little girl sobbed.

Frank started toward her but turned away in disgust. Frank Jr. was watching every move his father made, and seemed very upset by his actions. Angela sat in her swing watching the birds through the glass doors that led to the patio. "And I suppose you think it's alright for her to speak to her father that way, Regina?"

"I suppose her father should know how to handle her much better than he is, and should be able to recognize a distressed child when he sees one."

"I am trying to fulfill my obligation to her and that's the end of the story. I have my rights in black and white, and we are going by them, whether Eva likes it or not."

"I don't see Eva anywhere, Frank. I see three little children, all being unjustly dragged into a mess that they had nothing to do with; and may I remind you that sometimes grey is also a lovely color?"

Chapter Twenty
The Fat Little Old Lady!

The next couple of days were the same routine, Gabby crying every morning and every night, and watching her Cinderella movie every day. She would put her little high heels on and clutch her purse that held the figures from the movie, as if someone would take it away from her if she let go of it. "See my mommy, Sati?" she asked, holding up the figure of Cinderella in her ball-gown . "She is coming to get me soon."

"Yes darling, she is."

"Sati, you make sketti for my supper?" Gabby eyed the meatballs on the counter.

"Yes honey, I did."

"I love you to pieces Sati, you too much for one heart," the little girl played as she talked.

Frank came in from work and swung Frank Jr. high in the air, "Hey buddy, how was school?"

"Great! We had a lot of fun today and we learned two new Halloween songs. I taught them both to Gabby, but Angela just ignored me, so she'll have to wait until she's older. I am going to be Luke Skywalker for Halloween, Dad, and Gabby's being Cinderella!"

"Oh?"

"Yep, we got our costumes today and Angela's is going to be a Dalmatian!"

"So when do we get to hear the Halloween songs?" Frank Sr. loosened his tie, "And you don't look anything like a Dalmatian," he added grabbing Angela from her blanket of toys and kissing her.

Regina watched for any notice of Gabby and saw none. "Gabby is going to be Cinderella for Halloween," Regina repeated.

"That's great, honey," he patted Gabby on the head with far less feeling than he gave Monique.

"We're having sketti, Frank," the little girl answered.

"Daddy," Frank corrected, "You call me 'Daddy,' not Frank."

"We're having sketti for dinner tonight, Daddy," the little girl's lip quivered as though she was about to cry.

"That's better," Frank answered over his shoulder, on his way upstairs to change out of his work clothes.

"Gabby stuck her tongue out at him as soon as he turned the corner; and Regina was glad that both Frank Jr. and Frank Sr. missed her reaction."

Eva called, and Gabby couldn't wait to talk to her, "Meee!" She shouted and reached for the phone. Regina handed her the telephone and continued to put the final touches on dinner. "Me and Sati have a tea party today, and we eated a rabbit on toast.

Then Sati gave to me a blanket to eat and it get all over my mouth, so Sati wash my face. Frank Jr. no can put his big fat mice near me, because I don't like them. They are not Gus and Jack like Cinderella has. I played all day under the ocean with Frank and his friends! No. Sati no was there with me; she working in the house, but she come to check on us and to give us lunch. Okay. Okay. Okay."

"Mommy want to talk to you, Sati."

Regina took the phone to hear Eva screaming and almost in tears. "Why is she in the pool supervised by a five year old? And what cloth did she eat? She could choke, Sati! I don't want her eating rabbits, and what mice are being used to tease her?"

Gabby threw herself to the ground crying and kicking both legs in the air while calling into the phone to her mother. "Is that her screaming?"

"Now she is, but she certainly wasn't earlier," Eva.

"I am calling the police!"

"You are calming down, right now!" Regina did not raise her voice, but the tone silenced Eva. "Now, first of all, no child is ever, but ever near the pool without an adult! Gabby is talking about the basement, which is a huge playroom decorated in an under-the-sea décor. The rabbit that she ate, is Welsh Rarebit, a cheese sauce poured over toast; and how anyone can have a proper tea party in a Cinderella costume without it, is beyond me! The blanket that she ate, happened to be cotton candy, and the big fat mice are Frank Jr.'s guinea pigs who have been persecuted by your daughter because they cannot measure up to Gus and Jack!"

Eva was laughing and crying at the same time. Gabby, screaming and crying, reached for the phone, and Regina spoke firmly but quietly to her. "I will be delighted to hand you the phone, Cinderella, but you must first stop screaming. You will scare Gus and Jack!"

"And the lady mice," Gabby snubbed.

"Yes, to say nothing of the lady mice!"

Gabby calmed down and talked to Eva and Mercedes, then handed Regina the phone and began to cry softly reaching up to be held. Eva apologized to Regina and now cried softly herself, both from sadness and relief. Frank Sr. walked into the kitchen and glared at the phone. "Hang it up!" he ordered. Regina raised her eyebrows and finished her conversation. "I said to hang it up, Regina. Why did you keep talking to her?"

Regina did not answer, but carried Gabby into the family room and set up a small table so that she and Frank Jr. could watch Cinderella while they ate.

"Did you hear the lies that little brat was telling her mother? Did you hear Eva's response not even considering that she was being misinformed? What's the matter with you, Regina?"

"Picture Frank Jr. at Eva's house for a moment, will you? Now suppose he gets homesick and calls us. He might say something like, 'Hi Mommy and Daddy, a whole bunch of people were here today. They hung an animal up by a rope and took turns beating it with a big stick until it smashed open. Then we all got candy and small toys!"

"What would come to your mind?"

"That they're psychos, which is true."

"Would it dawn on you in the least that perhaps your son just participated in a piñata celebration? A celebration common to the culture of the people he was staying with!"

Frank walked over to his wife and spoke softly, "Regina?"

"'What's on your mind, if you'll excuse the overstatement,'" she answered tossing the salad.

Frank was stunned, but laughed in spite of himself, "That was very unkind, Sati, and I'm telling Abba!"

"Good! Tell Him what an infantile boob you've been, while you're at it!"

"Regina! Please let me hold you, I am so sorry. I don't recognize myself these last few days, but I'm trying to sort things out. Please help me," tears sprang to his eyes as he spoke. Regina put the salad aside and rushed to him. He held her as though he was afraid of losing her and sobbed quietly so the children wouldn't hear. "I'm a complete jerk and I don't know how to fix myself," he whispered.

"Well first of all, you aren't a jerk at all, and you certainly aren't broken."

"I resent Eva and her mother so much, Regina, and Gabby too for that matter."

"Frank, a very wise man once said, 'If you don't like something, then change it. If you can't change it, then change the way you think about it.'"

Frank wiped his eyes and smiled, "And what is that supposed to mean?"

"Exactly what is says! If you must endure a situation or a consequence for a lifetime, then accept it or change the way you view it. Nobody should be able to control your mind except you."

"I see this entire scenario as a punishment— a forced disgrace; and so my only way of getting even for being trapped, is to force visitation. Now I see the people that I love the most, that mean the world to me, being hurt by my decision, and Gabby too, I guess."

Regina did not answer, but waited for him to continue. "Help me, Regina. Help me through this. Please help me?"

"What if you looked at the whole picture differently, and re-evaluated the pros and cons of getting even?"

"Like how?"

"How do you truly feel about Gabby, Frank?"

"Like I wish she wasn't here. Like I wish she didn't exist."

"Then why not just be a responsible father and send the money on time every month keeping the lines of communication open, in case Gabby ever does need more?"

"I don't want to give her more, and they better not ever ask for more!"

"Frank," Regina could hardly keep a straight face, "I was referring to simply being known as her father, rather than as a mystery person. Many children come from homes where mommy and daddy don't live together, especially in this day and age. It's sometimes better for them grow up telling their friends, 'my Daddy lives in Bradington, and he sends me birthday presents and Christmas toys, and he comes to Florida and takes me and Mommy and Abuela to Disney World with my Sati and my brother and sister.' Rather than being taken from an airport kicking and screaming while their sobbing mothers board flights back home; and bystanders watch, aghast. Bystanders, who could very well be patients, by the way."

Frank was in deep thought; but he nodded and finally spoke, "Well, I guess I'll have to give up my selfish satisfaction of being compensated for being tricked."

"Hardly, sir!"

"What then?"

"By easing off with visitation, you keep your child support reasonable and give more when and if you want to. Do you think they're going to make any waves?"

"So, we should sign a new order agreeing to cap the child... why are you shaking your head no?"

"Courts don't like that Frank, and that's not really what you want to do either.

It just happens to work out so that you can view the situation in a way that you find it easier to live with. We will, of course, take good care of Gabby. They just won't be inclined to gouge you down the line if they ever got the bright idea to do so. Believe me, orthopedic surgeons can get nailed for some high dollar child support; and they can also subpoena all of your financial business too, so we need to watch our records carefully."

"So what do we do, Pollyanna?" Frank set plates out for their dinner.

"We simply tell the truth! We explain that we are concerned for Gabby's emotional well being, and agree to modify visitation as we all see fit in her best interest." Regina served the spaghetti and meatballs along with the salad and garlic bread. "I'm starving," Frank smiled and counted his blessings before picking up his fork.

Looking into Regina's dark brown eyes he saw nothing but love. Love for him and their children, love for Gabby and her family, and most of all, love for Abba. As they began eating Gabby came running into the kitchen crying, "I want my mommy, Sati, call her!" Frank looked at his little daughter and asked her what just happened to make her cry.

"I don't want to be here, I want to be with my mommy," she sobbed. Frank Jr. came in and explained that she was trying to put a meatball in her purse to take home to Mommy, and he told her that it would get sauce on her toys and rot in there by the time she got it home.

Frank Sr. laughed and reached to hold Gabby. She resisted at first but finally went to him. He hugged her and whispered, "Sati can put some meatballs in the freezer in a special dish for you to take home for Mommy, Abuela, and you too! They won't go bad that way, and you can all eat them in Miami."

"I go to Miami now, Daddy. I go to the airport now. Please."

"Sati will call Mommy and we'll tell her to come and get you, honey. You can come back whenever you want to, but nobody will make you come. Daddy and Sati and Frank Jr. and Angela will come to see you in Miami until you are much older. Okay?"

"Okay," the child smiled at her father for the first time since her visit. "Mommy and me and Abuela will be at my house, and you CAN'T PLAY, FRANK," she started crying again, and reached for Regina.

"How do you like that?" Frank handed her back, with an insulted expression on his face.

"The voice of a small, confused child, Frank."

"Well, I don't care. I don't want to PLAY with them anyway!"

"Make that two," Regina winked and whispered to Abba, thanking him as they finished their dinner.

Dishes were cleared and baths were drawn. Gabby burst out crying again when she realized that her Cinderella play figures were down in the basement. "They come in my bubbles," she wailed. "I will go and get them," Frank started for the door. "These Latin ladies are always hysterical! She gets that nonsense from her mother!"

Entering the basement/ playroom, he was drawn to the couch for a few minutes. He looked around the large bright room and marveled at what he had seen before, but never really looked at in detail. The room was decorated in an under the sea theme and it was absolutely enchanting.

The walls were done in 3-D in stucco waves of blues and greens with realistic off-white foam tops moving across the room. Sunlight drenched the scene, but faded under the sea, to portray different lighting and detail. Amazing! Truly amazing!

Mermaids were positioned on large under water "rocks" made from insulating spray foam and painted with beige granite spray to look like sand. Two were engaged in a beauty salon, one of them styling the other's hair, as a crab handed her curlers. Two more mermaids were at a treasure chest collecting bubble gum that had floated down from the surface, and putting it into their bags. They appeared to be having the time of their lives with large pink bubbles coming from their mouths (large beads painted pink).

Three GI Joe dolls were combined with Santa dolls for the head changes and clad in purple, teal, and royal blue sequin tails, holding fireworks (cocktail sticks with glittering strands of plastic that looked like colored fire). These fine men of the sea were Neptune, Triton, and Poseidon, and looked magnificent with their muscular torsos protruding in full splendor in their regal settings! A small bathroom wall shelf with two bottom shelves that swung out in opposite directions had been spray painted gold, and each god of the sea sat on one shelf, surrounded by rich colored shimmering chiffon that looked as if it moved gently with the tides. Orcas and dolphins were friends in this ocean, and waited patiently with chairs on their backs to pull the gods wherever they wanted to go!

Schools of resin fish in every color imaginable scurried across the walls to get where they were going, while an exquisite plaster of Paris octopus wearing pink eyeglasses, taught school in another section. The ABC's floated overhead, forming small words in the AT, ET, IT, and OT families, set among colorful coral.

Each group of primary colored words settled over the underwater house that they lived in such as, cat, pet, sit, and pot, and so on, for each family.

A sunken ship on the far wall housed treasures and another mermaid bathing in a tub filled with "bubbles," that sparkled from the glitter they had been sprayed with. Realistic GI Joe divers were on the scene for the boys' part of the playroom, along with the Coast Guard on the surface of the ocean. Seagulls perched on driftwood with french-fries and sandwich scraps that they had scavenged from the bathers; and finally the beach scene had white sand and adorable blankets and chairs filled with people out for a day in the sun. A little beach ball tossed in the surf and a pail and shovel stood by the water, temporarily neglected for a beach time snack. Last but not least, lifeguard stations kept watch over the huge pirate ship that was a wonderful fort for Frank Jr. and his friends to climb on and hide in.

Frank marveled at the room and bowed his head in prayer. "Abba, can You ever forgive me? I am such a fool! My wife is Your servant and I need to get back to work for You too, if You'll have me. Please help me to try to understand my daughter and not to hold grudges against her mother. I beg You for a second chance!"

Walking back upstairs he was met by, "Miss Al Capone," as Sati called her, with both hands on her little Cuban hips. "Frank, where have you been? Were you playing in my sea?"

"Daddy. You call me, Daddy, like Frank Jr. does, okay?"

"Daddy."

"Yes, that's much nicer! And no, I wasn't playing in the sea, but I had to swim under the waves to get your figures."

"You wet?"

"Well, no I am not wet."

"Hmmmm. Those are mine, Daddy," Gabby pointed to the figures.

"Yes," Frank said, handing them over.

"See my mommy?" Gabby held up Cinderella in her ball gown.

"Yes, I see her."

"See my Sati?" Gabby held up the plump, older woman, who was Cinderella's fairy godmother. Frank laughed. "Okay, then where's Abuela?"

"Right here in the purse," she explained holding up one of the little girl mice.

"Let's call Mommy," she began to cry out of nowhere and pointed to the phone.

"Now what got you crying again?" Frank shook his head in controlled frustration. "Can you please tell me, honey?"

"No!" Gabby dropped to the floor, and began kicking her feet and screaming at the top of her lungs. Regina calmly walked over to her, picked her up, and knelt to be at eye level with her.

"Bastante," (Enough!) she said in a firm voice. Gabby stopped the tantrum immediately. "There is no need to behave like that, Gabby; and I don't know about you, but I have never seen Cinderella carry on the way!"

"I want my mommy, and Daddy no let me talk to her."

Frank was furious, "I ….." he decided to let Regina handle the problem.

"Daddy was trying to help you, Gabby, but if you just start screaming, he doesn't know what you want and neither does Sati."

"I want my mommy, Sati!" the little girl cried, checking her little figures to be sure none were lost in the shuffle.

"I know you do, honey, and Daddy told you that he was going to call Mommy to come and get you, didn't he?"

The little girl just nodded. "Okay, then suppose we ask Daddy

nicely if we can call Mommy, and suppose we have no more hysterics. We cannot talk on the telephone like Princess Cinderella if
we are carrying on like that, can we?"

"No, no cry like that, Sati."

"Good girl. We will call Mommy and ..." the child interrupted in another burst of sobs, "I no go to bed. I go to bed in my casa
(house)."

"Okay that's fine; you may watch Cinderella, and 'no go to bed.'"

"Yeah, and remember what happened to Cinderella when
she abused her curfew...." Frank decided to stop when Regina
looked at him with what appeared to be double barrel shotguns
where the lovely brown eyes usually were.

The four visitors from Memphis were delighted to hear that they
were still not excused from their visit even though Gabby would
be leaving early! They planned to come as scheduled and have a
blast, as always. Eva was called and told that Gabby's father felt that
it would be best to end the visit early, as the child was homesick.

She spoke with Gabby, who was a very big girl, and did not
scream and cry. She was delighted to hear that she would go home
the next day, as soon as Eva and Mercedes could get coverage at
their jobs and change their flight reservations. Gabby added that
she did not have to go to bed, but was going to watch Cinderella.
She also, at the tender age of three, said that her father was a
big, mean, pig, in Spanish. Eva was very grateful to Regina and
thanked her. "Don't thank me, sweetheart; thank Frank and most
of all, let us all thank Abba!" Regina took a deep breath of relief.

Eva hung up the phone and danced for joy. "Gabby is coming home tomorrow! She will not be returning until she is much older, but they will call her regularly. When they come to Florida, we will ALL, yes ALL, be included in the visit!" Eva cried tears of joy. "Regina said that Frank was concerned about Gabby's emotional upset and that she is too young to handle the separation anxiety at her age."

"Oh right," Mercedes laughed and hugged her daughter. "You know who did that for her? Sati probably wouldn't let Frank treat her badly; the conceited pig!"

"Mama, Sati will not be one bit happy with us if we are rude to Frank, and it will only cause him to send for Gabby again."

"Well, we will be nice to his face, but I can't stand the sight of him!"

"Gabby called her father a big, mean, pig in Spanish on the phone. We probably shouldn't encourage that. I know that Sati will not want us to. We need to be nice to Frank for her sake as well as Gabby's."

"I will be nice to his face, and nothing more! He's a monster!" Mercedes said, deciding to have a nice cup of Cuban coffee to celebrate.

The next afternoon Frank and Regina took Gabby, Frank Jr., and Angela and went to the Memphis airport. Eva and Mercedes had already landed and were chomping at the bit to get their little one back. They could not get a plane back for three hours, so Regina suggested that they all have dinner.

"No," Gabby screamed, "I want to go home."

Eva was very gentle but firm, "Gabriella, there is no need to act like that. We are going home, but we are having dinner first. I expect you to act like a nice girl now."

"Like Cinderella," Gabby answered indicating the costume she wore.

"Yes, just like Cinderella." Eva winked at Frank Sr., who smiled back.

They dined at The Fantasy, a restaurant that was decorated like a rainforest and served every food imaginable. While they waited for their dinner, everyone chatted pleasantly. Gabby set her toy figures on the table and named them.

"Mommy," she said placing the lovely Cinderella by the salt shaker, "Sati," she said introducing the fairy godmother, "Abuela," she set the little girl mouse up, "Frank, my brother," the fat little mouse named Gus joined the setting, "Daddy," the little mouse named Jack was standing among the group as everybody including Daddy laughed; and last but not least, poor little Angela was a little piece of cheese.

"That is too adorable," Eva laughed with tears of gratitude in her eyes.

"Oh sure," Regina laughed, "you get to be the gorgeous princess and I am the fat, little-old-lady!"

"Yes, and I am a mouse!" Mercedes laughed along.

"I think she remembers when you were pregnant," Frank Sr. reasoned the choice for Regina's figure.

"No," Frank Jr. shook his head. "She calls mommy the fairy

godmother because she's the one who makes everything alright."
Regina looked startled but the other three adults jumped to their
feet and applauded. Eva and Frank hugged each other and returned to their seats, as the waitress served the dinner with a look
of curiosity.

On the way back to Bradington, Frank Jr. asked if they were stopping at Frances and Lamar's. "No sweetheart, it's too late, but
they are coming to our house for the whole weekend." Frank Sr.
was quiet but seemed much more relaxed. When they arrived
home, he put Angela to bed and whispered a prayer. "Thanks so
much, Father. I have three gorgeous children but one just happens to live in Miami. I have a wonderful wife, who I would swear
is an angel! Most important of all, I have You, Who I worship and
adore. I don't intend to lose sight of that again!"

Regina read two stories to Frank Jr. who stayed awake for
both. "Mommy," he sat up in his bed, "Gabby told me every time
she needed something that she was going to her fairy godmother,
and then she came to you. She did not choose that figure because
the little lady was a plump person. She chose her because she was
the one who able to fix things."

Regina hugged her little son, who was wise beyond his years,
and sat with him until he fell asleep.

Chapter Twenty-One
Shades Of Grey

The group from Memphis arrived late in the morning and were well received with huge hugs from everyone. Behind them came a surprise visit from Elizabeth and Dan, who pulled into the driveway just before noon! Elizabeth's initial concerns about intruding were put to rest immediately, as her daughter and everybody else was delighted to see them.

Observing the child walking in from the patio in a swimsuit, the Colonel asked Frank Jr. if he was aware of the fact that it was fall. "Why sure Grandpa," he laughed, "and I have two Halloween songs for you. I'm being Luke Skywalker and Angela is being a Dalmatian. My friends are all being Star Wars people too, and we're going to get tons of candy! Do you want to be the Emperor?"

"Regina Louise, please tell me that this child is not swimming this time of year!"

"Sir, yes Sir! We have a pool heater," she laughed and was glad that she told Frances and Hazel to pack swimsuits for themselves and their husbands.

Dan and Elizabeth came prepared as well, but Dan wasn't sure he was willing to brave the air itself. As everybody settled in, the long table in the dining room was covered with cold cuts, cheeses, rolls, potato and macaroni salad, deviled eggs, pickles, olives, cheese cakes and, a huge tower of Italian cookies. Regina had also made a spooky, chocolate sucker tree of ghosts, monsters, pumpkins, goblins and bats, which sent radar to every child in the neighborhood to come over for a sample!

Saturday or not there was a meeting at the town hall to discuss the country club policies and the blow up with the Solbergs. Bob Jenkins, Luke Hanley, Earl Turnbull, and Noah Cadence crowded around the coffee pot and then settled into their chairs.

Bob explained the importance of having a top notch orthopedic surgeon in Bradington, and elaborated on the characters of the Solbergs. After explaining the saga with the Gentry family on his own street, he sat back and opened the floor for discussion.

There was a moment of silence as the men contemplated the fact that the oppressed family's head of household had actually saved Bob's son's life.

"Well I aint gonna sugar coat it," Noah Cadence, the owner of the Silver Wheels Skating Rink, spoke first. "We need to be considering the risks of the NAACP comin' in here and fryin all our butts! We can have stricter rules to weed out undesirable patrons, but they need to go for black, for wahte, for everybody." Noah was a tall thin man with sandy colored hair and deep brown eyes. He had a pleasant appearance and a matching disposition.

"So you say now, buddy," Earl was his usual cantankerous self, "but what happens when the wahte folks refuse to let their kids skate with the black kids and your business takes a nose dahve?"

"Then I'll make the large amount of money that I've been loosin' from the black community; but I also know that very few of the wahte kids will pull out and that sooner or later they'll be back. Those youngsters go to school together, and folks will git real tired of hauling their kids to Memphis to skate. I'm ready to adjust our policies for my own protection."

Luke raised his eyebrows and nodded in agreement as Earl lit a fat cigar.

"You know Earl, you may also want to consider the fact that the Solbergs have a nice income and you just happen to sell cars for a living," Bob cracked his knuckles.

Earl was suddenly thinking about his own hide and leaning toward protecting it. "Well say, - just say, - we did let black folks into the club with strict guidelines," he looked at the other three men to analyze their expressions before continuing. "We could only take doctors, lawyers, dentists, etc. to be sure we keep our standards high."

"That's discrimination, Earl," Luke answered and Bob nodded in agreement.

"Your membership fee would be enough to ensure members of the upper middle class and wealthy folks. Impoverished or lower income people wouldn't be able to join anyway, black or wahte," Noah added, reaching for a donut.

"So are we all in agreement that we need to allow 'shades of grey' into our antiquated policies, for the protection of ourselves and the town of Bradington?" Bob asked the group for an on the spot commitment.

"I vote yes." Noah seemed to be glad of the opportunity to reach out to more customers.

"I'm with Noah. How about it, Earl? Do you want to sell Regina Solberg a new car or not?" Luke added laughing.

"That holier-than-thou wouldn't buy a car from me anyway," Earl flicked his ashes bitterly into a plant on the desk, "But I guess we have no choice."

"It's far better to initiate the updated policies ourselves than to be humiliated into doing it, and sued to boot!" Bob warned the group.

The vote was unanimous, 'shades of grey' in both the skating rink and the country club; the last two places in Bradington that were quietly continuing the unlawful practice of banning black people from their facilities.

"Do you think that the Solbergs will move the Christening party?" Noah asked Luke.

"I would like to think so, but more importantly, I don't think they would say anything about the reason they were not considering us to begin with. The Solbergs are anything but troublemakers," Luke recalled the delightful dinner he had shared with the new family in town.

"Okay, I'll speak with Frank and Regina today since they're my neighbors," Bob stood up and stretched.

"I'll tag along if you don't mind," Earl was always in the market for a prospective sale.

"So how do we let people know that we will take blacks now, the newspaper?" Luke was ready to remove the risks at hand.

"Shoot no!" Bob stretched again and turned in response to a determined woodpecker at the window. "We don't need to broadcast the fact that there was ever any banning going on here. We just need to fix it quickly, before someone gets the long overdue urge to fix us! Just send invitations for memberships to the country club to the entire community, and advertisements for the skating rink to the schools, to be passed out to <u>all students</u>.

Everyone at the Solberg residence was refilling their iced tea glasses and dessert plates, when there was a knock on the front door. "Bob, come on in," Frank was unusually jovial. Noticing Earl's presence he was obligated to welcome him as well. "We didn't realize you had company," Bob apologized.

"Really, well who did you think the other two cars here belonged to, Frank Jr. and the baby?" Frances was her usual no nonsense self, rising to shake hands with Bob whom she had already met, and to glare at Earl, whom she already disliked.

"You remember Lamar and Frances Mac Michaels, Leo and Hazel Gerehauzer, and Regina's folks, Elizabeth and Dan," Frank smiled with pride; then introduced Earl to all of them. Please come in and have some lunch. Bob saw the sucker tree and marveled at it while Earl looked around the table seeing dollar signs, and licked his fat chops.

"We came by to let you and Regina know that we now see 'shades of grey!'" Bob smiled and continued, "The Bradington

Country Club and the Silver Wheels Skating Rink are now open to all of our citizens, regardless of their race."

"Well, bully for you, Bucko! Where have you been hiding? You're not legally allowed to ban anyone from any public facility based on their race," Frances laughed, and Hazel followed.

"We certainly realize that, Frances, and we have come to beg pardon and see if there is any way Regina would change her mind about the location of Miss Angela's Christening," Bob blushed from embarrassment.

Earl could restrain himself no longer. Impressed by the status, size, and physical conditions of Dan, Leo, Lamar, and Frank, as well as their obvious wealth, the dining room became his stage.

"Ladies and gentlemen, I met the lovely Regina Solberg under extenuating circumstances. After reflecting on her deep respect for all human beings, I don't even see any grey area!"

"Must be looking between his ears," Frances referred to the grey matter of the brain, making no effort to muffle her voice, and causing great restraint among the others.

Earl continued unabashed, "Nope! I see black and wahte equally," and I thank you for bringing that beautiful view to our town, Mrs. Solberg," the bigot practically sang.

"I see black and "what" newspapers that will make you glad you did," Hazel added to everybody's surprise. It was crystal clear to both visitors, that Regina was well loved and not to be tampered with.

"So Miss Regina, will you have us back?" Earl got down on one knee. Regina was not impressed, but was aware of the fact that the man had feelings and would be utterly humiliated if she wasn't careful of her response. The dedicated missionary was also aware that the boundaries of un-necessary roughness, were closing in fast.

"Angela would be delighted, sir. We will have to use Master Chefs however, as I have already committed to them."

"Darlin, that is no problem whatsoever!" Earl rose, shook Frank's hand, and kissed Regina's. "Please let us take our leave of you fahne people, and forgive our interruption."

Bob shook hands and apologized as well. As both men left Earl commented, "How would you like to meet them in a dark alley?"

"I'll say, there big dudes!"

"Bob, I was referring to Frances and Hazel," he slapped the town manager on the back laughing, and reached for another cigar. "Regina's another one I never want to tangle with again. No, Sir! I'd rather stick maw tongue to a frozen street pole!" The bigot wondered if he would ever be considered for a spot on the Christening list, for no other reason than selling cars.

Leo, Dan, and Lamar laughed when Frank filled them in, and Hazel claimed her turn to hold Angela. "Well Pollyanna, you have been fast at work as usual," Lamar smiled with pride.

"I didn't do anything except plan my daughter's Christening!"

The missionary smiled innocently. "And provide a year of free ice cream to a little boy who was treated unfairly," Frank laughed as he hugged his wife.

"Well, how's the golf course here, son?" Leo contemplated switching their game to the club that was five minutes away.

"I've never seen it; Regina refused to patronize them," Frank laughed, "They call her 'Rosa Parks' at Frank Jr.'s school!"

"Well, now that they allow everybody membership at the club do you feel differently, Madame?" Dan asked his daughter beaming with admiration.

"Sure."

"Good, let's go for a ride!" Lamar suggested, while the ladies started clearing the table and gabbing about the Christening.

Elizabeth gasped with delight when she saw the Christening gown hanging in the nursery. It was a gorgeous long ivory-colored silk dress with flowers along the hem. Each bud was bedecked in hand sewn pearls from a piece of old jewelry that had been salvaged by Regina years ago. The long braded necklace had belonged to Ana Foglietta, Regina's late grandmother, and was to be tossed in the trash because it was so old that the strings had broken. Though she was a very young girl at the time, she selected the necklace because she felt sorry for it, and vowed to save it wrapped in a paper napkin and set in an old, tin, tea canister. Her late father, Michael Foglietta, was touched beyond words and had encouraged her to choose another piece of jewelry as well.

"I've made my choice, Daddy, and these little beads will be great one day, just wait, and you'll see."

The beads were beautiful and meaningful. Tiny slippers, and an adorable bonnet, also sprayed with the same tiny pearls complemented the outfit. Andrea and Brian had been selected as the god-parents, and the party was to include two-hundred people.

The four tier cake was being designed by Regina housing the same exquisite angels and tiny cherubs that were used for Frank Jr.'s Christening cake. The saying was to be written in pale pink, *Welcome Angela Dawn, God sent us the best He had!* White, pink, and yellow, chocolate roses on long stems were in the freezer awaiting their display. They were mint flavored, had pale green leaves, and looked too pretty to eat! The three older women were as impressed as though they didn't know Regina.

"Where did you find the time?" Hazel was astounded at the preparations that had been completed so far ahead of the event.

"A little bit each morning," Regina smiled, "It's really not difficult. We found the candy molds years ago, at a close out sale at Diamonds Department Store, in Miami. I bought a huge box full for twenty-five dollars! Some for every holiday, flowers, cameos, and sun, moon, and stars."

The ladies all discussed the menu and agreed that it would be perfect. There was chicken cordon bleu, tenderloin on petite rolls, honey baked ham, scalloped potatoes, linguini with parsley butter, spinach artichoke casserole, sweet baby carrots, asparagus with cheddar cheese sauce, and a salad bar. In addition to the cake there would be the white chocolate rose sucker trees and a huge assortment of Italian cookies.

Barry Walker sent Frank Jr. home from school with a lovely gift for the baby and let the young man know that he would love to attend the Christening. Frances read the card and laughed, "Nothing like inviting yourself to someone else's party!"

"Oh well, why should he be the only one in Bradington who's not coming,"

Regina laughed good-naturedly. She and the school principal had reached a mutual understanding and were now very pleasant to each other in spite of their rough start. He appreciated the help Regina offered the school and admired the control she was able to keep over the whole lunchroom full of students, while still being very kind to them. It was obvious that the youngsters loved and respected her.

Thunder storms whipped through Bradington for the next three days, accompanied by torrential downpours and hail. Trees were collapsing in submission to the saturated ground, and in many areas, blocking the passage of traffic. Such was the case with a delivery truck that was carrying supplies to the Bradington schools. When little Darrell went to select his ice cream he was told by Hilda that there simply was none. Watching the child's eyes fill with tears, she scolded, "well the truck caint git through! We have no os cream today!"

"I am telling my Regina tomorrow when she's here," the boy sobbed as he started to walk away.

"Mr. Walker," Hilda called across the lunchroom, "Could you please come over here?"

"Yeeeess?" The principal answered, as he changed directions to accommodate the new request.

"Darrell is upset because there is no os cream and he plans to tell Regina Sol… …"

"I'm on it, Hilda," the principal called over his shoulder walking quickly toward the disgruntled child. "Darrell," Mr. Walker called out on the way over to him, "Darrell, I'm sure we can work this out! You're a business man, aren't you?"

The boy nodded brushing the tears from his face.

"Well how about we go to the teachers' lounge and look in the vending machines there for another dessert – a better dessert?"

The boy nodded in confusion but accepted the principal's hand and walked with him.

"There now, we have king size M&M's and suppose I throw in a pair of Twinkies for your inconvenience? Would that let us off the hook for today's ice cream?"

"Yes, sir," Darrell smiled in response to far more than the sweets he'd been bribed with.

Mr. Walker carried the boy and his treats back to the cafeteria and was genuinely taken back when the child put his little arms around his neck and kissed him on the cheek. Unable to speak, the principal just smiled. Finally he said, "Now be sure you eat the good food first, okay partner?"

"Okay!" Darrell beamed. The other children smiled up at the principal with delighted amazement. When he addressed another little black girl's new Barbie lunch box, she looked up at him with shining eyes. The children, along with the lunch room staff, were watching his every move with deep admiration, and he was well aware of it. Suffice to say that a certain Mr. Walker returned to his office scratching his head and realizing that he had the opportunity to become a super star right in his own school!

The close knit friends from Miami were all coming to Christening celebration and Regina was relieved when Frances and Lamar, and Hazel and Leo split the housing! Wyatt, Sylvia and their five children would stay with Frances and Lamar, while Roger, Hyacinth, Chuck, Jeanie and their two kids, would stay with Hazel and Leo. Frank and Regina would house Dan, Elizabeth, Bub , Sis, and Andrea and Brian.

The friends were delighted to be together again and stayed up until the wee hours of morning gabbing and enjoying each other's children. Frank Jr. had his own social club going on as he introduced the triplets and his good friend Charlie to all of the kids on the block. The new babies were introduced in a very matter of fact way, since they were too young to really matter! Both Frank Jr. and Charlie had to admit that having baby sisters was not as bad as they had imagined it to be. The triplets were proudly introducing their twin brothers but Hyacinth made it clear that the girls still ruled by the seniority standards!

Angela's Christening was a smashing success and brought the Bradington community closer together! The Walkers were present with their twins, and socialized among the guests comfortably.

After the party was under way, Barry asked Regina if he might be permitted to see the soft sculptures that he had heard about through the grapevine. He was not shy about adding that he would gladly pay dearly to have the school library and lobby areas done. Regina was flattered and delighted to be fitting in better. She agreed to have the Walkers over for dinner and to discuss the new plans after her out-of-town guests returned to their homes.

Jeannie was also doing two sculptures in her new town, but Sylvia simply had no time for the art. The three ladies compared notes, as they did by phone on a regular basis. Regina loved her close friends, and felt sorry that Jeannie and Sylvia had not adapted as well as she was finally able to.

Elizabeth and Dan were admiring the cake when they simultaneously noticed the two guests in the doorway, arriving late to the reception. Elizabeth clasped her hand to her mouth and Dan struggled to keep his own composure. Dorothy and Raymond Solberg entered the country club and walked toward their son. Leo and Lamar stood in position to intervene if needed, and Frances moved swiftly from the buffet to grab Angela, as though the evil fairy had just appeared! Frank was startled and uncertain of his parents' intentions.

Suddenly all eyes were on Regina, who walked up to her in laws and embraced them. Both of the senior Solbergs burst into tears as Frances rolled her eyes. Dorothy hugged her son and asked permission to be seated with the other guests. Regina led the Solbergs to the place cards that were at the host's table "just in case," and introduced them to their friends in Bradington as though nothing was amiss.

Dorothy and Raymond were taken back when they saw Angela and even more so when they saw how much Frank Jr. had grown. The image of her own son, the little boy touched Dorothy's heart when he offered to show them to the buffet. Little Hyacinth looked at the Solbergs suspiciously and commented, "Hey, aren't you guys evil? What are you doing here anyway?"

Regina motioned to a stunned Sylvia that all was well, as Dorothy laughed and bent to the little girl who had just confronted her.

"We have come to see all of you, and to show you that we are not evil; just a little stupid sometimes. May we stay at this lovely party?"

Hyacinth put her arm around her sister and whispered something. "Well you can be in our club. Frankie and the boys are getting bossy but soon my twin brothers will be on our side too."

"Wow!" Raymond jumped in, "can I join in too?"

"Over there." Hyacinth indicated the boys section. "You cannot be in our club - because it's just for girls."

Raymond, delighted to have the tension in the air cut, continued, "But, I like little girls better than jelly donuts!"

"Do you have any jelly donuts for our club?" Holly was suddenly sparked to make friends with the enemy.

"No, but I can get some."

"When?"

"On the way home?"

"Well okay, but just tell everybody that you're a girl."

Raymond threw his head back and laughed, as he walked toward his own beautiful little grand-daughter and asked Regina for permission to hold her.

"The ceremony was lovely, darling," Raymond gushed. "We watched from the doorway and left before we were seen, but we couldn't leave Bradington without seeing you guys."

"Well I should hope not!" Regina smiled warmly. The rest of the twelve-pack, and Dan and Elizabeth followed her example and welcomed the Solbergs, as a misty-eyed Frank Sr. whispered a prayer of thanks to Abba.

Chapter Twenty-Two

A Penny For Your Thoughts

Dorothy and Raymond were planning to leave the Christening and head back to Florida, stopping along the way to spend the night at a hotel. Dan, at his daughter's request, convinced them to stay in Bradington for a few days instead.

"I don't know how to break the ice Dan," Dorothy whispered quietly.

"The ice has already been broken, sweetheart; you did that when you walked in that door. Come on over and see the kids' new home."

Regina was always a supporter of "let bygones- be bygones," and included Dorothy and Raymond in all of the wind down activities. The senior Solbergs were delighted to hear that Gabby was not in the picture as before, and marveled at their son's new home. The things that Dorothy and Raymond had made or bought for their son over many years past, and all of the family pictures were in place as though nothing had happened; and as

Regina predicted, Frank Jr. was only too glad to fill them in on any details about his former bedroom wall. The senior Solbergs were impressed by the advanced social skills that their grandson displayed, and even more so by how witty he was. They were still uneasy about the things that they had said and done to their son and his wife, but graciously accepted Regina's invitation back into the swing of things.

While the other family members and close friends joined in by making small conversation, they had no intentions of simply dismissing the past, as Regina was. Bub and Sis both supported Dan in reassuring the Solberg seniors to stay at the house.

"Oh do stay here," Sis coaxed, "there's plenty of room and you would miss all of the fun at a hotel."

"You can have my room," their blue-eyed grandson piped in with excitement; "I'm camping out with my friends down in the playroom –under the sea."

"Wow!" Raymond answered with genuine interest and continued, "What will you guys do if the waves get too big?"

"We are patrolling the waters for trouble, Grandpa. The whole block is coming and my friends from Miami. Not the babies though – it isn't safe for them."

"Well I certainly feel safer," Dorothy added with a nervous laugh hoping that she would be allowed to join in the game.

Frank Jr. walked over to her and put his arm around her, "If you have any trouble you just call on us. That's what we're here for. Grandpa Leo has trained us 'to serve and to protect!'"

"Wonderful! It's settled then," Frank Sr. said with feeling as he accompanied his father to their car to bring their luggage in. Frances and Elizabeth rolled their eyes simultaneously and Sis winked and nodded along.

Dorothy wanted to talk to Regina, but didn't dare to ask with Frances and Hazel on guard. The whole twelve-pack from Miami was reunited with the new babies, and Dorothy viewed the group as an absolute threat. All of the friends made an effort to make the senior Solbergs feel welcome, but they still resented them for what they had done to Frank and Regina.

After a huge dinner at the Lamar's house the next day, Dorothy was sitting outside by herself giving the friends their space together. She felt that she had no right to be among them and envied Raymond's invitation to play with the vast crowd of kids! She couldn't believe that she had been invited by Frances to attend dinner, and didn't want to wear out her welcome, which she was well aware was for Regina's sake rather than hers and Raymond's, to begin with. Regina walked over to her and sat down, "'a penny for your thoughts,'" she laughed.

"I'm not worth a penny, Regina," Dorothy sobbed.

"I didn't say you were," Regina laughed, when her mother-in-law responded with a shocked expression followed by an appreciative grin.

"I have messed up my whole life Regina, and everybody else's too."

"I don't think your life is messed up and I don't know that anybody else's is either. Besides, you don't have the power to mess up anybody else's life, Mom, and I don't think you would intentionally do that, even if you did."

"I'm a bossy, controlling, witch, Regina."

"The most well adjusted people that I have ever met are able to recognize faults within themselves and call them to the surface for correction."

"Meaning?" Dorothy looked over her designer glasses as she blinked away the tears.

"Meaning, that we all have faults which we can and should correct."

"You? Regina, what are your faults?"

"I haven't time to tell them all," the small-framed redhead whispered and laughed quietly.

"My son adores you."

"Your son adores you too, and he has missed you."

"Why hasn't he called us then, Regina? Because he's finished with us, that's why!"

"Because he's a man, that's why!" Come on Mom, you know how they are!"

"So what do we do now? How do Dad and I fit back in?"

"Well for starters, you are back in! You were never really out; just taking a break. We are cooking out tomorrow night at our house and we would be delighted to have a nice Caesar salad and some of your best crème puffs! Dad is one heck of a bar tender, so why don't you two just join in and make yourselves at home? We all want you to."

Dorothy hugged her daughter-in-law and cried. "I resented you so much, Regina; you can do anything!"

"I can't make a Caesar salad or crème puffs, like you do. I

can't be Frank's mother or Frank Jr.'s and Angela's grandmother. I certainly couldn't do what you do for animals, I don't sew, knit, or crochet, and I could go on forever if you like."

Raymond joined them and hugged Regina, "We've never had a daughter," he said as Dan walked over and joined in.

"Well count your blessings! They're very expensive and a lot of trouble. We don't call her Pandemonium for nothing!"

Regina loved him for what he was doing and hoped the others would follow his lead.

During the short visit things went very well, and Dorothy and Raymond were grateful to be reunited with their son, his wife, and their grandchildren. Although they were still awkward around Regina, they knew that nothing would be said about the past, and relaxed as they rekindled a relationship with her. Very little conversation about Gabby took place to Regina's relief, but Frances and Hazel were back and forth the next couple of days whether anybody liked it or not, to keep a check on things.

Regina was handing out Halloween cookies to the slew of neighborhood kids, when she noticed a deep look of sadness on Dorothy's face. She waited patiently for her mother-in-law to talk.

"You know, I always did these things for my boys and their friends," she nodded indicating the cookies and the suckers. "They don't remember, though. All of those acts of love have been wasted. They don't appreciate Dad and me, Regina, and it's our own fault. Adam never once thanked us for his education or for his office building. He comes over to visit us because he has to, not because he loves us. Marge hates us too and I guess I can see why."

"No act of love is ever wasted, and I don't think Marge hates anyone, Mom, I think she's just very quiet."

Noticing Dorothy's hopeful expression that she would continue, she did. "As far as your sons are concerned, I'm sure that they appreciate the things that you have done for them, right down to the earliest chocolate chip cookie! Frank has told me all about the snake cake that you made for Adam's eighth birthday. He even showed us pictures of it in his album."

"Did he really, Regina?" Dorothy sobbed.

"Really!"

"I knit them many sweaters, sent care packages to Adam in college, bought them whatever I thought would make them happy, and all with strings attached to satisfy my own insecurity of losing them one day."

"I don't know about you, but I know that I have been guilty of forgetting to thank people for kindnesses they have shown me, until it suddenly hit me that I had taken things for granted. I bet that is the case with Frank and Adam."

"We didn't do as much for Frank, because you were there."

"That doesn't mean that you weren't there too, Mom. It doesn't mean that you stopped loving your son because of a misunderstood relationship with a new daughter-in-law, or that you need to punish yourself by writing decades of love off because you may have been a little bossy at times."

"I just wanted them to succeed, Regina. I don't have a college degree." Dorothy put her head in her hands and cried.

Regina went to her immediately and hugged her. "So what, I don't have a college degree either. All of my siblings do, but I simply do not. The laminated plaques on walls are handy, and there's no doubt about that. Our abilities in life however, should go far beyond the four corners of a diploma."

"You do so have a degree, Regina," Dorothy laughed lightly in appreciation for the attempt to make her feel better.

"Really; in what?"

"You are honestly telling me that you didn't have any degree?"

"I'm honestly telling you that I still don't."

"How did you know how to negotiate the house that you have? Frank told us you did the whole thing."

"Actually," a sheepish smile spread across the missionary's face, "I learned from you and Dad. I do pay attention every once in a while, you know!"

Dorothy sat straight in her chair in amazement. "I thought Dan was kidding when he said that you had a degree from the school of hard knocks! Regina is it too late for us to have a relationship with you? Can you forgive us for all the things that we have said and done?"

"Done, and I would love to have a nice relationship with you. You raised the man I married."

"Your son is very like him, Regina."

"And how; they are identical except for the color of their eyes."

"Do you really think that my sons are aware of how much I have always loved them and that I only wanted them to succeed?"

"I certainly do."

Dorothy continued to talk, telling Regina the stories of how

poor the Solbergs were when they started out. "My greatest concern was getting Raymond educated and then both boys. I lived
hand to mouth for years, wondering where the money would
come from for Adam's braces and glasses."

Regina listened intently, trying not to laugh as she pictured
her geek brother-in-law in thick glasses and a "tin grin," if he ever
grinned, that is. Dorothy was an only child and had a very lonely
life, whether she brought it on herself or not.

After all of the guests left, and the sad farewells among the twelve-
pack were over, Regina set to work on Dorothy's feelings and solutions as to how she could help her. Both kids were fast asleep
and Frank was sitting in the living room eating the final remains
of the left over Christening cake. He stood when his wife entered
and went over to hug her. "We got them crawling back to us now,
sweetheart. They feel like crap and they should!"

"We do not want them to crawl or feel like crap, Frank,"
Regina laughed softly.

"Well I sure as hell do! They deserve to; and they're lucky they
weren't removed from the Christening reception by the police."

"That would be great for your image – headlines right here in
Mayberry – *Local Doc has his parents arrested for trying to attend
their new grandbaby's Christening.*"

Frank laughed, "Are you willing to just let them back into our lives?"

"Isn't it a little late not to, since they just spent four days with
us and our friends?"

"Who still hate them by the way; my parents should be bursting with gratitude."

"Funny you should say that, Dr. Solberg!"

"What do you mean?"

"I mean that I had a long talk with your mother when they were here, and she is hurt, Frank; really hurt!"

"Good, maybe she will learn to treat us with the respect we deserve," Frank reached for his empty plate and led his wife into the kitchen for seconds.

"Your mother feels that any good she did for you and Adam when you were growing up, is simply lost and will never be remembered. That's a sad, lonely feeling, sweetheart."

"Pray tell – exactly what "good" does the Nazi refer to!"

"All of the things mothers do for their kids; cookies, bedtime stories, knitting sweaters, providing a safe home, nice meals, et cetera."

"Oh! So what of that? She did what she was supposed to do – what any decent mother should do — and threw it up in our faces!"

"That's the part that she is so sorry about."

"What are you suggesting that we do as a cure, Pollyanna?"

"I was thinking that maybe you and Adam could chip in and send your parents on a cruise."

"Are you out of your mind?!"

"No. I think it would be nice. After all they did raise you two and send you to school."

"I recall being cut off and paying for a good bit of my schooling myself."

"So what Frank? It would mean the world to them and both of you can easily afford it."

Frank leaned against the counter and folded his arms. "And where do you think they deserve to be sent?"

"Oh, how about you send them all around the world?" Noticing the color drain from her husband's face, Regina decided to rescue him. "Can't have everything; how about a week to the islands then?"

"I'm not sending those two, anywhere! They can buy their own cruise, Regina. They're lucky we took them back. Just being allowed back with us is gift enough, as far as I'm concerned."

"A little appreciation never hurt anyone, Frank. You know that she realizes that she was wrong. Let her have this little reassurance that everything is okay now."

"Everything is not okay! Let's remember the puzzle in storage that was once our son's wall, shall we?"

"Let's remember how frightened they were to enter the Christening, shall we?"

"Oh yeah, I meant to ask you why there were places set for them?"

"Just in case they did exactly what they did."

Regina looked her husband straight in the eye as she handed him the phone. "Call your brother, Frank."

Frank called his brother only to learn that they were expecting a baby and had not told his parents yet.

"We won't be paying for any cruise, Frank," Adam stated matter-of-factly, "but if you want to, I'll sign the card for you so they think that we did."

More angry than he had ever remembered being, Frank relayed the message to Regina. He was flabbergasted by his wife's response, "That would be lovely; I will send the card for him to sign."

"Adam is a jerk!" Frank shouted as he checked the phone to be sure he hadn't broken it when he hung up.

"Confirmed," Regina answered folding her arms across her small chest.

"Well I'm not allowing him to sign the card unless he pays. I'll simply tell my parents that he chose not to!"

"Well done, darling! Very well done! We can have our very own family jackass contest – aaaand – you both win!"

"Are you suggesting that he be allowed to take credit for the gift that he refuses to chip in for?"

"I'm clarifying that the gift is to make your parents feel appreciated and loved, Frank, regardless of who chips in for it."

"Do whatever you want about this, Regina, but I am absolutely against the whole idea, and I will tell my parents so when they call here crying to thank us for the gift cruise!"

"Oh I bet you will," Regina thought as she fixed a plate of cake for herself and a second one for Frank.

The next day, Regina put the card in the mail to be signed by the loser, and bought a Barbie Cruise ship and a bottle of champagne to set into it. She bought two first class tickets for an eleven day cruise to the Caribbean Islands on the Seven Seas Ocean Liner, and put them together in a lovely package. When the card came back she had Frank sign it and mailed the box to the senior Solbergs. Three days later the phone rang as they were ready to eat dinner. Regina answered to hear Dorothy's voice, "Regina let us talk to our son, please."

Passing the phone to Frank Sr., she could hear the tearful thanks and the joy in their voices. "You and your brother are wonderful, Frank! So who's idea was it?"

"I figured, what the hell," their proud son who vowed to take absolutely no credit, gloated.

"We know that you put Adam up to it, Frank," Raymond sobbed and added, "and we love you for it, son."

Regina took the corn bread out of the oven as she winked toward the gorgeous sunset, "I figured 'what the hell,' my Abba! I love You this much!"

Frank Jr. was all ears but said nothing. His blue eyes twinkled as he listened to his father relay the words, knowing full well that his mother prepared and sent the gift. Angela was more interested in her high chair suction toy but laughed when her brother told her, "I'll explain all of this when you are older, Angela; much older!"

Distracted by the dinner being presented, Frank Jr. laughed and asked, "What happened to those chickens, Mom?!"

"What do you mean?"

"They shrunk a lot in the oven!"

"These are Cornish hens, honey," Regina laughed.

"Can I take one to school tomorrow; the kids will never believe this!"

"Absolutely," Regina hugged her son and asked him to say the blessing.

Chapter Twenty-Three
The Sandwich Ring

Frank Sr. came in from the clinic in a terrible mood. "I'm telling you, Regina, my partners will push me too far one day, and I'll tell them all where to go! They are lucky to have me running this branch clinic, and I want the full recognition that I deserve for the income that we are raking in!"

"What do you mean, honey?" Regina asked with great interest.

"I want more respect in the hospital for one thing. I said that I wanted spacesuit scrub attire for my hip surgeries, and a nurse had the audacity to giggle at me. She giggled, Regina,- giggled right in my face!"

Regina fought to keep a serious expression herself, and didn't dare to laugh as the rant continued. "I threw her off my case and we were delayed since they had to send for another circulator (the nurse who does not actually scrub in, but "circulates" to obtain and do things that are needed by the operating-room staff). Then the entire surgery schedule got botched because we were late. Administration called Memphis, and I hit the ceiling."

Regina, trying to remain as supportive as possible asked, "So what was the outcome of the call to Memphis?"

"Oh Mike Dougherty calls me and raises hell! He says that I need to watch the way I talk to the hospital staff, and that he has had other complaints from the nurses on the floor. I felt like I was a kid in a parent-teacher conference."

"Were you aware that there were nurses who had complained prior to the phone call of today?"

"Kinda sorta! They're so damn touchy, Regina. I don't have time for their southern nonsense. One complained in tears that 'Doc rolled his eyes' at her. Tough! She's an idiot, and I don't have time for idiots."

"Well the people here are very sensitive, darling, and you must remember that you are like a movie star on the hospital set. Everyone in the hospital wants to be treated nicely, especially by the doctors. They aren't used to the elaborate advances such as space-suit scrubs here, even though it was childish to giggle about it."

"So what am I supposed to do? Do you think it was right for me to throw her off the case?"

"Do you; in retrospect?"

"She humiliated me in front of the surgical team, Regina."

"And that was very inappropriate behavior on her part; but you – are the head of the surgical team, Frank. The master of the ship; and I should think it is your responsibility to see that things run smoothly no matter what. Is this nurse a good circulator?"

"Yes, she's excellent."

"Well, then perhaps there is some other way that you could

relay the message that laughing in your face was disrespectful, and that you certainly didn't appreciate it."

"It's too late now, I have already dismissed "Scarlet O'Hara" from all of my cases, and I hate her guts anyway."

"What does that do to the operating room schedule?"

"That's not my concern!"

"I beg to differ."

"So what am I supposed to do now, go kiss her fat southern feet and beg her to come back?"

"You might," Regina paused and smiled as her husband laughed. "Or you could call a meeting with the administration and the nurse who was involved, and explain your position."

"Yeah, I'll just tell her that she was out of line, and that she needs to provide me with a written apology, before she can come back on my cases."

"Why not address the situation with an apology for getting upset, and then continue by explaining that the supplies you requested are vital to the related procedures. You certainly could add that you were offended by her laughter."

"I'm not sorry, Regina, and I don't have to explain anything that I order!"

"Well I would consider pretending that you are sorry for hurting her feelings; and explaining, is a way of teaching. Surely you're sorry that the upset took place and made its' way to Memphis?"

"Yeah, and that's disrespectful in itself!"

"Too right you are, and you might bring that up calmly as well; first to your senior partner and then to the local administration."

"Maybe I'll call Mike Dougherty tonight."

"That's a good idea, and I'll finish supper. We're having por-cupines."

Frank shook his head and laughed as he hugged his wife. "What are porcupines, Regina?"

"They are rounded meatloaves covered with spaghetti stick-ing out of them. They also have olive noses and tiny caper eyes. Served with sweet carrots and corn pudding, they are quite a hit with kids. Twelve of them are eating dinner with us tonight."

Mike Dougherty apologized to Frank for jumping to conclu-sions and agreed that Bradington matters should be settled in Bradington. The hospital administrator was conference called at his home, and he also had a calmer outlook. He agreed to meet with Frank and the nurse who dared to "giggle" at him first thing the next morning. The issue resolved itself and while everyone didn't exactly hug and make up, they all realized that they must work together as adults, and decided to govern themselves ac-cordingly for the time being.

Thanksgiving was fast approaching and Frank Jr. felt compelled to meet with his father. "Dad, you know how you guys did some-thing nice for Grandma and Grandpa when you gave them that cruise? Well I was thinking that maybe you and I and Angela should do something special for our mom."

"Okay! You got it Buddy!"

"Why don't we make her something really special? Something just for her?"

"Leave it to me, son. I will take care of it," Frank Sr. answered, but did not notice the tears of disappointment welling up in his understudy's big blue eyes.

The four Solbergs were out shopping the next Saturday for Thanksgiving outfits. They would be traveling to Florida along with Leo and Hazel and Frances and Lamar for Thanksgiving dinner at The Montecello Restaurant, to include Regina's family, the senior Solbergs and Marge and Adam. After purchasing smart beige turtlenecks and dark brown slacks and jackets for Frank and Frank Jr., Regina found an adorable apricot-colored dress with a matching apron that was embroidered with tiny squirrels gathering acorns, for Angela. Little buckle shoes, tiny orange stone earrings, a gold bracelet and a delicate pearl hair bow completed the look beautifully. Regina already had an outfit that she was fond of at home, so the small hungry group decided to stop for lunch.

Settling into their seats at the International Deli, Frank Sr. winked at his son and whispered, "I took care of the special surprise." Frank Jr. looked puzzled as he had no idea of what the surprise was. When Regina's Reuben sandwich arrived, there was a gorgeous sapphire ring surrounded with small diamonds on it. She looked shocked at first, as she thought someone in the kitchen had lost their jewelry during the preparation process. Once she realized that the ring was for her, she was even more surprised.

Frank Sr. neglected to tell Regina that this whole thing was her son's idea, so the little boy just sat in his seat and smiled. Finally Frank Sr. asked his son what he thought of 'Mommy's new ring', and without a second's hesitation, Frank Jr. answered, "'I figured what the hell!'"

Regina knew instantly what had transpired, but Frank Sr. seemed to be in the dark.

Making no attempt to lower his voice, he scolded, "Young man, you don't use words like that. Apologize to your mother and I immediately!" Frank Jr. fought back his tears and apologized. When his father went to pay the bill he mumbled, "and it's 'apologize to your mother and me' – DOCTOR Solberg!" Regina put her arms around her son and hugged him tight.

"You are a very special boy, Frankie, and don't you ever forget it." Frank smiled and hugged his mother back. Having secured two extra bedtime stories, he answered, "That's what my Abba said," and turning to his baby sister he added, "I'll tell you all about this too when you are older. You know, like old enough to Trick-or-Treat, and chew gum and stuff." The infant responded with her usual laugh; kicking her little legs as if she understood every word that her brother had just said. The two blue-eyed, cotton-top children were beautiful, and Regina thanked God for them throughout every day.

Frank Jr. wasted no time collecting a large brown grocery bag full of craft items and shut himself in his room. He was planning to make his own special gift for his mother whether his father liked it or not.

"This time Dad won't know what's going on," he told himself. *"This will be from Angela Dawn and me!"* Coming downstairs

Frank asked for strict observation of the KEEP OUT sign on his closet, and went outside to round up his friends. Nodding in compliance Regina went to answer the phone.

Frances was a bundle of excitement about the Florida trip, and called to say that she had picked up a set of Pilgrim dolls for Angela and Gabby and a set of resin Pilgrims and Indians for Frank Jr. Regina was delighted that Frances had remembered Gabby, as she missed the little girl terribly.

Upon sharing the information with Frank however, her heart sank when he responded. "We are not seeing Gabby or the other two 'Cubes', Regina; we are going to relax and enjoy ourselves!"

Tears of disappointment and anger rolled down her cheeks. "Frances bought Gabby a set of Pilgrim dolls, honey. I guess she assumed that they were to be included in at least part of the visit."

"Well she should mind her own business because they're not going to be included in anything!" Frank walked into the garage slamming the door behind him.

Regina closed her eyes and called for help, "Abba, my dear Abba!" she sobbed, "Something is happening to my husband. Please help me to be understanding and please help him to communicate with me."

Frank came back in with a large envelope of paperwork. He walked over to his wife and held her. "I'm sorry," he whispered. "I have been so preoccupied with the problems at the hospital, that I didn't stop to think. I just wanted some time away for us this time, honey."

"Okay, but what has you so upset at the hospital?"

"I'm too big for Bradington, Regina. It was an excellent stepping stone but now that I'm a seasoned orthopod, it's time to move on. For one thing I'm worth a whole lot more money. In addition to that, there are multiple demands for positions all over the country."

"Frank we have not been here that long; surely you're not considering relocating."

"Not right now, but by next year."

Regina nodded noting that next year was weeks away, but said nothing. Stunned by her silence, Frank suggested that they talk more about the subject later. "Why don't I run out and get some Chinese food for dinner?" Frank waited for a happy response and got one from his son.

"Come on buddy, you can come with me while the cootie girls stay at home." Frank swung Angela into the air as she shrieked with delight. Handing her to her mother, the two "boys" were off to China Town Restaurant.

Regina went straight for the phone and called Frances. Her second mother listened as she relayed the story. Finishing with the sentence, "he said that he is too big for Bradington," she began to cry.

Frances was ready to strangle the "seasoned orthopod," and did not attempt to hide her feelings. "It sounds like he's too big for his breeches! I have noticed a real arrogance about him lately; a whole new obnoxious swagger!"

"I can't even think of moving again so soon," Regina sighed, wiping her eyes on a napkin.

"Where is the demi-god now?" Frances was happy to hear Regina laugh as she answered.

"He and Frank Jr. are off to get Chinese food for dinner."

"I thought you were making wine stew when we spoke this morning."

"Oh, I did. I'll just serve it tomorrow."

"Did the Bradington Big Shot clear his yen for Chinese food with you first?"

"Well no, he just suggested it."

"I was telling Leo the other day that I was disappointed in Frank and this snobby attitude that he's adopted lately, and he said that it's a normal phase that new young doctors go through."

"I do hope that you won't love Frank any less," Regina sounded worried.

"Right now I couldn't love him any less," the protective second mother snapped. "I love him for your sake and I will continue to act as though nothing has happened. I will also send Gabby her gift whether it pleases the Czar or not!"

Regina loved Frances and appreciated the fact that her attitude was more of a support for her. She had also noticed several looks from both of the older couples in Memphis the last time they were together, and prayed that this was only the phase that Leo described!

There were indeed many other opportunities for orthopedic surgeons, although Regina recalled how quickly Frank jumped at the current position, and hoped he would put more thought into the next possibility. Once the kids were in bed they talked about the different locations, agreeing to put all serious planning aside until after the holidays.

"By the way," Frank looked puzzled, "our son ask me to stop at Wal-Mart and spent twelve dollars from his savings jar on craft items. I asked what he was making and he answered that the project was 'classified.'"

"Well he earned $15.00 today for completely re-organizing the three bottom cupboards. He said he was looking for work to save up for something. He and Shawn Michael have their own business. Yesterday they earned $15.00 from Vernon for weeding the entire front of their house."

"Doesn't this concern you, Regina?"

"No, I think it's adorable and short lived. They were already complaining about being overworked at Vernon's and spent plenty of time snacking on the job here."

"What is this project? Shouldn't we demand to know?"

"Not as long as they are buying craft items with their profits. Any requests for napalm, and we storm the closet in his room," the smart aleck missionary smiled sheepishly.

"Okay, wise guy, but this is the stuff that parents are supposed to watch for."

"Engage the SWAT team at once, sir," the 'wise guy' hugged her husband and laughed. Frank laughed as well realizing that his suspicions were uncalled for.

Elizabeth and Dan were chomping at the bit to have their daughter home for the week of Thanksgiving and Bub and Sis were tickled to death to have the Mac Michaels and the Gerehauzers stay with them. Andrea and Brian were out shopping for their nieces and nephew and couldn't wait to play with the new toys they bought for them. Dorothy and Raymond were a little put out that Frank and Regina were not splitting the time between both houses, but accepted the difficulty of setting up in two places for the baby.

All of the ladies were wearing hats with their outfits as the popularity from Great Britain had traveled around the world. Frances and Hazel had pill box hats similar to what Jackie Kennedy often wore, Elizabeth, Sis and Dorothy had slightly bigger hats in gorgeous colors that matched their outfits. Andrea selected a smart beige hat with a subtle bird cage veil and Regina had a stunning peacock colored hat that would sit slightly to one side of her thick auburn locks. The telephones had been busy with talk of little else, causing the men to laugh and roll their eyes.

Marge had decided quietly to herself, that she was not wearing any "tacky hats," regardless of what Princess Diana or anybody else did! Pregnancy was difficult for her and she did not relish being around the senior Solbergs in the least. She was delighted that Regina was coming though, as she had always liked her, and wanted to see the children.

Tuesday before Thanksgiving the two large cars from Tennessee pulled into the driveway barely missing the welcome party! Angela was wide awake and smiled at everyone as they passed her from one to the other. Frank Jr. ran to Dan and after an "emergency secret conference," both went quickly into the den. "Your package will be safe in here, Buddy," Dan smiled at his grandson. "We'll not only put your sign on the closet door – we'll also lock it!"

Frank Jr. beamed at his grandfather, "I made this gift for my mother for Thanksgiving, and I made clothespin bookmarks for everyone else! They're from me and Angela, but she's just too little to help with the actual production."

Dan was touched to see how thoughtful his young grandson was and how well he handled himself.

The ladies grouped together to prepare for a cookout and everyone welcomed the senior Solbergs who arrived with a huge cookie bouquet, adorned with fall colored ribbons. The cookies were shaped like Pilgrims, Indians, acorns, haystacks, and cornucopias, and looked delicious. Marge and Adam had declined the invitation due to morning sickness which Dorothy described as "more frequent than not." Everyone had a wonderful evening, and Andrea was thrilled to be able to spend time with her sister, as the two had always been very close.

Dan, Leo, Bub and Lamar were making the den into a giant tent for Frank Jr. to sleep in and the ladies were gushing over Bradington's princess, Angela Dawn. "The kids at Frank Jr.'s school love her," Frank Sr. boasted, "and the principal won't put her down! He and Regina have done wonders with the kids from the lower income neighborhoods," he continued with pride.

"Regina will make a difference wherever she goes," Dorothy smiled and winked at her daughter-in-law. Raymond continued the subject of Bradington and how the clinic was running. Frank spared no details about how he'd outgrown the area and the mentality there.

"Frank, perhaps you should return here! The group in North Palm Beach is looking for a fifth partner, and your father handles their accounts," Dorothy added with excitement.

"We'll see, Mom, Regina wants to stay north and really isn't ready to move again at all, so we agreed not to discuss it any further until after the holidays."

"Well while you're home it can't hurt to go talk to them, Frank." Raymond persisted.

"Let's see what happens," Frank was ready to drop the subject.

"Regina, would you mind if we stole Frank tomorrow for a few hours to talk with the guys in North Palm Beach?" Dorothy was unaware of the piercing glare from across the room.

"Let's not talk business now, Dorothy, especially monkey business," Frances faked a laugh. "Surely you don't intend to accompany Frank on any interview at his age! Besides we are all here to visit and have fun!"

Although she made no comments, Regina had no intentions of moving close to the Solberg seniors or to Adam. Frank, well aware of her feelings on the subject, politely closed the conversation.

The remainder of the visit went extremely well and the Solbergs went home as the other group of four left with Bub and Sis. Dan and Elizabeth also decided to leave well enough alone for the night and simply enjoy the visit to the fullest.

Chapter Twenty-Four
The Top Hat

Thanksgiving morning Frank Jr. presented everybody with their clothespin bookmarks, which were absolutely adorable! Painted by hand and sprayed with top-coat to promote a lovely mate' finish, each had a plastic Thanksgiving figure glued to the top. He then asked Regina to close her eyes and went back into the den to retrieve his special gift.

"Okay you can open them now," the young boy commanded with excitement. Regina opened the large box and saw the beautiful hat her little son had made over the last few weeks. A firm paper plate with the center removed was the base, although disguised with artificial flowers and tiny birds in blues and greens. A long string of pearls wound in a zig-zag around the edges, and the center was covered with peacock blue satin ribbon glued into place in a sagging wavy pattern, to accommodate an upsweep, which was Regina's common hairstyle whenever she dressed for a special occasion.

Speechless at first, Regina hugged her son, "It is beautiful Frankie; the prettiest hat that I've ever seen!"

The grandparents all joined in to complement the gift and Leo especially elaborated. "I bet those ladies in England would be jealous of that hat! It's spectacular, young man!"

Dorothy and Raymond came over later and gushed over their bookmarks. They also raved about the hat but when Frank Jr. explained that he made it to match his mother's dress they quickly clarified their position.

"Now Frankie," Dorothy started, "I'm sure that your mother loves the hat and she will wear it some other time, but not to dinner today at the Montecello!" Since none of the other adults seemed to disagree, Frank Jr. hid his disappointment behind a quiet smile. He realized that his mother had already purchased a hat that matched her dress and would be wearing that one today.

Dan caught his grandson's eye and added, "She's probably going to save Frankie's hat for something very special; it's far too nice for just any dinner."

"You bet I wouldn't wear that hat just anywhere," Hazel added, "It is too glamorous!"

Noticing that Frank Jr. suddenly beamed with pride the group turned to see Regina walk into the living room with the hat in place, looking quite beautiful to the side of a gorgeous cascade of her abundant auburn curls. The dress matched perfectly and nobody would ever guess that a first grader was the milliner! Not that Regina gave a hoot what anybody thought or would think.

Dorothy opened her mouth slowly, "Honestly - ... .

"I wouldn't," Frances growled from behind her.

Regina handed Angela to Frank Sr. and asked her son to escort her to the car.

The Montecello Restaurant was packed with people who were dressed to the teeth. Many commented on Regina's hat and were shocked to learn that her son had made it for her.

"You know," Bub said in surprise, "You'd never guess that the hat didn't come from a top boutique in Palm Beach!"

"Huh! Palm Beach should be so lucky! I stand corrected," Dorothy smiled at her grandson.

Raymond shook his head and smiled, "How do you like that? Who'd ever have guessed?"

After Dan led the blessing and did a beautiful job of it, everyone went to the buffet. Frank Sr. escorted his son as Regina got the baby settled in. The two children were then left with the four sets of grandparents while their father escorted Regina to get their plates. Everyone raved about Regina's hat and asked questions about it. Proudly answering, Regina was glowing with pride. The extensive buffet included traditional Thanksgiving foods as well as international selections from all over the world, and the dessert tables seemed to have no end!

Dinner was a great deal of fun, and even Marge and Adam were forced to have a good time. Marge was delighted to be seated among Regina, Andrea, and Frances and asked many "baby" questions to which she got reassuring responses. Doting on Angela and Frank Jr., she decided that having a baby might be fun after all.

"I'm considering some books to help me with any difficulties that may arise after the baby gets here," she added calmly.

"I hope they're books about moving," Frances wasn't close to joking.

"Adam can't," Marge responded sadly, "but my mother is moving here a few weeks before the baby is due. Dorothy said that you guys may be relocating back here?"

"Dorothy lied," Frances squeezed lemon into her tea.

Regina laughed and nodded in agreement, "I really don't see us coming to this area," she added. "Quite honestly I love it where we are. It seems like we just settled in."

"Because you did just settle in," Frances added and continued, "and so did all of us. I'm personally hoping that no move takes place for a very long time. Frank also must consider the cost of tail insurance."

"Oh," Marge added slowly and cautiously, "because Dorothy has an appointment with the Orthopedic group in North Palm Beach tomorrow and intends to get their take on Frank joining them. What's tail insurance?"

Frances raised her eyebrows and answered quietly, "How sweet----- Mommy's going on a job interview for her son the doctor! Tail Insurance is a malpractice coverage that covers any possible suit that could occur after a doctor leaves an area. It's darn good and expensive."

"Well her son the doctor is not moving here as long as I'm his wife," Regina added. "I have absolutely no intention of living in North Palm Beach."

Marge laughed and silently regretted that Regina and Frank

wouldn't move closer. She admired Regina and hoped that Adam would stand up to his parents like his brother did.

Suddenly attention was requested and the restaurant came to order. The Prettiest Hat Contest, which none of the group realized existed prior to now, was being announced. Three winners would receive prizes and Frank Jr. walked over to his mother and said, "I didn't know about this, Mom, your other hat would have probably won," the young man said sadly.

"My hat is the winner, Frankie, whether they think so or not. I wouldn't trade it for one of Princess Diana's hats!"

Third runner up was a cornucopia hat, with fall colored beads around it. The prize was a $50.00 gift card to a local department store. Next was a burnt orange picture hat set slightly to one side of the winner's head, who proudly marched up to claim her prize of a Thanksgiving quilt. The first place winner was Regina, who had her son walk her up to claim a huge basket of fruit, nuts, cheeses and elegant imported chocolate Thanksgiving molds, including turkeys, Pilgrims, Indians, and cornucopias in colored frosted grandeur. As Regina accepted the basket, the announcer asked her where she had purchased the hat. When Regina responded that her young son had made it, the crowd stood and applauded, as Frank Jr. grinned.

Regina handed the basket to her son, and told him to be in full charge of it. Marge looked at Regina with tears in her eyes, "I hope motherhood is as wonderful for me as it is for you," she hugged her little nephew.

Frank Sr. enjoyed showing off his children and gladly accepted the praise for their remarkable behavior in the restaurant.

Even little Angela sat like a little doll and smiled contentedly. Leo and Dan both looked at Regina and then at each other.

"Do you have any idea why he wants to move so soon?" Dan nodded toward Frank.

"Not really, but I think he has a case of new doctor syndrome. I planned to talk to him about it after the holiday. Maybe we can get some details on the golf course tomorrow."

"Good idea. They just settled in Leo, and Regina is happy in Bradington."

"I know, Frances is ready to string him up," Leo laughed, as he buttered his sweet potatoes.

"She looks beautiful though, better than I have ever seen her; so I assume they are okay."

"Oh yeah, I don't think Frank and Regina are having any problems," Leo confirmed.

Friday was a very fun and relaxed day. The guys all played golf and the ladies shopped and gabbed. Andrea and Regina looked like a pair of high school girls; both were beautiful and glowing with happiness. The entire group was having Chinese food that night and Elizabeth had invited Dorothy and Raymond to join them.

After dinner Angela was bathed and put to bed, while Frank Jr. was permitted to play quietly until he got tired. Loud war whoops cut the peaceful setting as Leo and Lamar came out of the den in Indian head dresses and Dan and Frank Jr. fired cap guns, from the other side of the sunken living room. Frances and Hazel grabbed cameras while Elizabeth clasped her hands and laughed. Amazingly enough they didn't wake Angela, and settled their standoff in time for dessert.

Frank Jr. donated the "boring portions" of the prize basket, but secured the chocolate figures in a fort that he purchased at the mall that afternoon. The ladies poured coffee and set out numerous pies and mini cakes among the fruit and cheeses from the prize basket. Once everyone was settled quietly, Dorothy stood and made her announcement. "Cricket, you are hired on in North Palm Beach, and you have your father to thank! He spoke to David Crenshaw, the senior partner. You see, he plays golf with Dad, in addition to also being his client!"

Raymond motioned modestly and continued, "They will start you at $150,000.00 plus bonuses, and there is a gorgeous house for sale in your price range a mile from the Palm Beach Gardens Hospital."

The Solbergs, oblivious to the mouths that had dropped open, waited for their son to jump for joy. Frank sat in his chair in shock, and did not answer. Glancing at his wife, he finally collected himself. "Mom, I cannot make that decision right now, and I cannot make any decision without discussing it with my wife."

Dorothy's heel caught the leg of her chair and she temporarily lost her balance. Quickly recovering, she placed her hand to her chest and announced, "I tripped."

"Yeah, on the umbilical cord that should have been cut when Cricket was delivered thirty years ago," Frances blasted, making absolutely no effort to lower her voice.

Dorothy glared at Frances and then at her son, "What is your answer going to be, Frank?"

"Mom I can't accept that position as we are not ready to make any commitment yet. I haven't even spoken to my partners about leaving the group."

"Raymond, it's time we left," Dorothy pushed her chair from the table with such force that it fell backwards.

Dan spoke softly, "Come on now, Dorothy, nobody is saying that they don't appreciate what you tried to do for Frank. Don't walk out on such a wonderful holiday."

"Why don't you save your lectures for your darling daughter who is keeping everything on hold until she's good and ready to permit her husband to make his own decisions?"

Frances and Hazel looked at each other and then at Elizabeth, before all three laughed. Dorothy marched toward to the door and turned to order Raymond to follow her. Leo was on his feet in an instant, "Hold it! I hope that you don't think for a moment that you are taking your delicious spice cake with you, because I want some more."

Dan walked over to the Solbergs and gently added, "Please stay. It's just a little misunderstanding. Besides, that dish that your spice cake is on is very expensive, and I saw Hazel and Elizabeth both eyeing it; one of them might steal it!"

Everyone laughed and the Solbergs returned to their seats. The talk of the relocation stopped for the evening; but Regina and Frank silently agreed that there was no way they would be living close to his parents. Dorothy had also omitted the fact that David Crenshaw had telephoned Memphis and spoken to Mike Dougherty at his home.

Regina had spent the majority of the weekend talking to her dear

Abba, and thanking Him for her beautiful life, particularly her step-father, who she loved dearly. The Solbergs kept to themselves for the most part which delighted the other ladies. Bub and Sis both mentioned that is was a shame that Dorothy was such a problem, as it would be nice to have the kids come back home, especially since two children had been born since they had moved away.

Running out to walk Monique, Elizabeth noticed the car phone flashing and told Frank about it. He went out to the car and returned infuriated but flattered. Mike Dougherty had an emergency message waiting, begging him not to leave and raising the salary offer from North Palm Beach. The hospital administrator also called to apologize again to him and to reassure him that there would be no more disrespectful behavior tolerated.

The community in Bradington loved the Solbergs and nobody wanted that disrupted. Frank couldn't believe that his mother overstepped to the extent that she did, and as he picked up the phone to tell her so, Regina spoke softly. "Frank, the senior partner here had absolutely no right to contact Mike Dougherty. You did not seek a position with them, and he should have known better than to call anyone without both your knowledge and permission."

"Mike said that Dr. Crenshaw had called him for a reference."

Frances was livid and so was Leo, "They had absolutely no right to violate your personal space, son," Leo stated calmly but firmly.

"Your mother is a meddling buttinski," Frances added, sending Frank Jr. into rolls of laughter. She moved toward Frank and began to cry softly, "You can't take Regina away from Bradington or away from us, Frank. We all just settled in."

Frank was laughing softly as he responded, "I think you're right, and after all, my mother doesn't even have 'a license to meddle!'"

Regina closed her eyes and thanked Abba once again for His help. She had been asking all week to stay where they were, and sighed with relief now that they would.

Snow! They would also be seeing snow soon. Regina asked Frank as they were getting ready for bed if he was at peace with the decision to stay where they were. He scooped her up in his arms. "When were you going to tell me that you were unhappy about leaving? Why didn't you tell me that wine stew had been prepared when I got the inconsiderate idea to simply get Chinese food, without asking about dinner plans? Do you ever think that you count too, Pollyanna?"

"Yes."

"Do you ever take a stand where I am concerned?"

"Oh yes. I stand behind you and beside you, and I always will."

Frank held her for a long time, as he thanked God for all that He had blessed him with. As they drifted off to sleep, Frank whispered, "I think we should host Christmas at our house, Regina. Andrea and Brain can both get off, and you know your folks will come. Bub and Sis won't require much arm-twisting either. As for me, I can be the jackass in the manger!"

Regina laughed, but corrected him. "You are far from a jackass, my dear! You are the love of my life and I am grateful every waking minute for you and for our beautiful children."

Volume Three
The First Mrs. Solberg

Chapter One
Déjà Vu

Dropping a bag of groceries on the table to free one of her hands, Regina grabbed the phone. "Marge, what a pleasant surprise," she continued while setting Angela down. Her sister-in-law started crying so hard that she was barely able to talk. Regina listened patiently keeping her active daughter in her sight. Now a toddler, Angela moved quickly and quietly. Her thick blonde hair was in two curly little pig tails which jiggled as she ran, encouraging the action.

Marge, finally able to talk, continued, "The baby is two weeks late and they want to induce labor," she cried again as if they had sentenced her to the death penalty.

Frank Jr. handed his mother a note asking if he could play a little game with his baby sister, and was answered with a grateful smile and nod.

"Why does that upset you, honey?" Regina was far more concerned for the condition of the future mother than about the risk of the suggested procedure.

"I am petrified that something could go wrong, and of course Dorothy showed up at the doctor's office shooting off her big trap that you were induced with Angela, and then practically booked the birth!"

"First of all, it doesn't matter whether I was induced or not. This is a decision for you and your doctor. How did Dorothy know you were even going for an appointment?"

"Adam and his blaring mouth," she sobbed again.

"Marge," Regina continued softly, "schedule an appointment with your doctor and go to it alone. Don't even tell Adam that you're going. Explain the situation and ask that your case be kept confidential, as it should be anyway. Then tell Adam how you feel about his mother showing up for appointments."

"I wish I could! Adam won't stand up to his parents in any way, shape, or form, Regina. Dorothy's even got names picked out for a boy and a girl!"

"And what, pray tell, might those be?"

"Raymond Adam and Dorothy Janette."

Regina's laughter got Marge laughing and able to vent easier. "Marge, you need to do what is best for you, but I would not allow anyone else to name my child. Taking a stand is not as hard as it sounds."

"Well I'm naming my baby Talbert if it's a boy and Samantha if it's a girl!"

"That a girl! Once the baby is born they will ask you – not Dorothy or Raymond what the name is to be."

"I don't want Dorothy there when the baby is born, Regina," Marge started sobbing all over again.

"Sounds to me like you need to sit Adam down and have a heart to heart with him."

"You better believe it! He reprimanded me in front of Dorothy and Raymond this morning because I have gained fifty-eight pounds."

Regina listened to her sister-in-law sob, trying to think of solutions to the problems she described. Finally, when Marge was a little calmer, Regina made a suggestion. "Why don't you call Frank and ask him to talk to his brother?"

Stunned by the idea, Marge was silent at first. "Do you think Frank would do it?"

"Well, it certainly can't hurt to ask. Is your mother with you yet, honey?"

"Yes, and she despises Adam's parents, but loves him."

"Does Adam get along well with your mom?"

"Yes, he loves her."

"Those are two big pluses! Call Frank, Marge," Regina provided a direct number.

"Regina, I don't know how to thank you!" Marge sounded better already.

"Don't give it a thought, and definitely don't worry about inducing the labor, because that's done all the time. At Jackson Memorial Hospital, it's a requirement that once the water has broken, the baby must be delivered in twenty-four hours."

"Really?"

"Absolutely."

"Well then it must be relatively safe."

"Certainly!"

"Regina, I have always admired you, and I thank you again!"

"Call me anytime, Marge; anytime at all."

Regina hung up the phone and prayed that Marge would be able to talk to Adam and resolve the privacy issue with Dorothy, so that the excitement of the upcoming birth could be enjoyed to the fullest.

Turning to the sound of Angela Dawn squealing with laughter, Regina saw Frank Jr. and his two friends pulling her across the hard wood floor by Monique's leash, which was attached to the buckle of her pink Osh Kosh overalls. "Frankie, that's hardly playing with your baby sister!"

"Mom she's having a great time; she's in our game."

"And what game might that be?" Regina raised her eyebrows and crossed her arms.

"She's our calf, and we are taking her to the fenced area for grass and safety, but we have to lead her there because she's wild."

Regina couldn't help laughing, but unhooking the calf, she informed the three cowboys that this particular livestock needed to be fed and bathed. A large stuffed animal was substituted, and the cowboys were delighted that they could be a bit rougher with the new replacement.

Regina touched her stomach gently and asked, "My Abba, is it too much to hope that another little doll is really on the way?" Placing the note under her husband's pillow, she hugged a spaghetti-O covered Angela and prepared her bubble bath.

A native of Flushing, New York, Michele Menard has traveled all over the world, embracing different cultures along the way. She has four children, and following an exhausting seventeen year divorce battle, has managed to still love her former husband. Enjoying a very close relationship with God, she can usually find humor in almost any situation!

CPSIA information can be obtained at www.ICGtesting.com
Printed in the USA
BVOW09s1504151114

375240BV00003B/13/P